The Maker Series
Earth

Jeffrey Allen Bolling

Bollingsbooks—Fellsmere, FL
ISBN: 978-0-578-54536-3
The Maker Series: Earth
Jeffrey Allen Bolling
Available Formats: eBook | Paperback distribution

Dedication

- A special thank you to my mother, who always encouraged me to dare to believe in myself as much as she believes in me. To My Wife for always being my rock through many trials and tribulations. To My Lord and Savior Jesus Christ to whom I owe everything that I am blessed with today.

-I dedicate this book to my late father who showed me how an imperfect man can still be a great man.

Please take note that this is a book of fiction and I make no implication that Jesus Christ is not the one true Lord and Savior.

"To look out at this kind of creation out here and not believe in God is to me, impossible, ...It just strengthens my faith. I wish there were words to describe what it's like." — John Glenn

On a mountaintop, against an incredibly bright blue sky is a dish-like device. The device is sitting on top of a large brown building. It looks like the kind of dish that might communicate with a satellite. Attached to the building are large cylinders that resemble cooling towers for a nuclear facility, but smaller. A large hum is emanating from the building, and a small light comes out the dish-like device. As the frequency and volume increase, the light becomes more solid, eventually becoming laser-like, shooting into the sky; eventually, that light fades, but the humming remains.

Chapter 1

Gabe is leaving the kitchen with two glasses of red wine. He enters the adjoining living room, handing Rai her glass. He takes a seat, and they continue their conversation. Rai says, "Look, Gabe, (she has called him that since the day she met him and they started dating) you can try to keep your head in the ground like some silly ostrich, but Sophie is a grown woman now, she is 26 years old for heaven's sake!"

Gabe says, "You know they don't really put their head in the ground."

Rai says, "I know that."

Gabe says, "I know you're right, but the thought of our daughter getting married still crushes my heart. Can we please change the subject?"

Rai said, "Sure, how is work going?"

"It's going ok," he replied. Gabriel Dane is 46 years old, about 6 foot 1 inches, he is half black, half white with a fit build. He had gone through naval postgraduate school, had a Ph.D. in Science and studied Space systems. After leaving the navy, he was brought on as the new Director for The Space Network (T.S.N.) in Barstow, California. Gabe had met Rai when he was in the postgraduate program in Monterey, California and she was at the University of California where she got her BA in environmental studies. She was also 46 years old, and of Chinese and Korean descent. She was fairly tall with a thin build and dark shoulder-length hair. After a short marriage, they divorced because of career decisions and long distance issues.

Rai said, "Thank you for the wine, Gabe. I've got to get going but make sure you take some time to talk to Sophie about her future."

∞

The next day, Mia Russo was at the TSN where she was the Deputy Director reporting directly to Gabriel Dane. She hears a knock on her office door and says, "Come in." As the senior data technician enters the room, she notices a small stack of papers in his hand. She says, "Hello" to Robert Wall, who has been working at the TSN for about three years. Mia says, "What do you have for me?"

Robert replies, "Well, Mrs. Russo, it's an odd signal we received this morning. I wanted to pass it on to you and get your take on it." She thanks him and tells him she has a few calls to make and she will look at it later in the afternoon. With that, Robert leaves, and Mia picks up the phone. She talks to her husband Santos about their son who had a scuffle at school…they also talked about what they wanted to do for dinner that night. After a few more calls-one to the principal of her boy's school-she was finally finished with her calls. She takes out the stack of papers; on them are a series of numbers and characters-about fifty pages of numbers and character type letters. But she can tell right away that they repeat about every fifth page. She starts by trying to reference them against other explainable and identified signals and data she has filed away in her office. She is not able to match this data to anything they've seen before. At one point she thinks she is starting to work out a way to identify the meaning of the numbers and the characters, but then gets frustrated because she realizes it's a dead end. It is now about three o'clock in the afternoon and she decides to talk to Gabe about it.

∞

Mia calls Gabriel and explains what the Technicians found that morning. He asks her to bring the pages up to him, so she sets out to walk up to his office. Gabriel had always admired Mia; she was a little on the shorter side, a curvy Italian woman, 38 years old, who was very bright and strong-willed. The two of them had always kept their relationship strictly professional. As she entered his office, she walked to his desk and handed him the pages. Gabriel asked how her family was, and she asked about his. She and Gabriel had a few mutual friends, and they discussed some of the current issues with them. Mia says, "I need to get to my son's school." She and her husband needed to meet with her six-year-old son's teacher because of a fight. As she left, Gabriel began looking over the data. He saw the repetition quickly as well. He could see a mixture of numbers and what appeared to be letter-like characters, but not anything he was familiar with, he would need to do some research tomorrow. It was getting late, so he decided to leave for the day.

After their meeting with their son's teacher, Mia and her husband Santos decided to pick up some pizza on their way home. They sat with their son and talked about his issues at school. He explained how the other boy picks on other kids and how the boy started picking on him. The boy called him "beaner." It was something he didn't even know the meaning of. So, he pushed him down on the playground, and that is what the teachers saw.

3

They said that he should tell a teacher and not put his hands on other kids. A bit later at home, Mia was helping him with his spelling words when the phone rang. She saw that it was her job calling, and she thought, "That is odd; the whole time I've worked here, they've never called me at home at night." They asked her to come in, she considered calling Gabriel, yet she decided not to call him and drove to work. Once she was there, the night technician informed her of the incoming signal. She looked at it, and it was the same signal as earlier that morning. She decided to leave the new pages on Gabriel's desk.

Mia gets back into her car and drives home. Walking into the house, she says to Santos, "We have started receiving an odd signal and the night techs wanted to make sure I knew about it."

Santos asks, "What is the signal?"

Mia says, "We aren't sure yet. Gabriel is going to look it over tomorrow." Mia then goes into her son's room and kisses him goodnight.

∞

The next morning, Gabe is driving to work when Rai calls. She wants to talk to him about the current job she is on. She is a rural development specialist. Rai says, "The contractor doesn't understand the new policy the county put into place as it relates to septic tanks. He is being a real pain in the butt! He wants to proceed with the old regulation tanks, but I can't let that happen."

Gabe says, "Just set up a meeting with one of the County Commissioners and explain the situation."

She had planned on doing that. This was one of those situations that Gabe had not learned how to navigate yet. She just really wanted him to listen and not fix the problem. 'Nothing new,' she thought to herself. Just then, Gabe said he had arrived at work, and they each said goodbye.

∞

As Gabriel walks past his assistant, Bobbi, each says good morning, and then Bobbi says, "There is a new report on your desk." As he sits down, he looks over the new data waiting for him. It is the same data as before but with a different time stamp on it. It was late evening when it came in. Gabriel starts looking over the data. One thing that few people knew about him is that he has always had this ability to look over data and almost see a picture. He would pour over the data for hours and not even realize time had passed. This was one of those times. It was lunchtime when Bobbi called Gabriel and asked if he wanted anything from the sandwich place. He said "Sure, turkey and Swiss on rye."

After lunch, Gabriel calls Mia and asks her to come to his office. Once she arrives, they move the pages of data to a round work table he has in his office. Gabriel asks Bobbie for some coffee. Once she brings it, he asks her to stay and take notes as they discuss the data. He tells Mia that he had examined the data and used his normal ciphers and algorithms, but he had not been successful. He then recalled how the British mathematicians were able to break the German codes in World War II. As he set out along that path, he started to see a sort of pattern in the characters and numbers. He was trying to put it to an alphabet, but it was not working. He knew that Mia had gone through the Undergraduate Major Program for linguistics at M.I.T. which is why he quickly hired her after she had done a little volunteering about ten years ago. He asks her what she thinks. She picks up his notes and sees where he is going with it. She starts examining the information he has so far and tries to run it through the languages that she is aware of. After a few hours, she starts to make some sense of it. She tells Gabriel, "It looks like old Biblical or Classical

Hebrew; it's not all matching up but it's close enough." Because some of the characters are slightly different, it is enough not to be able to make full sense of it. It is now about 5:00 pm, so they decide to come back to the data tomorrow. He asks Mia to get with the Data Technician Team and start trying to trace the signal's origin. They each say "goodnight" and leave for the day.

Meanwhile, at Rai's townhouse, Sophie and Rai are talking at the counter separating the kitchen from the living room, one on each side of it drinking some iced tea. Rai looks at her; she is amazed at how beautiful her daughter has turned out. She is tall like Rai with larger breasts. She has a round figure and almost golden skin. Her eyes are shaped like Rai's, but she has larger lips like Gabriel. She has a BS in Education and is a 1st-grade teacher in Fresno, California. Sophie was talking to her mom about a few of the kids in her class. She was frustrated because she felt like she was forced to be more of a parent and less of a teacher. She told Rai about a few of the parents and how young and frankly, how selfish they were. Rai talked about some of her work issues and then she asked how Sophie and Hayden were doing. "Honestly mom, "Sophie says, "we are great." Haden is a tall man of Chinese descent. He is a top chef at a high-end restaurant in Fresno. "Mom," Sophie continues, "we are in love, and I think he is going to ask me to marry him." Rai had a feeling this was coming so she told Sophie that she and her dad had discussed it as well. Sophie was happy that they had discussed it; she didn't want to be the one to spring it on her dad. They had a great relationship, but he was always protective of her, and no man was good enough. Just then, Rai's cell phone rings. As Rai lifts it, she can see it is Gabe. As Rai answers her phone, Gabe asks how things are going. She tells him a few things about work and some things she and Sophie had discussed, yet refrains from talking about the relationship discussion she and Sophie were having. Gabe starts telling Rai about the odd signal they had gotten, that he is sure that it is some kind of hacking job. Rai asks if he has contacted his old friend Dan over at H.E.T. I. Gabe states that he has not, but he thought it was a good idea, even if it was to bounce a few things off of him. Dan is the President and CEO of the Hunt for Extraterrestrial Intelligence or HETI.

Rai puts down the phone and Sophie asks," Was it, dad?"

Rai says, "Yes." Just then, Sophie got dizzy and had to sit down quickly, Rai rushed to her and asks, "Are you ok?"

Sophie says, "Yes, I have been really busy and just felt tired and run down." Rai gives her a glass of water and a cool cloth and puts it on her forehead. Sophie says, "Mom, I'm fine, just tired. I'll be ok." After a while, she feels better and says goodbye to Rai, as they hug, Rai notices that she has lost some weight.

"Sophie," Rai says, "Have you lost some weight?"

"A little" Sophie replies,

"Well, eat some food, please, and maybe see a doctor?" Sophie replies, "I'll make an appointment." Sophie leaves, but Rai is worried about her.

The next day Mia, Gabriel, and Bobbie meet again in Gabriel's office first thing in the morning. They pick up where they left off. Mia has been looking at the old text from the night before and wants to try something. She looks at the repetition of the characters and starts to see her mistake. She spends the next two hours, with Gabriel's help, going over each passage and each character. Finally, working on a dry erase board, they come up with an M, a half hour later they get an A, later an S, then an H then an I, next to an A, then a C and finally an H. Gabe spells it out.

Mashiach

The three of them look at the word on the dry erase board. Bobbie and Gabriel are clueless. They are not aware of what the word means. But Mia, she knows, she is utterly confused. She is looking at the data again, spelling it out again. Finally, she looks at the word on the board one last time. She looks at Gabriel and says, "It's a Hebrew word." Then under Mashiach, she writes,

Messiah

Gabriel breaks the silence and says, "This has to be a hack job." Gabriel asks Mia to please double down and figure out who is doing this and why.

∞

Mia goes to Robert's office and asks if he has time to discuss what data he has on the origin of the signal. He says, "Sure," so they go into his office and she takes a seat across from him. He starts by telling her how they had spent much of the day yesterday. First, they tried to isolate the frequency, with which they had no real luck. It was a signal, unlike anything they've seen before. However, they were able to isolate a type of radio wave. The signal, if all of their calculations were correct, came from an undiscovered yellow dwarf star in the Proxima Centauri system. Mia said there has to be another explanation. Mia wants Robert to examine other options. Mia says, "I want to know if we were hacked somehow, that maybe someone is in-putting the data and sending us on a wild goose chase.

∞

Gabriel calls Dan Henry, his old friend who works at the Hunt for Extra-Terrestrial Intelligence or HETI. Dan has been there for about 30 years. He is a slightly overweight, 60-year-old man with a wife with whom he has had three children. Dan lives outside of Mountain View, California. Dan answers his phone and was very surprised to See Gabriel's name on his phone. "Hello, Gabriel." He answered. "How have you been?"

Gabriel says "Great." He asks Dan the same thing.

Dan says, "I am doing well. how is Rai?"

Gabe replied, "She is well." He tells him a few things that Dan was not aware of, for example, Sophie is teaching now; Rai has been promoted at work. Dan tells Gabriel about a few things his kids are doing. Finally, Gabe say she has something he needs to talk to him about. They decide to meet for lunch. Dan says he will drive down to Barstow. Gabriel stops in and tells Bobbie he will be meeting Dan for lunch and he would be back soon.

Gabriel pulls into the Sandwich shop in Barstow. He walks into the restaurant and gets a table. About two minutes later Dan walks in and finds Gabriel quickly. They shake hands and sit down. Dan starts by asking more about the family. He asks about Rai and how the two of them are getting along. Gabriel and Rai are still very close. Neither one of them had dated after the divorce, and they talked almost every day. Dan asks how work has been going, and Gabriel says, "That's what I wanted to talk to you about. A little less than a week ago, we started getting a signal, an odd signal, and it repeats every twenty-two hours. There is also repetition within the signal. I wanted to know if your team has received anything in the past week."

Dan says, "I'm Sorry Gabriel, but, no, we've not received any signal."

Gabriel says, "Ok, well, I am confused about the whole thing. We have decoded it and what we've found makes no sense."

Dan says, "Gabriel, look, some governmental stuff binds me, but I am going to be honest, we have received a signal, but we have not had success in decoding it."

Gabriel replies, "Really? When did you receive the first signal?"

Dan says, "A little less than a week ago as well."

"Ok," Gabriel says, "Let's get some people together in a room and see if we can figure this out at some point."

"Sounds good Gabriel," says Dan. Gabriel thanks Dan for driving to meet with him. They say their goodbyes and each of them drives away.

∞

In a room, there is a man; he is sitting at what appears to be some type of computer. He leans in and starts to enter information into it by way of a keyboard. Once he is finished typing, he flips a large switch on a console and then presses a key on the board in front of him. Again, a loud hum starts and a light comes out of the dish on top of the building, eventually turning into a laser type light but more solid than a traditional laser. Then it eventually disappears, but it is obvious there is still some activity happening.

∞

The next morning, Mia knocks on Gabriel's door and opens it at the same time. Not waiting for an invitation to enter, she rushes into his office. Gabriel looks up in surprise from the pages of data and says good morning to her. Mia says, "Gabriel, there is a change in the signal."

"Oh?" he says.

Mia says, "We are working on deciphering it, but it is different for sure." Gabriel looks surprised and confused at the same time. "Also," she continues, "we have been working hard on tracking the signal."

"Ok," says Gabriel, "and what have you found?"

"Well, here's the thing, we've run every test available, and our systems say Proxima Centauri. It led us to a yet undiscovered dwarf yellow star just like our sun. That is what we have so far."

Gabriel says, "No way this is real, we are getting hacked." Mia leaves a bit deflated. She had been so excited she didn't expect Gabriel to react that way. She heads down to Robert's office. Once she arrives, she finds Robert at his desk, continuing the work he has not stopped. When he sees Mia, he asks, excitedly what Gabriel had to say. She tells him, "He doubts the information we have given him and wants us to focus on hacking attempts to our system." Robert is also let down. He thought Gabriel would go through the roof with excitement.

Meanwhile, Gabriel calls Dan. "Hello Gabriel," Dan says.

"Hello, Dan," Gabriel says.

"What's up?" Dan says.

Gabriel says, "Well, my team has more information, I have been remiss in giving you all that we have found. I want to talk to you. Can we meet again?" Dan says he will come to Gabriel's office.

Gabe pulls up to Rai's driveway and walks up to her door, knocks, and she opens the door. She greets him with a hug and a kiss on the cheek. After their divorce, they've continued a close relationship since they decided to split years ago. At the time, Gabe had gotten the offer to run the T.S.N., and Rai had just started her new position at Rural Community. While they cared for each other, each wanted to pursue their career, and they thought divorce was better than trying to maintain a long-distance relationship. They each figured if it was meant to be, it was meant to be. They did decide to set aside a date night once a month, and tonight was that night. They got into Gabe's car and drove to their favorite Italian restaurant. As they drove, they talked about Sophie and what was going on in her life. Once they arrived and were seated, Gabe asked Rai how things were going at work. Rai says. "Well, I think I have that contractor straightened out, the one that didn't want to follow the new regulations for septic tanks."

Gabe says, "That's great!" Gabe knew that Rai was extremely passionate about the environment and taking the new position in her company, while not directly in the field, she was able to affect more change as it related to new construction. Rai figured if she wasn't able to stop the growth, she would do all she could to make sure that companies would be held accountable for every step in the process. Rai asks Gabe how his job is going and Gabe replies, "Strange."

Rai says, "Oh, why?"

"Well," Gabe says, "The signal I told you about, we keep getting it, and now, as of this morning, it has changed. My team is working on deciphering what it says now."

Rai asks, "How did your talk with Dan go?"

Gabe says, "It went great. He held his cards close at first, but eventually he said they had gotten a signal about the same time we did, only they've not been able to decode and decipher it, but we have."

Rai, shocked, says, "What!"

Gabe says, "Yep, we figured it out, and what it says is crazy and ridiculous."

Rai asks, "Well, what does it say?"

Gabe says, "Messiah, but it was originally in an old Hebrew text. Mia was able to translate it, roughly, to English."

Rai says, "Where is it coming from?"

Gabe says, "My team says Proxima Centauri, but I am sure it's a hack job."

She asks, "Why?"

Gabe says, "It's just too crazy."

Rai says, "Gabe, for as long as I've known you, you've always been a dreamer, you've always looked up at the stars and wondered, is there life out there." She continued, "Do you remember laying on the beach at night, when we were both much younger, and how you would point the stars out to me, and then you would point out the planets and even the galaxies?" Rai finished by saying, "Gabe, just don't forget that part of you." As they finished their meals and Gabe paid, he asked if it was an early night or if she was coming back to his place.

Rai said, "Let's go back to your place, it's been a while."

The next morning Gabriel walks into his office and says good morning to Bobbie. He says, "Please clear my schedule this morning, Dan Henry will be driving down and should be here in about half an hour."

When Dan arrives, Gabriel says, "Good morning Dan, come on in."

Dan enters, and they take a seat at the round table where Gabriel and his team had been working to figure out what the data meant. Dan is looking around at the mess of paper and the information on the white erase board. Gabriel had left everything in place. Dan starts by saying, "Gabriel, my team tracked the signal to Proxima Centauri." Gabriel confirmed that his team had tracked it to the same place. Dan continues to say, "While we don't know what the message is, I did sit down with a team of physicists and my communications team to ask them, hypothetically, how you could communicate from such a distance quickly." Dan pulls out a notebook and says, "They came up with a couple of possibilities, entangled photons that involved tachyon particles, essentially creating a message on one end and creating a twin at the other end of that message. Or, using tachyon particles to travel faster than light, and finally using wormholes to send a message. Again, this was all hypothetical."

Gabriel said, "Well, here is what we have come up with…we developed an algorithm, and eventually, Mia was able to decipher the code. It was an old form of Hebrew." Dan was shocked that they had been able to crack the code. He had met Mia a few times and was impressed with her, and he was kicking himself for not trying to entice her to come to HETI. Gabriel continued, "We came up with one word, Mashiach or translated, Messiah."

Dan sits in silence, running the information around in his head. Finally, he says, "What do you think of it, Gabriel?"

Gabriel says, "I think we've been hacked."

Dan, silent again, finally says, "That has to be it, the alternative is impossible."

Chapter 2

Rai is driving to a spot on the coast where she has been working with the school system to teach school kids about the importance of our role in taking care of the environment. She had been volunteering for an ecological restoration company for many years. She was currently working with the kids in the classroom as well as in the field where they were removing invasive plants and replacing them with locally appropriate plants. When she arrived at the site, she was heartsick and appalled by what she was seeing. She walked out to the beach where eight pacific dolphins had stranded themselves. The kids had just arrived, and they were distraught by what they were seeing. She called the authorities in the area to help them. Meanwhile, she and the kids were trying to keep the dolphins wet by pouring water on them. She could tell that they were getting weaker and that something had to happen soon.

About an hour later a team of people pulled up, but it was too late. All the dolphins had died from the exposure to the sun. The kids were upset...some of the kids were even crying, so Rai tried to make this a teaching moment. She was explaining to them that the oceans of the world were dying because of climate change and the rise of CO_2 in our atmosphere. She told them that the ice caps had been melting for over a decade and they were melting faster than anyone thought possible...this was altering currents in the oceans and causing the oceans to rise as well. She told them that fresh drinking water in some countries was almost nonexistent and that people were forced to buy water from other countries just to survive.

After lunch she finally took the kids to their site they had been working on and she could see a renewed vigor in their work. She thought to herself, 'Maybe I am making a difference in this world after all.'

Gabriel sits in his office. Dan has left so he is alone. As he looks over the pages of data and all the information on the board, he decides to leave for the day. He walks out and stops to tell Bobbie that he is leaving and he will be back tomorrow.

Later he finds himself on his back porch at home, overlooking the California desert. As he drinks his iced tea, he reflects on his conversation with Rai, and for the first time, he allows himself to at least be open to the possibility that this could be real. The signal could be real and there could be life on another planet. The thought was almost too much for him to comprehend. If it is real, it will change the world as we know it. Also, the message itself is perplexing and the language used…again; he couldn't make sense of it. Maybe Messiah in their language means something else? Maybe it means friend or enemy? But, if it translated to their form of Hebrew, it would tip the entire world over. Gabriel had been agnostic all his life; this would force him to rethink that. He walks into his home and starts to move some things around in a drawer. The television is on; and he overhears the reporter talking to the news anchor. The reporter continues, "Yes that's right Jill, sea levels have risen to new heights and are forcing many resorts here to close their doors for good."Finally, he finds it, Rai's old bible. She has been a Christian all of her life, or at least as long as he'd known her. It was and is a continual point of contention in their relationship. Gabriel hears the news anchor again; this diverts his attention again. Jill says, "Today the Prime Minister of Canada was announcing new rules on the exportation of water to other countries,"-cut to the Prime Minister at a news conference, "We will be adding an additional tariff on the exportation of our fresh water supply. I understand that there is a water crisis happening around the world, but I would not be putting our country first if I didn't try to bring us out of our national debt and this is the most logical way to do it." Rai had stopped trying to make a believer out of him a while ago. He opens the bible and looks for the New Testament. Mathew 1-This is the genealogy of Jesus the Messiah, the Son of David, the son of Abraham. He read for about an hour then Sophie called and said she had some news and wanted to have dinner with Rai and him. They make arrangements to meet the next evening at the Italian eatery in town.

The next Morning, Gabriel walks into his office after saying good morning to Bobbie. He takes a seat at his desk and picks up his phone and calls Mia. He asks Mia to meet with him when she has some time. About 45 minutes later she knocks on his door, and he says come in. She enters, and each says good morning. Mia says, "Why did you leave early the day before?"

Gabriel says, "I had a meeting with Dan from HETI yesterday." Gabriel continues, "He drove down, and we divulged to each other what information we had on the signal, He has met with some experts on physics and communication, and they came up with some hypothetical ways for long distance faster than light to communicate, and I gave him the information we had."

Mia says, "What, why did you do that?"

Gabriel says, "Because it's the right thing to do, Mia. I am tired of secrecy and worrying about who's going to publish a paper first."

Mia is slightly confused and asks, "What are you talking about Gabriel?" Mia continues, "If you think we are just being hacked, then what paper is anyone going to publish?"

Gabriel says, "I had dinner with Rai, and we had a long conversation, about the signal and she reminded me of how adventurous I used to be, about how I used to appreciate the stars above."

Mia leans forward and says, "Go on."

Gabriel says, "I left yesterday, and I went to my home; I just sat in silence on my back porch. I can't tell you the last time I did that."

Mia says, "So, what revelation did you have on your back porch, Gabriel?"

Gabriel says, "There wasn't a revelation, maybe just time to give myself permission to wonder again." Gabriel continues, "Mia, the reason I asked you to meet me, is I wanted to ask you a question, and that is, what if this signal is real? What if there is life on another planet?"

Mia says, "Gabriel, I've been wondering that since we received the signal. I think it is going to turn this world upside down."

Gabriel says, "Ok, I agree, and that was the first thing I thought about too, but then, I took it a step further. The fact that there could be life on another planet is crazy enough, but then factor in the message itself. If you have translated it correctly and the message says Messiah, imagine what that means. Not only could there be life on another planet but they must have a similar society."

Mia had not let herself consider much past life on another planet and the ramifications of that. Gabriel says, "I think I would like to call Dan, can you stick around?"

"Sure," Mia says.

Gabriel calls Dan at HETI, "Hello Dan," Gabriel says, "It's me Gabriel, and I have Mia with me here on speaker."

Dan says, "Hello, how are you both? What can I do for you?"

Gabriel says, "First I wanted to see if you all have made any progress."

Just then, Robert comes into Gabriel's office and says "Mia, I have an update on the most recent message we have received. We used your cipher and finally figured it out. It is Moshia."

Mia thinks about it and says "It means Deliverer or it could mean Savior, which is a common translation in the bible."

Gabriel and Mia are at a loss for words. Finally, Dan says, "Guys, I don't know what to say other than, I think we need to work together on figuring out who is doing this. I am proposing that both facilities eliminate any way for an outside entity to infiltrate our systems. I am proposing that we take our systems offline."

Gabriel finally takes his eyes off the desk in front of him and looks at the phone and says, "I agree, it will take the question of hacking out of the equation."

Robert is still in the room, so Mia asks him, "Robert, what do you need to sever the connection and take us offline so we are picking up all signals via our system and computing independently?"

Robert says, "I need another 500 terabytes, and I have a few programs I'll need to download that I normally run through a separate server off-site."

Mia says, "Ok, get it done."

Gabriel says, "Dan, have you thought about this past the possibility of our facilities being hacked?"

Dan says, "Briefly Gabriel, but it is a bit overwhelming to think about it. I mean the possibility of life on another planet, the ramifications of that, I have no idea how the nations of this world would respond. But let's not get ahead of ourselves. Let's see what happens once our systems are off line."

Gabriel says, "Sounds like a good plan; I am so thankful for your input and collaboration on this, thank you, Dan."

Dan is a little taken aback by this approach by Gabriel. While he considered him more than just a colleague, he usually had his guard up when talking "shop" with him; he knew that he was usually looking for the next paper to publish. He didn't blame him, most everyone in this field was the same way, even Dan himself used to be driven the same way, but he was in the golden years of his career and wasn't as worried about that stuff anymore. "Mia, let's get going on this plan and let me know when we are ready to sever our connection and go offline." Dan says, "Gabriel, let me know when that happens, and I'll let you know when we do the same."

After saying goodbye, both parties hang up the line. Dan calls Annbella Smith, his Astrobiologist. She answers and Dan says, "Hello Ann, I just got off the phone with the folks at TSN, We have agreed to sever all online connections and run independently. Can you please talk to the techs and make all of this happen?"

Ann says, "Sure thing, any other news?"

Dan says, "As a matter of fact, while I was on the phone with them, their senior data technician interrupted the call and said they had decoded the last signal. They said it was Moshia which translated means Deliverer or Savior."

Ann says, "Dan, what do you think? Who do you think is doing this?"

Dan says, "No idea, but we need to eliminate this crazy notion that the signal is authentic. So, please get the lines disconnected and our systems running independently."

Ann says, "I will get right on it." Each says goodbye and hangs up.

∞

Gabriel's phone rings. He and Mia are still talking after their call with Dan.

"Gabe" Rai says, "Would you be able to come over tonight?"

Gabe says, "Sure, what's up?"Yet as he was saying it, he realized something was wrong. He knew her tone, and this tone was serious. Gabe says, "I'll be there around seven o'clock this evening if that's ok?"

Rai says, "Sounds good; I'll see you then, bye."

Annbella Smith, a woman around forty years of age, is married with two teenage kids. She has worked at HETI for four years and is currently an astrobiologist. As she hung up the phone with Dan, she picked it back up and called her I.T. guy and talked to him about what Dan wanted done. She hung up the phone and pulled out the data that they had for tracking the signal. She knew the signal (if real) was coming from Proxima Centauri and that the yellow dwarf star was not charted yet, She thought to herself, "How had they missed this star? She recalled though another close star that had just been discovered because of a perfect alignment of the asteroid belt, different stars and planets that obscured earth's view of it." She wanted to learn more about it. She knew that back in 2017-2018, there were about twenty newly discovered stars and that most of them had a rocky planet orbiting them. Over the decade that has passed, they found that few had enough or any oxygen to sustain life. So she decides to contact Rashad over at The American Space Agency (T.A.S.A.) who oversaw the exoplanet exploration program. She makes a quick call back to Dan and informs him of her plan, and he gives her the ok.

Gabe arrives at Rai's home and knocks on her door. She answers the door and is visibly upset. He hugs her and sees Sophie seated in the kitchen. He walks in, and Sophie stands and gives him a long hug. Rai asks him to sit down. Sophie begins, "Dad, I've not been feeling well, and I told mom about it. She asked me to see a doctor, and I did. Dad, they ran some tests and found that I have stage three cervical cancer."

Gabe is typically a very analytical man showing little emotion. However, nothing can prepare you for this. Hearing that your child has cancer. His response was typical, "Are you sure? Should you get a second opinion?"

Sophie responds, "Daddy, I can do that, but my doctor says time is of the essence and that I need to start treatment as soon as possible…that if I start soon, I have a good chance of beating it."

Gabe, silent again for a minute finally hugs her again. Gabe says, "Baby girl, we will get through this. Anything you need, just say the word. Rides to the hospital, meals, whatever you need."

Just then, the doorbell rang. Rai answers the door, and It is Hayden. He is greeted and welcomed in by Rai. When Gabe sees who it is, he is a little miffed. "What was he doing here?" he asked himself. This was a family matter.

Sophie and Hayden hugged and turned towards Gabe. Hayden says, "Mr. Dane, it is great to see you again." Gabe stuck out his hand, and the two shook hands. Sophie stepped up towards each of them and then stood next to Hayden. Sophie says, "Dad, I need to tell you something else, Hayden asked me to marry him and I said yes."

Gabe says, "Oh, Oh, Ok," Turning to Hayden Gabe asks, "When did your propose?"

Hayden says, "A few days ago, but sir, it was before we knew her diagnosis, I don't want you to think this is a pity proposal. I love Sophie and I want us to spend the rest of our lives together. I am hoping you'll give us your blessing."

Gabe turned to Rai, she simply walked up and hugged him, he realized he needed to be there for her, this must be killing her and now was not the time to act all high and mighty. He needed to be the man she needed. Gabe says, "Can we talk?"

Rai says, "Sure." and they went to her back patio where she had a small pool. They stood arms around each other.

Gabe sighed and said, "So much to take in, I am honestly happy for them. I am scared to death of losing her, but she is a big girl, and I need to let her live her life."

Rai pulls him closer. Rai says, "Where has this man been all of this time?"

Gabe says, "Rai, there is so much going on right now. To be honest, I am struggling with what might be true because if it is, I have so many things to rethink."

Rai says, "What is going on?"

Gabe says, "Another time honey, I think we need to be there for Sophie right now." Gabe turns and pulls her to him and looks into her eyes and says, "Rai, I need you to hear me, I mean really hear me, I love you." Rai, kissed him, deeply, they kissed as they had all those years ago when they were much younger.

They separated and walked into the house and sat with Sophie and Hayden in the living room. Sophie started, "Dad, I so appreciate you being here and offering all your help and I am sure I will need you, but Hayden will be helping me through treatment."

Gabe simply says "Ok, so when do you start treatment?"

Sophie says, "Monday morning I go in for my first chemo treatment. Hayden will be driving me home, but if you want to meet me at my house later, I would love that."

Gabe walks up and shakes Hayden's hand and says, "Please take care of her." He then walks up to Sophie and hugs her, and after a moment of silence between them he says, "It will be ok baby; it is in God's hands." He kisses Rai goodbye and leaves. If he had looked back as he left, he would have seen the two women he loved most in this world standing in absolute shock. They had never ever heard him even once refer to God. Rai made a mental note to talk to Gabe and see what was going on; this was a different Gabriel than she'd ever known, so connected and expressive of his emotions. She hugged Sophie and Hayden, and they left as well.

∞

Annbella was talking to Rashad about learning more about the newly found dwarf star in the Proxima Centauri sector. She was seated next to him in his office. Rashad Basak was an Indian

American whose parents moved to America before he was born. He was a handsome man and very intelligent and was a post-doctoral research fellow at TASA. They were sitting in front of three oversized monitors that were interconnected so you could move things from one monitor to another. Ann says, "Ok what are we looking at here?"

Rashad says, "Well, these are Hubble and James Webb telescope images with some of the highest pixel count you can get. I'll need the coordinates for the new star."

She pulls a file from her bag and opens it to the pages she needed. "Here you go," she says.

As he is entering the information into the program she looks at her phone to see some of the texts she had gotten while talking to Rashad; she sees that Dan had texted her and wanted her to call when she could. Rashad says, "Ok, the information has been entered, so we need to let the program work. I requested a few months of images; it will help us determine a few things about the star." Just then, the first of the images becomes clear on the middle screen. It looks like any other star she has seen. Rashad loads a month's worth of the same image, and It begins to play like a slow video. She and Rashad are watching, and he says, "There! Do you see it?"He replays it, and then she sees the star move, just a tiny bit.

She says, "Yes, I do, it moved." Rashad says, "Yes, that's a wobble, it's from the gravity of another body orbiting around the star that makes the star move just a tiny bit."Ann says, "So you are saying?"

Rashad says, "There is most likely a planet or planets in orbit around this star."

Ann is excited about the information; she thanks Rashad and promises to stay in touch and leaves. She calls Dan on her way to her car. Dan says, "Hey Ann, any news from the I.T. guys?

Ann says, "Sorry, I've been meeting with Rashad and have some news. I'll get with them as soon as I get back."

Dan says, "Ok thanks, what's the news?"

Ann says, "Well, the star we've discovered has a wobble, meaning…"but Dan interrupts her and finishes her sentence and says, "There's a planet orbiting."

Ann says, "Yes, there probably is."

Dan says, "Ok, stop in when you get back, and we can talk some more. Are you ok if I talk to Gabriel about your findings?"

"No problem," Ann says.

Gabriel arrives at work and walks past Bobbie without saying his usual good morning, so Bobbie follows him into his office. Bobbie has worked for Gabriel for about five years, and she knows him well, enough to know something is very wrong. Bobbie says, "Gabriel, are you ok?"

Gabriel replies, "Not really, it's Sophie, she has stage 3 cervical cancer."

Bobbie is knocked back and sits down. She has tears almost instantly. Bobbie says, "Gabriel, I'm so sorry."She stands and starts to walk towards him, but he moves behind his desk. He is one not to mix business and pleasure, but then, realizes maybe she needs some sort of comfort. She has known Sophie awhile, and this must be horrible news for her, so he walks back around the desk towards her and hugs her. Bobbie needed this comfort, although she thought she was comforting Gabriel, then she realizes this was probably the second time in the five years she's known him that he has hugged her. Something is different about him. They separated, and Bobbie says, "If there is anything you all need, just let me know."

Gabriel says, "Thank you, Bobbie. I think we are good for now, but if you could keep this between us, I would appreciate it."

Bobbie says, "Not a problem" and leaves his office.

Gabriel sits down and calls Mia. "Hello Gabriel," Mia says, "How are you?"

Gabriel says, "Ok, I wanted to check in and see how we are progressing with the disconnect."

Mia replies, "I think we are going offline at 10:00 this morning."

Gabriel says, "Ok, I'll be downstairs at 10:00."

Gabriel calls Dan and tells him they are going offline at 10:00. Dan says, "Ok, I think we are about to sever our connection in about an hour."

Gabriel says, "Ok let's stay in touch." Gabriel agrees, and they hang up. Meanwhile, Gabriel calls Rai to check on her. Rai answers the phone, "Hello?"

Gabriel says, "Hello, how are you holding up?"

Rai says, "All things considered, I am ok." Rai continues, "I am glad you called, I was wondering if we could have dinner tonight?"

Gabriel replies, "Sure, I would love to. Seven o'clock tonight, I'll pick you up then?"

Rai says, "Sounds good; I will see you tonight at seven"

Gabriel walks downstairs and finds Mia and Robert. Robert is at his computer and looks at both Mia and Gabriel and says, "Ok, we are ready."

Mia looks at Gabriel, and he nods, Mia says, "Ok, take us offline."

Robert punches a few keys and sits back, he watches the program and says "Everything is working; it will just be a matter of time now."

Dan calls Gabriel and says, "Gabriel we are offline, how about you?"

Gabriel replies, "Just now."

Dan says, "Ok, stay in touch."

"Will do," Gabriel says.

Chapter 3

Everyone had waited for about 30 minutes at their respective facilities with Gabriel and Dan calling each other a few times, eventually agreeing to contact each other if anything happened. Gabe decided he would go home and get ready to meet Rai, so he said goodbye to everyone and told them to call him immediately if anything happens. Mia said she would, and Gabriel left. Eventually, everyone followed suit except for Robert and Mia, but even Mia left 30 minutes later. Robert sat looking through his phone and occasionally looking up at the monitor only to see a blank screen.

Mia arrives home and was greeted by her husband and her son. He had made dinner, and they sat down for, as of lately, a rare dinner together because she had been working so many hours. Mia looks at Santos and says, "Thank you so much for putting up with these crazy hours and picking up the slack. Dinner is delicious."

Santos says, "No problem sweetheart, so what's going on at work?"She tells him more about the signal they've been getting lately and how they just cut the connection to the server, and now they are waiting to see if the signal continues…if it doesn't then it means we were being hacked, and if not…she sighed. Santos was able to put the pieces together and was nervous about the idea of it being a true signal from some far away world. After cleaning the dishes, her son ran in and asked if they could watch a movie, she said sure, and they settled in for a family movie night.

A tall, slim, dark-skinned woman with long, jet black hair walks into the room where her husband is seated in front of a large screen. As she walks up, she places her hand on his shoulder and says "Hello husband."

Abarron replies, "Hello Liala."

She asks, "Will you be finished soon?"

Abarron replies, "Yes my love, the system is just about to come back online; I will send the next message and then let the system rest until tomorrow. He types in Mefalti, flips a large switch on a council and then presses a key on the board in front of him. He waits until the system builds up the energy and the message sends. He is still amazed at the amount of energy needed to send the message. He stands and wraps his arm around his wife's waist, and they exit the room.

∞

Gabe arrives at Rai's home at seven o'clock and walks up to her door; she greets him there. They leave for the restaurant. While driving, Gabe asks how Sophie is doing today, she says, "Ok." She tells him that the school she was teaching at was willing to work with her and her medical leave and would hold her job if needed. Gabe is happy about that.

They arrive at the restaurant, and they are seated. It is one of the regular places they go. The waitress asks for their drink order. Gabe asks for a bottle of red wine. The waitress brings it and pours a small amount in a glass. Gabe tastes it and nods, so the waitress pours them both a glass and they order their food. After the waitress leaves, Rai reaches across and takes Gabe's hand - this gets his attention, and he looks into her eyes. Rai says, "Gabe, tell me what's going on."

Gabe replies, "Um, my daughter is sick, and she is engaged?"

Rai says, "No, with you, what is going on with you? The way you have been acting, the way you responded, to…everything, was so out of character for you. So, what is going on with you?"

Gabe sits quietly for a minute; then, starts talking. "Well, you know the signal we've been getting at work? It has not stopped, and the message changed. It is still possible that we were hacked, but, I am having serious doubts about that. We have had some of the best I.T. guys in the state of California looking into this, and they've not found anything, not even a virus in our system. My gut tells me it is real. I can't shake this, it is on my mind a lot Rai, I know this sounds crazy, but I think another world has contacted us."

Rai is calm but quiet; she is processing the idea and then says, "That is incredible."

Gabe says, "Rai, it is not only that, but the fact that we were able to decode and translate the messages. It is Messiah and Savior."

Rai says, "Messiah, Really? Messiah?" Gabe nodes yes. Rai says, "Wait, are you sure that it is a literal translation?"

"That is not something I'm sure about, but if it is, do you know what that could mean?"

Rai says, "Yes I do."

Gabe says, "I've also been thinking about my life and the decisions I have made, were they the right ones?" Gabe waits and then says, "Anyhow, we've severed our connections to our server and any outside lines, and we are running on just our internal systems. We are waiting to see if the signal continues or if it stops."

Rai asks, "How long has it been? And when was the last signal?"

Gabe says, "We cut it at about ten o'clock this morning and haven't seen any signal since."

Rai says, "Oh, well there you go, it was a hack job then."

Gabe says, "We will see, I am not giving up yet. You have to remember that our processing power is much slower now that we aren't using external computing power."

They finish their meal and decide to go back to Gabe's house. Just as he pulls into his driveway, he gets a call. He sees that it is Mia and he answers it. Mia says, "Gabriel, we have a signal."

Gabriel says, "Ok, I will be there in a bit, but Rai will be with me," he hangs up his phone. He looks at Rai; he has tears in his eyes. She's only seen him like this twice before, once when they got married and then again when Sophie was born. Nothing was said, she reaches up and caresses his cheek, and he shifts the car into reverse, and they head to TSN.

While in route to TSN Gabe calls Dan. Dan answers, "Gabriel, I was just about to call you."

Gabe says, "We have a signal, do you?"

Dan says, "Yes we do."

Gabe replies, "Ok, I will call you once I get there and see what is going on." They hang up.

Gabriel and Rai arrive at TSN and rush into the large control center. Mai and Robert say hello. Mia and Rai hug saying it had been a long time. Gabriel walks up to the large screen that Robert was working at and there it was, just like before.

Mashiach

Moshia

Gabriel stands there for a moment, and then finally says, "You're sure we are completely disconnected from any external sources to our system?"

Robert replies, "Yes sir, I am sure."

Gabriel steps away and calls Dan. Dan answers, "Hello Gabriel, I am at HETI, and I am looking at the same two messages we have been seeing."

Gabriel replies, "We are looking at the same thing."

Dan says, "Ok, look...first off, we need to treat this as highly classified. Up until now, I had serious doubts about this signal, but now I can't deny what I am seeing. Can you bring your team here to Mountain View in the morning? We need to put our minds together and decide how to move forward."

Gabe says, "Absolutely."

Each says goodbye and hangs up. Gabriel looks at everyone and informs Mia and Robert that the three of them would be driving up to Mountain View where the Hunt for Extraterrestrial Intelligence (HETI) facility was located. It made sense because it was a bigger facility and had ties with TASA. Gabe also says, "One more thing, from here on out, this is highly classified, and we should not be talking to anyone about it."

Gabe turns to Rai and says, "Sorry I will have to take you home." He turns to Robert and Mia, shakes Robert's hand and thanks him for all his work. Then he hugs Mia and thanks her as well. Gabe turns and says goodbye to them and tells them that he will see them in the morning and that he will drive them to Mountain View.

He takes Rai by the hand and walks out with her. As they get into the car he says he will take her home. Rai says, "Gabe, I would like to spend the night with you if that is ok?"

Gabe hesitates. He knew that there were some things he needed to learn about what is right and wrong according to the Bible; he had gotten married to Rai in a church and exchanged vows, but they were divorced. In Gabe's heart though he had never stopped loving Rai and he thought God knew that. So, his reply was simply a caress on her face. He started his car, and they drove to his home. When they got home, Gabe asked his smart system to play Dave Mathews. Rai looks at him with a smile and says, "Vintage stuff?"

Gabe replies, "It's still our band, right?"

Rai grabs him, and they hold each other, just standing there. Rai says, "I still love his live stuff."Eventually, a slow dance between them starts, just holding each other, rocking back and forth. It was unlike anything they had experienced before. Gabe knew this was the woman he would love until the day he died. She was his everything. At this moment he never wanted to let her go, he wanted to melt into her and become one person. They continued to touch and caress each other with the lightest of touches, almost a tickle. He pulled away from her and began to undress her; slowly he lifted her shirt, and she raised her arms to assist, he knelt and began to lower her skirt, he stood and ran his eyes over his beautiful bride, he had never stopped thinking of her that way.

Rai began the same process with him. He pulled her to him and again they just held each other with their flesh pressing into each other. It was less sexual and more about their love for one another…it was like nothing they had known until now. She pulled away and looked up at Gabe and pulled his face down to hers; they kissed deeply and passionately like it was their first kiss. They moved to his bed where they made love as they had never done before, each just trying to get closer to the other, holding tighter, nothing but love in each kiss, until they finally released their love. They lay wrapped up with each other, tied in a knot, each telling the other how much they loved the other. Gabe thought about why this was so special, and he realized that he felt the presence of God.This whole time he could feel God's love present between them. It was so much more meaningful than he ever thought possible, then they fell into a deeper sleep than either had gotten in years.

The next morning it was early, but Gabe was already showered and dressed and ready to leave. He sat on the bed where Rai was still sleeping. He sat there for a minute, then leaned down and kissed her cheek. She woke slowly realizing Gabe had kissed her, and a smile spread across her face. Gabe handed her a key and told her to keep it. Gabe says, "Stay as long as you want baby. I would love to see you again tonight."

Rai just smiled and said, "I would love that."

Gabe says, "Great...I will let you know when we are on our way back."

As Gabe left, he stopped and looked back at her saying, "Rai, I love you"

Rai was so happy at hearing those words and replied, "I love you too, Gabe."

∞

Gabriel arrives at TSN just as Bobbie was arriving. Bobbie walks up and says, "Good morning Gabriel, here early aren't you?"

Gabe replies, "Yes, Mia, Robert and I are heading to a meeting. Could you please reschedule any meetings I have today?"

Bobbie replies, "Sure thing boss."

Gabriel and Bobbie walk inside together, and Bobbie heads upstairs. Gabriel heads to the control room where he finds Mia and Robert. Gabriel says, "Good morning, are you all ready?" Both reply yes and they walk to Gabriel's car. Gabriel says, "I got gas this morning and Donuts and coffee if anyone wants some."

They say "Great!"They each take a donut and a cup of coffee and with that Gabriel pulls out of his space and begins the drive to Mountain View. For awhile, there was little talking, but as the coffee started to take effect, they started to talk about all of the events taking shape over the last few weeks. Gabriel asks them both, "So, what are your thoughts on God?"

Mia replies, "Gabriel, I've been thinking about this. I am not convinced that these messages are what you think they are. I mean, yes it's amazing that we are getting messages from another world, but that they have a messiah and that it has anything to do with the one that our world knows is a million to one chance and by the way, to answer your question, I am a Christian, but I am realistic as well."

Robert speaks up saying, "I am Mormon and this whole thing is just crazy; I mean, we are talking about getting messages from another world! Why would that be their first messages to us or anyone?"

Gabe listened and calmly said, "I have no answers, but for the first time in my life I am going with my gut, and It says they know God."

Finally, they pull up to the HETI gate and given access inside. They pull up to a large building and park. Dan walks outside hurriedly, and greets them stating, "Come inside; we have something to show you." The four of them walk into a large control room with many screens; some are at least eight to ten feet long. As they walk in, they see it right away. The word,

Ahavah

Gabriel looks over at Mia with a look of a question; she looks at the word and thinks for a minute and then says, "God's love for his people."

Dan says, "Very good Mia, we got it about an hour ago."

Annbella walks up and says hello to the group along with Rashad, who Dan introduces to the group. Dan starts to walk and tells everyone to follow him to their meeting room just off their control room. Once inside Dan says, "I had refreshments and snacks brought in; please help yourself; we will be in here for awhile."

Everyone gets a drink, and something to snack on and Dan finally asks everyone for their attention. He turns on the large monitor that is mounted to the wall and has the protocol that they were all familiar with; it was the Declaration of Principles Concerning the Conduct of the Hunt for Extraterrestrial Intelligence. Dan says, "Just to get us all on the same page we have been getting three different messages repeated every 22 hours. This message is coming from the Proxima Centauri area, but it is a different star. We need to name it and would like Gabriel to do that since his team caught the message first."

Gabriel looks at his team and says, "Mia, what is Hebrew for God?"

She says, "Yahweh."

Gabriel Looks at Dan and says, "Yahweh Centauri."

Dan says, "Very well we will refer to this star as Y.C.1." Dan continues, "Ok, next on the list, I will be contacting Washington D.C. to inform Benjamin Williams, the current TASA Administrator, that we have confirmed contact from the newly named Y.C.1 star and a yet to be named planet. My assistant is attempting to conference him in when he gets a hold of him. Until then, we should continue. Next, on the agenda, I would like Rashad and Robert, with your approval Gabriel, to work together and head up a task force to isolate their means of communication to see if we can replicate it and send a signal back. As it is, even if we send a message today it would take about five years traveling at the speed of light to get a message to them."Gabriel says he is fine with them working together on it. Dan continues, "Ann, I would like to learn as much as we can about this region of space. Why haven't we detected this star before? What do you think you would need to accomplish this?"

Ann Says, "Honestly, I would like to partner with Rashad on this as well."

Dan says, "Rashad, what are your thoughts?"

Rashad replies, "Sir, I can do both. It might be good for the three of us to work together on both tasks."

Dan says, "Very well, I like the idea. Gabriel, what are your thoughts?"

Gabriel says, "I think it's a great idea, we can make our facility available or Robert can work here if needed."

Dan says, "Ok, great, we can work out the details later." Dan continues to say, "Ok, next we ha..." but before he could finish his sentence, his assistant had entered the room and started to tell Dan that Dr. Williams from D.C. was on the phone. Dan reached down, turned the speaker phone on and said, "Hello Ben, I mean Dr. Williams."

Benjamin and Dan had gone to school together and were old friends. It was a time like this where Dan needed to show respect for Ben's position. Dan says, "Sir, I am here with a team of people from both the HETI facility and the TSN facility. I have you on speaker phone right now. I need to tell you of a series of events and wanted to do it with all of these folks in the room because they are the ones that have done the work and will be able to answer your questions."

Ben says, "Hello Dan and everyone else in the room, what is this all about?"

Dan starts, "Well, honestly, I would first like to introduce you to Gabriel Dane, the director of the TSN."

Gabriel says, "Hello sir, actually we met at a conference a few years ago."

Ben says, "Yes I remember, it is great to talk to you again."

Dan says, "Gabriel, can you start with the series of events that have taken place at the TSN and then I'll pick it up from the time you contacted me?"

Gabriel says, "Sure, so a few weeks ago, the team at TSN detected a signal that repeated every 22 hours. We were pretty sure that our system had been hacked, so I directed my team to track who was infiltrating our system. After a few days, we were able to start to decipher the code thanks to Mia Russo my Deputy Director, a renowned linguist, who was able to begin a rough translation and determine it was an ancient form of Hebrew. The first message was Mashiach or translated to Messiah. At this point, we were all very confused, why would someone hack our system only to deliver this message? So, I was worried we had missed some sort of Trojan horse virus; and I had one of the best I.T. consultants in the state come in and examine our entire system only to find nothing. At this point, I decided to call Dan and see if he had anything like this happening at his facility."

Dan spoke, "Ben, Gabriel and I met and had several discussions about what each facility was experiencing; ultimately, we each decided to begin the process of taking our systems offline, which meant acquiring massive amounts of memory and downloading programs that are traditionally run offsite. Once we did that, we had silence for almost 10 hours. Then it started again. We started getting signals - all offline - with no way for anyone to send us data except for the designation of space that our team said the signal was coming from. Since the first message, we have also gotten two other messages. The second message translated to 'Deliverer,' and the third was 'God's love for his people'. The signal is coming from space, Ben, and the area is Proxima Centauri. Ben, Gabriel and I agree that this signal is authentic; another world has contacted us. I declared this highly classified and the only people who know this are in this room."

Ben sat in silence for a while, trying to take everything in. Finally, he spoke, "Ok, well, first, thank you for doing such a good job following protocol. I feel I need to call the president and I am sure she will want a cabinet meeting. I would plan on both you, Ben and you, Gabriel, to fly to Washington in the next day or so to give a briefing."

Ben Replies, "Ok sir, we will do that."

Ben says, "For now continue with your work and keep me updated. Once I talk to the president, I will have a better idea of when I will need you two up here. Thank you to everyone." Ben hangs up the phone.

Dan hangs up their phone and looks up at the collection of people assembled in the room. He feels good that the people here are some of the best and most uniquely qualified in their fields. He couldn't think of a better group of people to do this work.

Chapter 4

Gabriel had driven back to Barstow in the late hours of the night. He dropped everyone off at the TSN and told them he would see them in the morning. He had so many things running through his head the whole drive back; there was so much work to do, so many unanswered questions but, above all, his thoughts kept coming back to Rai. It was like a new love like they were kids again. He was leaving work, and he called her just to let her know he was leaving and would be home soon. Rai was tired but up waiting for Gabe. She had worked that day but had gone back to his place to see him after his meeting. Gabe pulled up to his house, walked in and Rai greeted him. She wore a light flowing pink gown with an Asian flair to it and her hair was still damp from her shower earlier. She handed him a glass of merlot and said, "Hello baby, how was the meeting and the drive?"

Gabe says, "The meeting was long but at least we have some direction. The drive was also long and, honestly, even with everything going on, my thoughts kept coming back to you and us. I can't explain it, but where we are now seems like a brand-new relationship but at the same time it's not."

Rai says, "I know exactly what you mean; I've been thinking about you all day."

They sat and talked for a bit longer. Then Gabe says, "By the way, I have to fly to D.C. tomorrow, just for the day. Sorry that I can't tell you more." They drank the rest of their wine then Gabe stood and said he was exhausted. He reached for her hand, and they went off to bed where they simply held each other the whole night. It was where they both knew they belonged.

The next day, Sophie had just had her first round of chemotherapy and she was getting sick. Hayden was there, and he was on the phone with Rai. "Yes, she is reacting pretty badly to the drug. The doctors say that people react differently to it and she is, unfortunately, reacting badly to it." Rai then said she was on her way anyways and would be at the Dr.'s office shortly.

After hanging up with Hayden, she called Gabe to let him know what was happening. Gabe answered the phone and Rai says, "Hey baby, I just wanted to let you know that Sophie is having a real hard time with the chemo and she is getting sick right now." Gabe said he would tell his team he needed to leave.

Rai arrived; and Gabe was there about ten minutes later. Sophie was in a chair reclined back. She was pale with sweat soaked hair. Rai was holding her hand, and Gabe was caressing her shoulder. Hayden took a step back letting her parents comfort her. Gabe looked at Hayden with a measure of more respect; he was there for his daughter, and he was happy Sophie had found someone who cared so much for her. Gabe motioned Hayden over, and Hayden took Sophie's other hand while Gabe put his hand on Hayden's shoulder. Gabe said he wanted to pray for Sophie. Rai and Sophie were both shocked but happy to pray. Gabe started as they all bowed their heads, "Lord, God, I've never done this, but I wanted to ask you to please be present in this room, be present on Sophie's journey through this sickness.Lord, please use your grace to help us all through this, thank you for bringing Hayden into our lives and for giving Sophie someone who loves her. It is in Jesus' name that I say these prayers, Amen."

As he raised his head and his eyes focused again, he could see tears running down everyone's face. He said nothing, just pulled everyone together in a big family hug. They all spent the next two hours there until Sophie was able to leave. Hayden helped her to the car, Gabe and Rai told Hayden to call if they needed anything and they pulled away. Gabe wanted so bad to be the one doing everything for her, but he knew it was their life to live and he needed to step back and let go yet still be ready to catch them if needed.

∞

Ben had hung up the phone with Dan and his team and called a few people. Eventually, he was waiting to be connected to the President of the United States. Finally, a voice came onto the phone that said, "Sir I am putting you through to the President now."There was a pause then a voice, "Hello what can I do for you?"

"Madam President, hello this is Benjamin Williams with TASA. I am calling to tell you I need to meet with you immediately. I have top secret information that you need to be aware of."

∞

Abarron was leaving a room filled with a group of people who were all seated on square white cloth on a dirt floor arranged in a circle. He walked back to his domicile where he met his wife along with his two daughters and his young son. He sat with them and shared a meal. Once finished, he talked with his wife about the next message he had been instructed to send. He then walked back to his workstation. He took a seat and started typing in the message; he then began the process of sending the message. This usually took a fair amount of time. Once the process was complete; he repeated the process as he had done before and the message was sent. He shut the machine down and went back to his family.

∞

Ben was now seated in the Oval Office; also present was the Secretary of State and one of the President's aids. Sarah Murphy was in the second year of her first term. She was as close to a moderate Republican as you could get since there had not been a truly moderate Republican since the late 1970s. She was extremely

41

smart and beautiful, especially for a woman in her 60's. She was average height about five feet seven inches and had graying red hair; you could see her Irish heritage. Having served in the Senate for twelve years, she was now proving to be a great president who reached across the aisle on many issues but stayed true to her party on the big issues. She was sometimes called a Libertarian because she was often fiscally conservative but socially liberal. The domestic situation was showing signs of improvement; and she was gaining much respect internationally as well. Ben had sat in on a few cabinet meetings and spoke to her on a couple of occasions but not privately like this; he was surprised that he was actually nervous.

Ben began telling President Sarah Murphy the events leading up to this meeting. She was attentive and engaging; he was thankful that she was able to put him at ease as he continued to explain everything. Ben was still talking, "So, as I understand it, Madam, they've currently received the three messages that I told you about. We are currently trying to figure out their method of communication so we can replicate it and return a message. They estimate that it will take five years with our current communication abilities to reply."

Sarah, just like everyone else who had heard this for the first time, sat in silence, trying to make her brain accept this as a truth. Ben could see her thoughts as they flashed through her brain and then finally, she spoke. "Thank you, Ben, for bringing this to my attention; I'm sure you'll agree it sounds like a fantastic story. Yet if you are telling me that the TSN, HETI, and TASA have all confirmed this, then I am going to have to believe you."

She turned to her aid Phil and said, "Phil, could you please cancel my meeting with the good Senator Eduard Blake and ask my full cabinet if they can convene in the cabinet room in 30 minutes. Let me know who can make it and who cannot."

Phil Says, "Right away Madam President."

Sarah turned back to Ben and asked if he would like a cup of coffee or something and he said, "That would be great."

She asked him to walk with her, and to his surprise, they walked into a kitchen on the same floor, and she began to pour him a cup of coffee. He couldn't believe he was being served a cup of coffee by the leader of the free world.

∞

Gabriel and Dan had caught a plane the next morning; Ben had his assistant arrange to have them flown to D.C., but it was the red eye, so they left that evening and had arrived in D.C. at 6:00 AM. They were met by a driver at the airport and whisked away to the nation's capital in a government vehicle. Once they arrived at the Whitehouse, they went through a metal detector and then they were searched. They were asked for their ID, and there was a quick background check done on both men as well; once they were cleared, they were escorted up to the cabinet meeting room where they were met by Ben and the President. Ben greeted the two and shook their hands. Ben then took the liberty to introduce the two of them to the President. 'Madam President I would like to introduce you to the two men responsible for detecting and decoding the messages we have received."

Sarah greeted them warmly, shaking their hands. She says, "I trust your flight was ok?" They both said yes. Sarah thanked them both for coming, and they continued into the meeting room. Once in the room, the cabinet members that could make it on such short notice stood as she entered and sat when she did. Sarah began by thanking them all for coming to the meeting then asked Gabriel and Dan to introduce themselves. Dan stood first and introduced himself, then Gabriel did the same and sat down. Sarah then asked Ben to explain why they were all there. Ben stood and went to the front of the room and began, "Ladies and gentlemen, what we are about to say must stay in this room. About two weeks ago, Dan and Gabriel's team each detected a signal; I am going to ask them to explain their findings of this signal."

Dan and Gabriel each looked at each other and Dan motioned Gabriel to start, much the same way they told Ben the whole story. Gabriel stood and began talking, "Well, about two weeks ago, my team came to me with a signal that had to have been hacked; we had some of the best people in the state come to review all of our systems and didn't even detect a virus in our systems. My team and I worked for several days, and with the help of some great people at TSN, we were able to decode and translate the message. I then contacted Dan, here, to see if they had gotten the same message." Dan stood but before he could say anything the secretary of defense asked what the message was. Gabriel looked at him and the rest of the cabinet and said, "Well, two things were odd about the message. First, once we decoded it, it was in an old style of Hebrew; luckily my Deputy Director and renowned Linguist Mia Russo was able to translate it fairly quickly. The message was translated to, Messiah."

With a hushed gasp in the room, suddenly everyone was talking to each other. Finally, Sarah asked everyone to please quiet down, and she had their attention, Sarah then said, "Please continue gentlemen."

Gabriel continued and said, "We have gotten two other messages. The first translated, Deliverer followed by a word that translates to God's love for his people."

It was now that Dan began speaking, "At this point both teams were working on triangulating the potential source of this signal, although both Gabriel and I still felt we were being hacked. Our teams came up with an undiscovered star, a yellow dwarf near Proxima Centauri and we know now that there is a potential planet orbiting this star. We are calling the star Yahweh Centauri, and It's about four and a half light years from us. Our next task was to eliminate the hacking possibility, so both facilities were outfitted with the proper programs and upgraded memory, because this is traditionally done on a different server. Once that was complete, we took all the systems offline and operated locally only. After about 12 hours, each facility started detecting the signals again and have continued to get them since then, as always, every twenty-two hours. Ladies and Gentlemen, we are here to tell you that we have confirmed a signal from another world. We are currently working on a way to communicate a signal back, but even if we sent a signal today, it would be almost five years before they got it. We are exploring other methods to speed up the signal."

Sarah stood and walked up to each of them, she shook their hands and turned to the group and asked if there were any questions. The Secretary of Defense asked, "Do you detect any hostility from these aliens?"

Dan answered, "No sir, we have not."

Then the Secretary of State asked, "Can you provide us with a list of all the people that are working on this project and what agency they are with?"

Gabriel answered, "No problem."

They waited, and there were no more questions. Sarah turned to them both and thanked them for all their work and told them that the driver would take them to their hotel for the night and then she would send a car for them to take them to the airport in the morning. The group thanked them, with pats on their back and handshakes as they made their way out of the room, and then they were left out in the hallway alone. Shortly after, a man approached them and escorted them down to the waiting car, and they were off. Gabe called Rai after they got to the hotel. Gabe asked how Sophie was. Rai says, "The chemo is not getting any easier, she's really sick, but the doctors say she needs to stay the course to kill the cells. Sophie is talking about using a holistic

45

approach, but I keep telling her that it is too risky, and she should stay on the chemo regimen. What do you think?"

Gabe says he would need to do some reading and talk to Sophie before he could comment on it. Rai asks how the meeting went. Gabe explained what he could without divulging any confidential information. Rai listened to everything that Gabe had to say; she was surprised how he had responded to her about Sophie, but she had to respect him for being supportive of Sophie. She was also still getting used to the new Gabe. He was attentive and loving but still the analytical man he's always been.

After Ben and Gabriel left the Cabinet room, Sarah went back to her seat and began speaking, "Ladies and Gentlemen, I want everyone's response, right now. I want your personal response, not your professional opinion or what you think you're supposed to say or what you think I want to hear; I want your raw response, what are you thinking?"

The group sat in silence at first; like everyone else who had heard this information, they were stunned, but finally, the Attorney General is the first to speak, and she says, "Well, I am scared and excited at the same time. Scared because we don't know what these beings are capable of, yet we are excited because if they have good intentions, imagine what we could learn from them!"

Next the Secretary of Defense William Jones spoke up saying, "Well, all I can say is, maybe we should increase the defense budget, what if they come here and try to take our planet over!"

Sarah simply sat in her chair, listening to everyone speak; they spoke of their fears and their excitement. Ultimately, people were excited to learn more about the beings who were contacting earth. She asked Julia James her Secretary of State to begin drafting talking points for the United Nations. Sarah says, "I don't plan on making this public yet and I am making this information highly classified, this is not to leave this room." She thanked them all for their time and says that they would be having a full cabinet meeting again once her aids could line up everyone's schedules.

∞

Deep inside North Korea, Young Ra-il asked, "How is the progress coming on the new installation project?"

Song Mi-hyang replied, "It is going as planned, Great Director of the Military. We have completed the final stage of excavation into the mountain, we are about to increase the pitch of the machine. It is at a steeper angle than the machine has ever gone, if successful we will go further underground than we have ever gone before, great Director of the Military."

Young Ra-il said, "Excellent Song Mi-hyang, you have done well so far. Do not disappoint me; the Dear Leader will not accept failure on this project. If you find an issue with the machine's attempt then fix it; you have an almost unlimited budget, so make it work."

∞

Gabriel and Dan had flown back the next morning and even though they had gotten some sleep they were both exhausted when they got back to California. They separated at the airport parking lot, and Gabriel began his long drive home. He was happy he could finally get back to his family and back to work. Earlier he had called Bobbie and told her that he would be taking the rest of the day off and that he would see her tomorrow. Once home, he found a note from Rai welcoming him home, that she missed him and she couldn't wait to see him tonight. Gabriel took a quick shower and put on some comfortable clothes. He was so messed up with all the travel and realized it was after lunch and that he was hungry. He made himself a sandwich and took it out to his patio to eat. He was taking a long drink of his iced tea; he was in deep thought about everything that had changed in his life in just a few short weeks. For the first time, he was reflecting on the changes that Rai was seeing in him. He was staring out at the California desert. His back patio was one of his favorite spots in the world. It was the reason he had bought the home. As he looked out, he caught a white puffy cloud trying to form just over the hills in the distance. It was a rare site especially this time of year. The sky was a bright blue; and the cloud was trying so hard to form in the desert heat. It changed shape, grew and moved further over the land. Eventually, unfortunately for the little cloud, the heat proved too much for it, and it eventually disappeared. As he reflected on this insignificant event, he thought about how that cloud paralleled himself and others as insignificant people on this planet. The cloud had potential and had it been born in a different place; it could have grown to provide needed rain on a drought-stricken area, or it could have grown to a huge storm and possibly destroyed a home and shattered a family's life. This little cloud could have also grown to provide shade for some kids playing in a park. Or a cloud could form and just as quickly fade away, seemingly having no purpose, unless someone is sitting on their back porch watching its form, needing a message from God that there are no mistakes. Everyone has a purpose, some huge, some small but still a purpose. Gabriel decided he wanted to learn more about God and Jesus. He knew a little about the Bible, but he wanted to talk to someone. He knew there was a church in town and decided he would be attending their service the coming Sunday. He decided to lie on his couch and watch a little TV.

Charles Veers, the anchor on the screen was talking about the new policy that Canada and a number of other countries were imposing - new taxes on the exportation of their water. They were raising the tariff from 5% to 25%. It was going to make this water inaccessible to many poor countries. President Sarah Murphy was on the screen chastising the Canadian Prime Minister for thinking of only themselves and not the good of the world. That was the last thing Gabriel heard. The next thing he knew, Rai was waking him up with a light kiss on his cheek. Rai says, "Hi baby, I missed you."

Gabe says, "Oh baby, I missed you so very much. What time is it?"

Rai says, "4:30, what time did you get in?"

Gabe says, "After lunch, I ate a sandwich and laid down. I guess I was more tired than I thought."

Rai says, "I brought Chinese for dinner, I hope that's ok?"

Gabe says, "That is great." They talked some more and had dinner later. Gabe couldn't remember the last time he had been so happy.

∞

Sarah is in the sitting room of the private residence of the White House. She is sitting with her husband, Timothy. He is her rock in this life; they have been married for 37 years. They had been high school sweethearts but split when she went to college, and he had gone into the Navy. They led separate lives for a while until a chance meeting at the grocery store. It just so happened that they both had just gotten out of relationships and they have been together ever since. Sarah was talking to Tim about her meeting with the cabinet. She was still reeling from it all and needed to talk to Tim. Tim was talking and says, "Well, It's a big universe out there. I think it was just a matter of time that this happened. Now, the crazy thing is, it sounds like everyone is focused on the other world part of this. I would submit that there is a bigger, deeper aspect to it all. The messages sound very familiar to our knowledge of religion here on earth. Imagine if it plays out like that, what are other countries going to do? How will they react? I think you should start thinking about that as much as the other world discovery."

Sarah responds, "Tim, you are so right, I was so focused on the first part that I wasn't even thinking that much on the implications of the content of the messages. I love you, and I am so lucky to have you in my life."

Tim says, "I love you more."It was their little saying between them. They both got up and went to the dining room to have dinner.

Chapter 5

Michelle says, "Dad, please tell Junior to pass the potatoes."

Her dad Jordan says, "Michelle, He's right next to you, ask him yourself."

Michelle Says, "I did, but he ignored me."

Jordan sighs and says, "Junior, please pass Michelle the potatoes."Junior looks at Michelle and passes her the potatoes. Jasmine asks Jordan how his most recent case is going. Jordan was a criminal defense lawyer in Atlanta, Georgia. His wife Jasmine was an accountant for a Cola Company. They lived in a nice home in Marietta, Georgia which was a little north of Atlanta. They were one of a handful of black families that lived in this neighborhood, but they had never had any problems in the area. It was a long way from where Jordan Delmar had come from. He was born to a prostitute mother, and his father was an alcoholic. They were poor; and Jordan had been all but forced to join a gang. When he was 18 years old, he got to vote for the first black president and that was when he knew he had to change his whole world. He was determined to get out of the "hood" and make something of himself. He was inspired by the new president and figured if he can be president I can at least get out of here. So, he got his GED and went to a community college where he met Jasmine. She was going to school as well but was stripping to pay her way. Jordan convinced her to stop. They both applied for some grants and took out some loans and finally got through college. They had both gotten into the University, Jordan had a law degree, and Jasmine had a B.A. in accounting. They were both smart and excelled in their careers. Their first born was Jordan Michael, III, who they called Junior, and then Michelle was born three years later. They were fortunate to have such great kids and to be able to give them the life they didn't have growing up.

∞

Junior is watching the news; the reporter is talking to the news anchor. The reporter continues, "Yes, that's right Jill, sea levels have risen to new heights and are forcing many resorts here to close their doors for good." His son walks in and says, "Dad, can I borrow the car, Lisa needs some help with her homework."His dad hesitates; Jordan knows he hasn't had his license that long so to sweeten the deal he says, "I'll take Michelle with me."

Jordan finally says ok; he knew she only lived about 2 miles away and it was residential driving and no highways. He says, "Make sure your mom knows where you two are going." Jordan tells Michelle they are going to Lisa's, and she is excited to get out of the house. His dad gives him the keys and says, "Be careful, no texting and driving and let me know when you get there and when you are leaving."Jordan says ok, and the two of them leave the house. Jordan knows his son is a responsible kid, and so is Michelle.

When Jordan gets to Lisa's house, he texts his dad telling him that they made it. The two of them knock on the door and Lisa opens it. Jordan introduces Michelle to Lisa, and the three of them enter the house. Lisa introduces the two of them to her parents, and then three of them sit at the kitchen table and begin working on their homework. Michelle brought her work as well; she figured she might as well get hers done at the same time. It was not a big deal that they were in a white family's home. Many of their friends were white, and neither Junior nor Michelle gave it a second thought. After about an hour of work, it was now nine o'clock, and they needed to get back home. They say goodbye to everyone and get in the car. Before he leaves, Jordan gets his phone out and texts his dad that they are leaving and would be back in a few minutes.

About a block into the drive, Junior sees police lights switch on and then pull in behind him. He is at a loss as to why he was being pulled over. He was being very careful about everything he was doing. He knew he wasn't speeding; he had used his signals and fully stopped at the stop sign. He pulled over and started to look for his license; he remembered his dad had said the registration was in between the seats, so he was looking around in there when the officer walked up. He backed away and said, "LET ME SEE YOUR HANDS!"Just then Junior dropped the keys on the floor, so he went to pick them up and the officer, who had already drawn his gun, shot Junior. The bullet entered the base of his skull, and he was dead instantly. Michelle was screaming, and the officer was yelling at her to get out and get on the ground. She was hysterical but finally got out and followed the officer's orders; she was handcuffed and put in the back of the police car. Once she was secured, the officer called for backup and told dispatch that shots had been fired and to send an EMT. Sixteen-year-old Jordan, III was dead. Upon investigation, they found there was no weapon and that Junior had been picking up his keys.

Jordan was getting worried; his kids should have been back by now, so he takes his wife's car and drives towards Lisa's house. Jordan sees a bunch of lights up the road and as he got closer he could clearly tell it was his car on the side of the road yet it didn't look like there had been an accident. He pulled off the road and started walking towards the police cars. At this point, he realizes there was an ambulance as well. Jordan was confused, and he had a really bad feeling about this. He told the first officer that this was his car and his kids were the ones that had been in the car. He asked, "Can you tell me what is going on?"

The officer says, "One minute, sir. I will go get my supervisor."

After a few minutes, a large black officer walked over to him and said, "Sir, I am Sergeant Coles, I have some bad news for you. Your son was driving your vehicle and was pulled over. We are still investigating the series of events, but ultimately, your son was shot in the head and was killed instantly."

It was like he had not heard what he said. Jordan took a step back and said, "Wait, where is my son? What Happened?"

Sergeant Coles again said, "Sir, your son is dead."

It took a few seconds for his brain to accept what was said…it was then that it hit him. Like someone had punched him in the stomach. He bent over and fell to the ground; he was sitting on the ground, a pain where he had never known pain before was piercing him, he didn't know you could hurt this bad. All he could do was sit there and cry. His amazing boy, who had such an amazing future ahead of him was gone, just like that, dead. Then, Jordan snapped out of it, he stood up and said, "Where is my daughter?"

Sergeant Coles says, "She is in a squad car, we will release her to you in a few minutes."

Jordan looks squarely into his eyes and says, "You will release her to me, NOW!" Something had switched inside Jordan. All the years of trying to do everything right and still something like this happens. He wanted justice, but not the kind of justice he knew, not the kind that he tried to practice every day at his job but the kind he had left behind him many years ago, he wanted street justice, an eye for an eye. He wanted to kill the person who killed his son.

Gabe and Rai were walking into the hospital. They had gotten a call from Hayden that Sophie had passed out at home. He found her on the floor when he had gotten home from work. Once they found the waiting room, they saw Hayden. He saw them, and he hurried to them. Gabe says, "Have you spoken to a doctor yet?"

Hayden said, "No."

Just then, a nurse found them and asked them to follow her. Sophie was awake but drowsy. Gabe, Rai, and Hayden all said their hellos and hugged her. They were so glad to see her awake, the Doctor walked in and said she had low glucose levels when she had gotten there. Once we started an I.V., she responded quickly. Just make sure she eats, and she should be ok. After about an hour and a substantial amount of money, they were all headed home.

Gabe and Rai were driving to Gabe's house, and he says, "Baby, I'd like for us to get away for a day, what do you say we head over to Santa Barbara Friday night and maybe come back Saturday night? I would also like to go to that church down the road Sunday morning; would you care to join me for that as well?"

Rai thought he couldn't surprise her anymore but this, once again made her stop and stare at him. Rai said, "Gabe, I would love to, but can I ask why?"

Gabe simply said, "I have questions, and I figured what better place to have them answered."

Friday came, and once they were both home from work, they packed a small bag and headed for the coast. Once there, they checked into their hotel got cleaned up and changed for dinner. They ate at the Harbor Restaurant on the pier. Their conversation focused on Sophie and their jobs. Once they finished eating, they went for a walk on the pier. The weather was always perfect there, and the sun was beginning to set. Once they reached the end of the pier, Rai leaned on the railing and expected to see Gabe do the same, but he didn't. She turned and didn't see him, that is, until she looked down. There was Gabe, kneeling in front of her, on one knee. She took a step back; she couldn't believe what she was seeing. Rai finally stepped back up to him; a few people had noticed what was going on and started watching the scene unfold. Gabe spoke, "Rai, I love you; you are without a doubt the one person that I am supposed to spend the rest of my life with. I would like you to be my wife again, forever. Will you marry me?"

Rai touched his face and said, "Gabe, I love you more, and yes I would love to marry you and be your wife again, forever.

He placed the ring on her finger and stood and kissed her long and deep. They hadn't noticed that several people were clapping as they kissed. They separated and thanked everyone. They began their walk back to the car, hand in hand, both the happiest they had been in a long, long time.

Annbella and Rashad were heading up a team of people with the goal of building a way to send messages faster than the speed of light. There were many theories to work from, but there was no technology that existed to achieve this goal. It was like trying to invent the car in medieval times. There had been weeks of meetings, all of which had to be top secret. They were working at the HETI facility, but the security had upgraded and there were armed guards posted everywhere. Rashad told Ann, "Ok, I know we keep working on entangled photons that involve some sort of tachyon particles but what if we try something totally different?"

Ann says, "Like what?"

Rashad says, "Folding space. There has to be a way to send data through some sort of wormhole."

Ann says, "And how do we do that?"

Rashad was silent, they both sat there for a few minutes when suddenly the monitor lit up, it was the message repeating, at least that is what they thought. Rashad just glanced at it expecting to see the repeating messages, but that is not what he saw. He told Ann to look at the screen, she saw it as well. A new message was flashing on the screen. It was of course coded but they had seen the old code enough to know this was different. They started the process of decoding the message. By this time there was a team of people to do this work, so it went much quicker. After a few hours, they had the Hebrew word on the screen. There, on the screen, was the newest message from a world they knew nothing about. It read,

Yeshua

Ann and Rashad looked at each other a little confused. She took out her phone and called Mia; Mia answered, "Hello."

Ann said, "Mia, we have a new message."

Mia asked what it said; Ann spelled it out, Yeshua. Mia says, "Are you sure?"

Ann replied, "Yes I am sure."

Mia blurted out, "Jesus!"

Ann asked, "What is it?"

Mia says, "No, that's the word, Jesus." Mia was excited and terrified at the same time. How could this be? How could they know the name, Jesus? Mia thanked Ann and hung the phone up.

Gabe was driving back to the hotel when his phone rang. He answered it; all Rai heard was, "Hello, Hey, how's it going? Yes, Oh, ok, and what did it say?" Then he slammed on his breaks and said, "Can you repeat that! Oh, ok, right, I'll call Dan and let him know, thank you, ok, I'll see you Monday."

Rai asked, "What was that about?"

Gabe had pulled into a parking lot. He turned to Rai and said, "Look, I can't get into details, but we just got a new message and it was one word, translated from Hebrew, it was Jesus."

Rai went cold. It was unbelievable; literally, she couldn't believe what she had heard. "How could it be? How could a world, light years away, know about Jesus?"

"I have no idea," Gabe said.

∞

Michelle walked up to her dad accompanied by an officer. She just collapsed into her father's arms. She started screaming, "They shot him, just shot him for no reason, daddy!" Jordan held her as she cried, he cried as well. Now he had to make a phone call; he had no idea how he was going to be able to tell Jasmine that her son was dead. As they made their way to Jordan's car, he told Michelle he would be back in just a few minutes. She got into the car and watched her father walk a few yards away from where they were parked and pulled his phone out. She watched as he pressed her name on the contacts and waited. Finally, he saw his mouth moving, so she knew he was telling her mom that her son was dead. Michelle saw her dad crying as he spoke. He pulled the phone from his ear and walked back to the car wiping the tears from his face; he opened the door and told Michelle he would be right back. Jordan turned and went back to the sergeant he had spoken to before and he said, "Who the hell did it! Who killed my son in cold blood! Who murdered him damn it!"

Sergeant Coles simply stood there as he berated him and once he was quiet he said, "I sent the officer back to headquarters to be debriefed and give a statement."

Jordan said, "I want his name and badge number."

Coles said he would need clearance to give him that information.

Jordan said, "Nope, not good enough; I want his name!"

Coles said, "Look, I cannot imagine what you are going through; please let me have your information, and I promise I will follow through with what you need but not right now, sir."

Jordan thought about it and said, "Fine, but if you don't call me tomorrow morning I will be at that station demanding answers!"

Coles nodded and turned away. He got into his squad car and left. Jordan walked back to his car and drove home where the three of them spent the worst night of their lives. Jordan was locked in his office contemplating his options. He wanted justice for his son, and he wanted to be the one to deliver it. He needed a name; he needed the name of the man who murdered his son.

Sarah was in the oval office and was on the phone with Huan Ji, the president of China. Huan Ji was a humble, quiet man who had the respect of many leaders around the world. He had been president for five years and was making allies of many countries in the west and Sarah was very fond of him, and it helped that he had spent time in London, so his English was great. He had proven to be someone who she could trust, and she found herself seeking his counsel when she needed it. Sarah says, "Huan Ji, how is your wife Xi Mingze?" Xi Mingze is the daughter of the past president of China and had married Huan Ji who won the favor of Xi Jinping; once he had passed away Huan Ji took his place temporarily until the next election at which point he became the next official president of China.

Huan Ji said, "Oh, Thank you for asking, she is doing well. She asks about you often."

Sarah said, "Oh do tell her I said hello, please. Anyhow, I need to talk to you about something very important, but I am not comfortable doing it over the phone."

Huan Ji said, "Well, we have the summit coming up in two months, can it wait?"

Sarah said, "No, no it can't wait. How about Tim and I come to your country? Would that be ok?"

Huan Ji said, "Absolutely, we would love to host you here!"

Sarah said, "Great! I will get my assistant to make the arrangements, does next week sound ok?"

After hanging up the phone, Huan Ji was very curious and he thought to himself, what could bring the President of the United

States just to talk? Huan Ji walked out of his office and told his assistant to have his car brought up; he would be going home to discuss something with his wife.

Ben had just gotten off the phone with Dan; he was sitting in his office, in silence, trying to bring all the events together in his mind. Now, Jesus? How? How could a world, billions of miles away from earth, know who Jesus was? Ben had to snap himself out of his deep thoughts; he had to call the president and let her know about this new message. He walked out of his office and told his assistant to hold all calls and clear his schedule. He had a feeling that his day would be spent in meetings for the rest of the day. He walked back into his office and sat at his desk, picked up the phone and made the call.

∞

Sarah was talking to Tim about her call with Huan Ji just an hour earlier when she got a call forwarded to her; it was Ben from TASA, so she took the call. She said, "Hello Ben, how can I help you?"

Ben says, "Madam President, I have just received information regarding the most recent message we've received from the other world."

Sarah was silent, and then says, "Ok, what was it?"

Ben says, "Madam again, just one word, it was Yeshua or translated to Jesus."

Again, silence; actually, a long silence. He knew she was deep in thought so he just waited. FinallySarah spoke, "Thank you so much, Ben; I will be calling another cabinet meeting in the next day, will you be available to attend?"

Ben said, "Absolutely, not a problem Madam."

They both said goodbye and hung up their phones. Sarah turned to Tim, walked up to him and hugged him, she spoke

60

softly and said, they got another message, and It was translated to Jesus. Tim stepped back with a puzzled look on his face, he said, "Jesus?" She shook her head yes. They sat down holding hands. Tim was an incredibly smart man, one of the smartest men Sarah had ever met, but more than that he was wise, he knew how to step back and look at the big picture. Tim simply said, "We need to pay Huan Ji a visit sooner than later."

Sarah said, "You are right, can you clear your schedule? Maybe we could leave the day after tomorrow, making it a Friday flight, spend the weekend and come back Monday?"

Tim said, "Sure, no problem."

Sarah then called Huan Ji back and said, "I am so sorry to bother you again President Ji but something has come up, and I know this is unprecedented but would it be possible for Tim and I to come this weekend? The matter is extremely important."

Huan Ji said he would clear his schedule for her. They would be staying with him and his wife as honored guests. It was set then; they would be leaving for China on Friday. She then called her assistant and said, "Please assemble my full cabinet for a meeting tomorrow no excuses, I want them all there." She hung up the phone and turned to Tim who was himself calling people to reschedule appointments. She waited until he was done; once he hung up his phone she said they would be leaving Friday for China and that they would be staying with Huan Ji and Xi Mingze as their honored guests. Tim said, "Great, I'm looking forward to it."

Sarah walked up to him and hugged him, she said, "Thank you, I am so lucky to have you in my life, this last message, while exciting, could incite some ill feelings from a handful of countries. I am just not sure how this is going to play out, but I know I have you, so, I am thankful and know I love you, Tim."

Tim said, "I love you more" with a wry smile on his face.

Chapter 6

Faizan Baqri was walking alone along Moorland Lane in Bethesda, Maryland. He had just left his new friends house where they had discussed parts of the Quran in a way that Faizan had not done before. He was beginning to question his parent's decision to leave Pakistan to come to America. He was learning why capitalism was not in line with what the Koran taught. He arrived home where his parents were waiting for him so they could eat dinner. Faizan was 18 and about to graduate high school. He had an older sister who was already in college so that just left him and his parents. The more he learned from his new friend, the more he resented his parents. That didn't mean he didn't love them, he did, but he couldn't understand why they made some of the choices they did. He wanted to learn more about his home country and more about the teachings of Mohammad. Faizan wanted to discuss this stuff with his father, but his new friend told him not to, that his parents would cloud his brain with untruths. So, Faizan decided not to discuss anything with his parents. As he sat down to dinner with them, His father, who was an aerospace engineer, could tell he was behaving different, so he asked Faizan, "what is wrong with you tonight Faizan?" Faizan simply said he was tired and had more homework to do. His mother began to serve them chicken curry with naan bread. They ate with some minor conversation; once done Faizan helped clear the table. His father went into the living room and turned on the news. He heard the news Anchor Jill say, "Today the Prime Minister of Canada is announcing new rules on the exportation of water to other countries," cut to the Prime

Minister at a news conference, "We will be adding an additional tax on the exportation of our fresh water supply. I understand that there is a water crisis happening around the world, but I would not be putting our country first if I didn't try to bring us out of our national debt and this is the most logical way to do it."Faizan then left his mother to clean the dishes. Once he was in his room, he texted his friend. He asked when they would meet again because he had many questions. His friend replied, tomorrow afternoon and be prepared to take his commitment to Islam to a new level. Faizan was excited to learn more from his new friend and teacher.

∞

Abarron was back in the sanctuary that the elders met in. He was kneeling in front of the group of men and women and was waiting for permission to speak. The Elders had many things to review, but now it was Abarron's time to speak. He looked up and started speaking, "Praise God, he is mighty, and I am blessed to speak to you all. I have sent much information to the new world, but I am getting no signal back. I fear that they have not yet been informed as to how to build the device; I would like to send them the way but need your permission first. I ask this in the name of Jesus."

There was silence; then the elders told him they would be discussing his request, they needed to pray before giving him an answer. He stood, bowed his head and left. As he walked back, he thought to himself, how strange was that? I am usually the one telling them what I am sending but this was different, so he understood the need to pray; God always had the answer. Abarron was a Prophet, he was known throughout the world. His conversations with God were clearer than any other Prophet alive today. All people had conversations with God, but only the purist of hearts heard him as a Prophet does. Abarron was a patient man who studied the life of Jesus and tried to live life in his footsteps. So, he would follow the laws set forth by God. He walked to the shade of a tree and sat on the earth; he always took time to pray to God or as he liked to call him, the Maker and he usually wanted to be connected to the earth when he did. He was thankful to God for the life he had given him and all the beauty he created. Abarron was not sure how long he had been in prayer; when he did so, he would be in a trance, and It was one of his fellows that broke his prayer to tell him the Elders were ready to speak to him. Abarron stood and put his hand on his fellow's shoulder and thanked him. He then proceeded into the sanctuary and sat before the elders. Silence first, and then the spokesperson told Abarron that he was to send the way to the device. Abarron bowed and thanked them, he then stood and left. He knew that it would take a tremendous amount of energy to send them this message, but once they had it, the information would be much clearer, only then would they be able to exchange their love of Jesus.

Gabriel and Mia are at his meeting table in his office discussing the last message when, Mia asks him, "So how are you and Rai doing?"

Gabriel says, "Actually, Mia, I asked her to marry me again."

Mia said a little louder than she had planned, "What, really? That is so great Gabriel, congratulations!"

Gabriel said "Thanks, we have found a love for each other that was probably there, but it is different now. We are planning a ceremony soon; you'll be getting an invitation, I hope you can make it."

Mia said, "Oh I wouldn't miss that for the world. Anyhow, back to work, have you heard from Dan and how Ann and Rashad are making out on their project?"

Gabriel said, "Yes, I spoke to him yesterday, they've made little progress."

Mia said, "I am not surprised, I am not even sure if it is possible."

Gabriel replied, "Well if it is, those two will figure it out."

"Agreed," says Mia.

Sarah was walking into the Cabinet room where she would be talking to her full cabinet about the new message and what she would be doing as they move forward. Sarah walked in and took her seat. She said, "Ladies and Gentlemen, this could be a long meeting, I would suggest you take advantage of the refreshments and snacks, I will have lunch brought in as well."

All the cabinet members looked at each other with surprise but then one by one, people got up and grabbed some water or coffee and a bagel and sat back down. Sarah began speaking, "Ok folks, as most of you know, there was a signal detected by our agencies from an unknown area of space. I've asked Ben to sit in on this meeting, so I will let him get you all up to date on everything that has happened since the first signal. I want you all to listen with an open mind. This is not a go through the motions type meeting today. I need you all to listen, process it, and then I will need your counsel and suggestions."

Ben stood, and a power point showed up on the large screen monitors located at each end of the room. Ben began bringing everyone up to speed; he decided to start from the beginning because some of the members who were present now were not present at the first meeting he had attended with the cabinet and the President. He told them about the first message and the other ones after that, then he said, "We have concluded that these are messages from another world. We have isolated our systems to rule out any hacking possibilities. We have tracked the message to a star in the area of Proxima Centauri (Ben had some nice graphics that were playing on the monitors that oriented everyone as to where the system was and where the newly discovered star was located). Gabriel Dane, Director of the TSN, was given a chance to name the new star as it was he and his team that first discovered and translated the first message, they chose the name Yahweh Centauri. We have a team working on a way to reply to this message in a way that will get the message there in an expedited manner. As it is, our reply will not get there for almost five years. Ladies and gentlemen, we have several confirmed messages from this world, the messages arrive in an ancient form of Hebrew, and we just received the most alarming message a few days ago. It was translated to -JESUS."

Ben thanked everyone and sat down. Sarah spoke next, "Thank you, Ben; I would like you to stay for this meeting if you can in case we have any questions for you throughout the day. So, now everyone is up to speed on everything that we know about the messages. I am going to be calling the United Nations President and convene a meeting about this. I think all nations need to know about this. I am not sure how it is going to impact our world, but I think we need to be prepared for anything."

Sarah noticed David, her Vice President, and William, her Defense Secretary, were having a side conversation, so she stopped talking and asked them if they had anything to add. They both looked at her and said, "Well, we have had some conversations about this, and we have some concerns. If this is all true, we are not as concerned about the actual message as we are the reaction of other nations, like North Korea, Iran, China, and Russia. All of these are nations that have leaders who are almost revered as God-like and those leaders might feel threatened by this information. They could pose a serious threat to our security and the security of the world. We should be ready to intervene if needed."

Sarah said, "Thank you for adding this to the conversation. I agree with the concerns about Iran and North Korea, these are countries that have a stranglehold on their people, but Russia and China aren't quite as firmly held. I have better relations with them as well. As a matter of fact, I am heading to stay with Huan Ji and his wife for the weekend. I want to talk in depth with him as he has close relations with North Korea."

Betty Smith, her Attorney General, spoke up and said, "Madam President, maybe we should consider holding off on announcing this, maybe we should not announce it at all."

The Secretary of Interior, Alex Jones spoke as well, saying, "That might not be a bad idea Madam."

Sarah was getting impatient and said, "Look, eventually someone else is going to pick this message up...hell, I'm sure someone already has, so I think it is important to get this information out as soon as we can. After that, I will be holding a press conference."

David spoke, "Sarah, I mean Madam President, do you think that's a good idea?"

Sarah said, "David, I ran for president, and when I did, I said I would be transparent, and that is what I am going to do. No closed-door deals, no typical politics. I meant what I said to the American people and you when I asked you each to be a part of my administration. You are all here because I felt you would support my approach to the presidency. I was raised to have integrity in all things I do, to do the right thing even when no one is around to see it. So, yes, I will be contacting the U.N., and I will be disclosing what we know to the world. If there is anyone who is having second thoughts about this approach I will understand but will ask for your resignation, not because I don't like or respect you or will hold it against you but because I have to have one hundred percent of your support when it comes to this aspect of this administration. If I am about to make a huge mistake or if I am wrong about a decision, please I am asking you to tell me, but I will not budge when it comes to this, is that understood?"

The members of her cabinet all either said yes ma'am or shook their heads yes. Sarah said, "Very good, thank you, everyone, now let's get back to work."

Faizan walked up to the door of his new friend's home. He was a little surprised when he arrived and saw two cars in the driveway that he had not seen before. He knocked on the door, and his friend opened the door. He said hello to Qadeer. As he entered the home, he could see two other men in the home as well. Qadeer introduced them to Faizan and offered him a drink. Faizan took a hot tea, and they sat down with him. Qadeer told him that the two men were from his motherland and that the Americans, the infidels, were responsible for the state of the world, their capitalistic ways had poisoned the world and that they needed to pay. They said Allah was directing them to exact revenge on the infidels and that Faizan was to be a key part of the revenge of Allah. Qadeer then says, "We are to take you to Pakistan and train you in the ways of the brotherhood of Islam. That is all we can tell you."

Faizan was scared and excited at the same time. He says, "Why me?"

Qadeer says, "Brother Faizan, you came to us, first by your interest in the Quran and then when you spoke to a friend of mine at the Mosque, he thought you were very bright with massive potential."

Faizan said, "But that was three months ago, you mean that you have known about me that long?"

Qadeer says, "Yes, we have, and you have not disappointed us."

Faizan sat silently thinking. Finally, he spoke, "I am happy I have met your expectations. I am willing to do the will of Allah and for my brothers in Islam."

Qadeer said, "That is great. I will contact you after you graduate, next week. Then you will tell your parents you are going to go on a cross-country trip before you start university, but you will be going with us. We will provide you with everything you need, you are an investment for us, we will take good care of you, but from here on out, until you come with us, you will have no more contact with us. It is getting dangerous for us to be here so we will be moving on. You need to remain as you were before you met us. Until we meet again young Faizan, be well."

"Goodbye," Faizan said.

Rai and Sophie are packing up Rai's home. Rai and Gabe decided it was silly to be maintaining two households so they agreed that it would make sense for her to move into Gabe's house. Sophie says, "Mom, I am so happy for you and Dad, I always kind of knew you would get back together someday."

Rai says, "Thanks honey, I am so happy with him, I can't believe how different he is now, it's like Gabe but different, just, balanced and full of love. Anyhow, how are you feeling? You have one more chemo, and that's it?"

Sophie says, "Yes, one more, they say the cancer is almost gone. I am so tired of being so tired; I am however, so thankful for all of the homeopathic diets you put me on. I am sure that helped me kick this quicker."

Rai says, "I am glad and thankful Sophie. I love you so much, and I knew you would get through this."

Sophie says, "So, when is the wedding day?"

Rai replies, "We are thinking about two weeks. Just a small ceremony and a short stay on the coast after."

Sophie says, "That's great! Where will you have it?"

Rai said, "Gabe and I have been attending service at the church down the road from us, and we are thinking about having it there if it is available."

Sophie says, "Ok, well, let us know, and Hayden and I will be there."

Rai turned to her and said, "Actually, I would love it if you would be my Maid of honor."

Sophie said, "Mom, I would love that!"

They hugged and Rai called Gabe to tell him the news.

Sarah said, "Ok everyone, look, I know it's been a long day, but this was a very productive meeting. I appreciate all your candor and openness today. If anyone has anything they want to add or bring to my attention, please don't hesitate to contact me. I will be leaving Friday for my weekend with Huan Ji so please wish us luck."

Everyone was talking and walking towards the door. From across the room, she could make out someone saying, "She is going to go down as one of the great presidents, she has great leadership abilities." Sarah just smiled slightly, she was very happy with the team around her. Now, to get home and speak to Tim about this weekend.

∞

Gabriel was walking into the First Baptist Church where he and Rai had attended a few times and met a few of the people that attended there regularly and liked them a lot. So, Gabriel decided he wanted to ask some questions of the pastor. He was not sure that he would even be here at the end of the day like this but thought he would give it a shot. He knew Rai wouldn't be home for another two hours, which gave him time to get dinner ready before she got home. He walked up to the doors, and they were unlocked, so he went in. He was familiar with this part of the church, but he had no idea where the offices were. He found another door which led to a hallway; he could see there was one open door with some light coming out of it. He walked up to the open door and found the senior pastor at his desk. "Hello sir," which startled the man at the desk, "my name is Gabriel Dane."

The man walked around his desk and shook Gabriel's hand saying, "Hello my name is Gary Manns. I am the senior pastor here at First Baptist, how can I help you?"

Gabriel said, "Well sir, I have been agnostic all my life, but there has been a series of events that has convinced me that God is real and that I should be following Jesus. I have a few questions though…would you be able to talk with me for a few minutes?"

"Of course," Gary said, "I always have time to talk about Jesus!"

Gabriel and Gary sat down in his office, and Gary said, "Ok what is on your mind?"

Gabriel said, "Well, I guess I am confused about a few things, first of all, one of the reasons I have never pursued or studied Jesus is because religion seems to contradict what I do know about Jesus. All I have ever heard about Jesus was he was all about love, and religion doesn't always seem to follow that teaching. I, as a mixed-race man experienced some bigotry at the hands of 'Christ-loving people'. So, could you explain to me the role of religion as it relates to Jesus?"

Gary said, "Wow, that's a profound question, but you are right, religion gets in the way of what Jesus wants us to do with our lives. You are right when you say Jesus wants us to love our neighbor as we love ourselves and when we ask ourselves the question, who is our neighbor? Well, the answer is simple, everyone is our neighbor. We are supposed to love everyone. It is not for us to judge, there is but one judge, and that is the all mighty God."

Gabriel asked, "So what do you do here? Why do people come to church then?"

Gary said, "Well, the church is not about a building, it is not about me. It is about the people that come to church, and it's about what happens between Sundays as well. You see Gabriel; I am just here to speak the word of God. I teach people about the Bible and how it can help you in all aspects of your life, but I am just a man like you. I have faults and am full of sin just like you as well. The church is about finding people who love Jesus and being a family for each other. We help each other, and we do our best to help people outside of this church. God wants us to go out and be his disciples but not go out and beat people over the head with our Bibles. We go out and show people the love of Jesus. We help where help is needed. That is what Jesus wanted; He would rather we go into a bar and strike up a conversation with an alcoholic rather than sit in a country club with our friends talking about our new car or the next house we are buying."

Gabriel Says, "So you are telling me, live the way Jesus wants me to live, and I go to heaven?"

Gary says, "Well, that is part of it, but first you have to invite Jesus into your life. You have to actually say a prayer and it goes like this: Dear Lord Jesus, I know that I am a sinner, and I ask for Your forgiveness. I believe You died for my sins and rose from the dead. I turn from my sins and invite you to come into my heart and life. I want to trust and follow you as my Lord and Savior."

Gabriel said, "Ok, I want to do that, you see, I have knowledge Gary, and I KNOW God and Jesus are real and that Jesus died for my sins, I am ready to say that prayer."

Gary, responded with a happy look on his face, because Gabriel represents why he became a pastor. Nothing makes him happier than to see someone come to Christ, so he said to Gabriel, "Ok here, I have the prayer typed out," and he handed Gabriel a small piece of paper with the prayer on it. Gary continues to say, "You can either say it to yourself or out loud."

Gabriel thought briefly, and then he said, "I want to say it out loud if you don't mind." So he started reading, "Dear Lord Jesus, I know that I am a sinner, and I ask for Your forgiveness. I believe You died for my sins and rose from the dead. I turn from my sins and invite You to come into my heart and life. I want to trust and follow you as my Lord and Savior." Gabriel was not one to show his emotions, but he couldn't help himself, once he finished he couldn't contain his emotions, he had tears in his eyes as he finished reading and then sobbed, like a little kid who had been lost in a store and finally found his mother. Gary came around the desk and hugged Gabriel, something that he normally would have pulled away from but not this time; he needed that human touch and so they stood in the office of the small church with Gary hugging Gabriel for a minute. Gabriel was finally able to contain himself and stepped back from Gary. Gabriel was a new man, he couldn't explain it, he was free, and he could feel the love of Jesus running through him. Gabriel said happily, "Gary, I can't thank you enough for taking the time out to talk to me and to help me find Jesus."

Gary simply said, "Gabriel, we are now brothers in Christ, forever, even when our life here on earth is over, we will see each other in heaven and will be brothers there as well."

Gabriel shook his hand but then stepped in and gave him another hug and thanked him again. As Gabriel was walking out of his office, Gabriel stopped suddenly and just stood there for a few seconds then turned slowly to Gary and said, "I just realized something, If God and Jesus are real, then that means that so is Satan."

Gary said, "Yes Gabriel, he is indeed very real, he tries every day to work his way into everyone's life and turn them away from the light of God." Gabriel felt a cold chill run through his body, he thanked Gary again and left the church.

Chapter 7

Tim walked back into the cabin on Airforce One holding two coffee cups; he says to Sarah, "Here you go love, I asked Paula to cut us two pieces of that chocolate cake they served with dinner."

Sarah says, "What? Tim, we shouldn't," with a grin on her face.

He said, "I know, but hey we can indulge every once in a while, right?"

He sets her coffee down and sits next to her. Sarah says, "So, I've been thinking about a couple of things."

Tim says, "Like what?"

Sarah says, "I was thinking, about all of the countries that probably know about the signals and I am thinking India and Germany. They have been at the forefront of space exploration as well as China. As much as I like Huan Ji, I am not blind to the fact that he is not one hundred percent honest with me, but I still like him and think he is a great leader."

Tim says, "So, talk to me about your thoughts on the reason we are going over there."

Sarah says, "Oh, you mean the signal?"

He says, "Yes."

Sarah says, "Well, I am a little nervous about it, I mean, now we know that God and Jesus are real. So, I ask myself, have I lived my life the way that he wants me to live it? I think I have, but you never know, do you?"

Tim says, "Actually, it is possible to know whether or not you've lived the life Jesus wants us to live."

Sarah says, "I know, but you know me, I always doubt myself. Anyhow, I am still having a hard time wrapping my mind around the whole thing. The idea that God created two planets and created people on both planets is just crazy."

Tim says, "Why? I mean the more I think about it, the more it makes sense, He is such an awesome God that can do anything he wants, so why not?"

Sarah says, "Right now, what I need to do is figure out what I want Huan Ji to do or actually what I need from him. I need to figure out what the rogue nations might do and if it is an aggressive reaction, what that looks like and what we might need to do."

Jordan is at the Marietta police station talking to the Chief of Police. In actuality, Jordan was arguing with him. Jordan yelling, says, "How can you not press charges against this officer? He killed my son in cold blood! He is a murderer and murderers belong in jail!"

Chief of Police Scott Glazer calmly says, "Look, sir, I completely understand your frustration and your anger. But I have looked at all the statements, and unfortunately, the officer had told your son, to show him his hands and he reached down beneath the seat making the officer think your son was going for a weapon. His reaction, as he was trained to do, was to eliminate the threat. I can't fault him for that sir, so I will not be bringing charges against him."

With that statement, Jordan got up and left the station, got into his car, and started driving. He drove west on Interstate twenty. He was full of rage and he knew the system was rigged and that his son would not get justice through it. He, Jordan, would give him the justice he deserved. A few hours later he was in Birmingham, Alabama and he pulled into a shop that sold guns. He got out of the car and walked in. He approached the counter and instantly the man behind the counter recognized him. It was one of his boys from the old days. Jordan says, "What up my man?"

Darnel says, "What the hell are you doing here bruh?"

Jordan says, "Well, I got a situation man, I got to take care of something, and I need your help."

Darnel says, "We are brothers for life, whatcha need man."

Jordan says, I need a piece, but I need it now, and I can't have it traced."

Darnel says, "I got something man, it is just a nine millimeter, but it was hot when I got it. You can have it bruh."

Jordan says, "Here's a grand man and you know that if you get in any kind of heat, I got you."

Jordan takes his new nine-millimeter handgun and walks out the door, gets into his car and heads home. He calls Jasmine and tells her he will be home late. She is and has been distant and shut down. Junior's death has affected her in a way that Jordan had not anticipated. She was almost dead inside, just going through the motions of life but not engaging at all. He was going to make the man pay for what he did to their son. He was full of hate and was determined to right this wrong. He had no idea what would happen after that but right now his heart was dark, it was as dark as it had ever been, back when his pops was telling him he was good for nothing and would beat his butt for no reason. That was nothing compared to this hate that filled him right now. So, Jordan drove east, back to Atlanta and then home. He would need to pick up Michelle from her friend's house, and then eat dinner. After, he would be planning out how he was going to take care of everything.

Robert Calls Mia and asks her to come into the new message center. It was a new addition to the TSN that was designed specifically for the new signals that were received. Congress had voted to increase their budget to give them the tools they needed. There was a new program that automatically deciphered the message and then translated it to English. The addition also came with additional funding for more personnel and thousands of terabytes of memory, and that allowed much more processing power. It was so much equipment that it filled a whole separate area the size of a house. The main challenge was keeping it cool, especially in the desert heat. Mia answers her phone as she tells Robert that she will be there in a few minutes. The computer that he was working with was new, and he had been working with a team of people that were extremely qualified for the work they were doing. They were finally getting the programs to work together and now, that they had finally booted the last system up, they were getting message after message. It was like they must have been getting just small amounts of the messages that were getting sent. Mia walks into the center after she swipes her card to enter. Robert says, "Hello, come on over, we just got the systems on and working together. We are getting messages at a higher rate. There was more information in the messages we were getting; now we have the increased computing power to get more of the message. It still didn't make a lot of sense, but it was more information than we had before."

Mia looked at a readout of the first message they had gotten. Because the message repeated, it always started with the first message they had received and then the one after that, etc. So it read, "Our Lord, thankful, Lord God, Messiah, he is." That was what they had from the first message. It would be a little while before the next message would come through, so Mia stepped out of the room and called Gabriel. She told him of the progress they had made. He said thank you and that he was on his way to meet with them.

Tim and Sarah are in the car with Huan Ji and his wife, XiMingze. Huan Ji says, "It is so great to see you Madam President and you as well Tim. I will have dinner served when we arrive, I hope that is ok."

Sarah says, "Yes that would be great. I am so grateful to you and Xi Mingze for hosting us this weekend. I want to talk to you after dinner if that is appropriate."

Huan Ji said, "That would be fine."

Sarah thought Huan Ji seemed to be distant; they are usually more inviting in their interactions together. The car arrived at the Zhongnanhai Compound; as they entered the home of the Chinese President they noted the opulence and detail of everything. They left Huan Ji and were shown their quarters. Once alone Sarah said to Tim. "Huan Ji seems a little different to me, he seems distant."

Tim says, "Maybe he is just nervous or suspicious about why you are here?"

Sarah replies, "Maybe you are right."

After about 40 minutes they were summoned to come downstairs for dinner. As they walked into the dining room, they were again impressed with how lavish and luxurious everything was. They sat at a large table but only the two couples were present so they ate across from each other at one end of the table. It was a five-course meal, and It was all amazing and delicious. The conversation was light but, still, Sarah couldn't help but feel a distance between them. They finished their dinner and went outside where there was a nice fire in a gas-lit pit. A table and some chairs were around the area. Huan Ji motioned them forward to choose where they would sit. She chose a few chairs that were close to the fire as she was a bit chilled outside. Once they were all settled in, Sarah looked at Huan Ji and said, "Huan Ji, I feel like something is bothering you, like there is a distance between us that has not been there before. Is there something that I have done or my country has done to make you feel unsettled?"

Huan Ji said, "As a matter of fact, there is something, I am greatly concerned about the state of affairs concerning several countries around the world. The water shortage is affecting so many, and this notion that countries with a surplus will be selling and benefiting from it is sad and not smart. It is going to cause a lot of trouble around the globe. I am frankly disappointed in the lack of reaction from the United States, especially as it relates to your friends to the north."

Sarah sat silent for a moment, and said, "Huan Ji, you are right, I should have been stronger in my reaction. I want you to know that I share your concerns and I will stand side by side with you on this issue, that is a promise."

Huan Ji was visibly pleased, and she could tell he instantly started to relax. Huan Ji smiled, stood and walked towards Sarah bowing, Sarah bowed as well, but then she hugged him. Sarah was so happy they were back to their old selves, she knew she would need him and his support for what they would be talking about next. Tim had moved over to talk to Xi Mingze, leaving Sarah and Huan Ji to talk. Sarah had been sitting a little sideways facing just slightly away from the Chinese President but after Tim moved she squared her position towards Huan Ji and she said, "Huan Ji, it is time we talked about the reason Tim, and I made this trip. I have to ask you something first though; have your scientists found any messages with an origin other than this planet?"

Huan Ji said, "Well, we did detect a message but figured it was a hack of some sort and discarded it, why do you ask?"

Sarah said, "Huan Ji, we had several departments in our country discover this and were able to not only discover its origin but the series of messages, as well as decode and translate them."

Huan Ji says, 'Hmm, ok I see, and what were these so-called messages?"

Sarah replies, "Huan Ji, let me say that I will allow your scientist to review our methods and all our steps to ensure that this is indeed an authentic message. It was sent from an undiscovered yellow dwarf star near Proxima Centauri, and the messages have been different names for Jesus as well as the actual name of Jesus. All messages are decoded into an ancient form of Hebrew then translated into English."

Huan Ji instantly said, "That is not believable Sarah! Not possible, I mean, a message from another planet and they come to us with the message of Jesus!"

Sarah said, "I promise you, we have isolated all systems and taken the possibility of outside influence out of the equation. The messages are real, and we keep getting updated messages. We have the most up-to-date state of the art equipment with our best people working on this. Huan Ji, listen to me, this is real, we are getting messages from another world, and I need your help and council before I move forward."

Huan Ji says, "Ok, say I believe you; what would you do next?"

Sarah says, "I plan to go to the U.N., only it will not just be the U.N. I want to invite all heads of all nations to a world meeting and reveal all we know. Then, I want to go to the people of the world and tell them all that we know."

Huan Ji says, "I have known you long enough to know there is no changing your mind, so I will not try, but with that being said, why did you need to fly all the way to my home?"

Sarah could see he was not convinced, but she thought over time he would be. Sarah said, "Huan Ji, I am worried about adverse responses by some of the rough countries around the world. Who do you think will respond negatively to this information and what will they do?"

Huan Ji says, "Hm, definitely North Korea, Iran, Syria, and Cuba but also a few countries in Africa as well, I am thinking Somalia and Libya. But the ones you will have to watch are Iran and North Korea. I could see them teaming up and taking action."

Sarah said, "Thank you for talking to me Huan Ji. I am so thankful for your wisdom and friendship. Do you mind if we relax for a bit before we discuss this more? I am exhausted and would like to visit for a while if you don't mind."

Huan Ji says, "That would be wonderful, would you like a drink? Some warm sake perhaps?"

Sarah says, "That would be great."

Huan Ji calls for their servant and just as he does, he stops and turns back towards Sarah and says, "Forgive me, but might I ask, have you asked Germany or India if they have received any messages?"

Sarah says, "No, you are the first person outside of my government that I have talked to about this." Sarah pulls her phone out and calls Ben.

∞

Lee Suk-park walks into the office of Song Mi-Hyang and bows; he stays that way until addressed. Song Mi-hang says, "You may speak."

Lee Suk-park says, "All important assistant, I am here to inform you that we are ready to begin the inspection. If all is to your satisfaction, then we will be ready to accept inventory."

Song Mi-hang says, "Very good; I expect you have a vehicle ready for me."

Lee Suk-park bows deeply and says, "Yes great assistant, it is right outside."

Lee Suk-Park follows Song Mi-hang outside and gets into the driver seat and starts toward the large mountain. As they approach, there is a canopy of trees, and under that, a metal roof structure. The cart starts to decline and the daylight converts to artificial light. They drive into the mountain for about a mile then the decline increases. They drive for about another mile, and they come to a stop in front of a massive door. They get out of the cart and walk to a smaller door surrounded by rock with three different security devices. Song Mi-hang presses her eye to a camera while pressing her finger into the clear pad on the wall; the system then asks for a code, and the door opens. As they enter, there is a massive empty space; as tall as a skyscraper and several thousand feet long. They walked across the room that seems to take about five minutes. Once across the room, there are several doors and a very large window that looks into the room. They step through a door, and there is a large control room with lots of equipment and computers with monitors attached. Song Mi-hang walks around with a list on a clipboard. She checks all the equipment, making sure it was all in proper working order. She checks for all the supporting equipment like the external drives and the cooling equipment. After about two hours the work is done, and they exit the room and drive back up to the surface. She briefly acknowledges Lee Suk-park and tells him he did well. She is pleased and steps into her office and calls Young Ra-il, the phone rings; he answers. She instantly tenses up; she knows that if anything went wrong that she would not only lose her position but most likely her life. Song Mi-hang says, "Most honorable Young Ra-il, I am informing you that the new installation facility is ready. I have inspected all the systems and everything is in working order."

Young Ra-il, says, "Most excellent Song Mi-hang you have done well. The supreme leader will be pleased. You will go far as we progress our position in the world." She says thank him and hangs up her phone. She smiles and leans back in her chair. She is pleased and wishes she could talk to her parents about everything she is doing.

∞

Faizan is in line to step out onto the stage; he had worked hard to fit in at his school, he made good grades and had several friends in his class. He wasn't the most popular, but many people liked him. He had been instructed from the beginning of his dealings with his new friends to fit in and act as "American" as he could. His name was called, and many people clapped and shouted his name including his parents and a few lady friends that liked him. He was, after all, a tall guy with dark skin and good looks. He walks up to the principal of the school, and he hands him his diploma. He shakes several hands in a lineup of staff and teachers then moves across the remainder of the stage and back to his seat; as he walked back he raises his diploma towards his parents and raises his fist. He sits down and is very excited. Many people were showing the same emotions, but Faizan was excited for a different reason. This marked a major milestone for him, and It had nothing to do with education. He would be bringing a major city to its knees. This day meant he would be contacted by his friends and would be going off to training for his mission. He was very excited and focused on his mission.

Ben has Dan on the phone and asks him, "Dan, I believe you had a colleague in Germany correct?"

Dan says, "Yes, why do you ask?"

Ben says, "I can't go into detail, but the President asked me to investigate a few countries and see if anyone has found the signal besides us. We both know that Germany is at the forefront with their new space program."

Ben asks, "Who is your contact there?"

Dan says, "His name is Gerhard Fischer, He is Director of HETI Germany, he will have knowledge of any signals, but that doesn't mean he will divulge anything."

Ben says, "Ok, give him a call and see what he has to say then call me back."

Dan replies, "No problem, I'll talk to you in a while."

Dan first calculates what time it would be in Germany, realizing it's about 11:00 AM. He then calls Gerhard. Gerhard answers the phone and says, "Ah, my old friend, how are you doing?"

Dan says, "I am doing well Gerhard, how is your family?"

He says, "Great, my girls are doing well in university; to what do I owe the pleasure for your call?"

Dan says, "Always to the point, arent you? Well, this is an odd question, but by chance have you encountered any odd signals at your facility?"

Gerhard says, "Yes we have, we have been trying to decode the data but have not had a lot of luck; it is rather odd for sure though. Why do you ask?"

Dan says, "Well, we have the signal as well, and we have decoded it and translated it. I am not at liberty to divulge that info yet, but we will."

Gerhard says, "Well, I look forward to that; thank you for the call, Dan."

Dan says, "It has been a pleasure, and I will be talking to you soon old friend, goodbye."

Dan hangs up his phone and calls Ben; Ben answers his phone and says hello. Dan says, "Hello, I talked to Gerhard, and they have received the signal but have not successfully decoded it." Then, Ben thanks Dan and they hang up their phones.

∞

Gabe and Rai are sitting on the back patio of their home enjoying a sweet glass of red wine. Gabriel says, "So, Rock View Nature Park? You are sure?"

Rai says, "Yes, that is where I want to say my vows to you. There is a little gazebo there where we could do it, jus ta few close friends and us."

Gabe says, "I have been there, and I think it's a great idea baby."

Rai says, "I am just going to have Sophie stand up for me; who will be your best man?"

Gabe says, "Well, I have given it some thought, and I was thinking Dan, but I could be persuaded to ask Hayden. He has been a Godsend for Sophie, and I have gotten to know him prettywell. What are your thoughts?"

Rai says, "I think it is up to you, whatever your heart tells you to do."

Gabe says, "Ok, I will ask Hayden then. Let's invite them over for dinner and ask him."

Rai says, "Great idea. I will make some dinner, and we can pull out that bottle we've been saving for a special occasion."

Gabe sits back as Rai gets up and calls Sophie to ask her if they could come over for dinner that evening. Gabe is learning to pray, so he closes his eyes and thanks God for all that he has given him. Rai turns just in time to see this; the transformation moves her. She thinks to herself; maybe I should start doing some praying myself. Rai calls Sophie; she answers and Rai says, "Hello baby, how are you feeling?"

Sophie replies, "I have been a little sick but I am feeling a little better this evening."

Rai says, "Well, we were wondering if you and Hayden had plans for tonight?"

Sophie says, "No we are just in for the evening, why do you ask?"

Rai says, "We would like you to come over for dinner, would you be up for that?"

Sophie says, "Sure we would love that."

Rai asks, "Great, does 7:00 sound ok?"

Sophie responds, "Sure, we will be there."

Chapter 8

In the city of Gwadar, Pakistan, Omer Abad sits on a beautiful beach with his wife Karimah and his two kids. As he relaxes he gets a call, he tells Karimah that it is the office and he needs to take it. Omer gets up and moves away from his family. He says, "Ok, I can talk, how are things progressing?"

Qadeer says, "Sir, the package is ready to go, we have everything lined up to move it."

Omer says, "Very well, make it happen. I trust you have an untraceable phone?"

Qadeer says, "Yes sir."

Omer says, "Very well, bring the package and the rest of our family here, and we will proceed."

Qadeer says, "We will depart immediately, sir."

∞

Huan Ji opens the door, Sarah and Tim step outside followed by Xi Mingze, then Huan Ji. Huan Ji pulls Sarah to the side and says, "Sarah, I want you to know that I am taking your claims seriously. I apologize if I seemed flippant when you first told me of your messages, it just seems so incredible. Anyhow, I would like to take you up on your offer to send a few of our scientist to your facility to see what you have discovered."

Sarah, says, "I understand Huan Ji, and when you want to send them just let us know. Also, I will be calling for a worldwide meeting to let everyone know what we have discovered, then I will have a news conference. It would be prudent if your scientist could be up-to-date before that meeting because I would like you to stand with me at the Nations meeting and the news conference."

Huan Ji says, "I will do my best, and I would be honored to stand with you."

They all say their farewells, Tim and Sarah are off to the airport. Huan Ji walks back inside his home and calls his Vice-president, Zou Hailian, and asks him to meet him at his residence.

∞

Rashad says, "First, let me introduce Annbella Smith, our Astrobiologist at HETI. We have been working together for a few months to figure out the best approach for this task and we have landed on creating a wormhole to send data through." Rashad was talking to a room full of people. All Ph.D.'s and experts in their field, they were given an almost unlimited budget and had access to the smartest people the United States had to offer. Rashad continues, "Let's get started, as you all know, theoretically, a wormhole is a passage through space-time that could be used as a shortcut through space. Also, you know that Einstein and Rosen used the theory of general relativity to expand on using wormholes as a connection through space creating a hypothetical shortcut. The wormhole, however, needs a mouth at both ends, and that is our challenge. We need to be able to create those openings at each end of those areas of space. We also need to explore the theory of using "exotic" matter to help stabilize the wormhole."

Dr. Adriana Rodriguez from TASA-Florida stood and said, "That is preposterous! There is no way we are anywhere near something like that."

Ann steps forward and says, "We are perfectly aware of the challenges in front of us, but we have been given the task of trying to communicate with a world five light years away in an expedited manner. This is the most plausible theory we can come up with. If there is something anyone wants to contribute, any suggestions, a new line of thought, now is the time to say something because we are wide open at this point."

Mia, who has been sitting outside of the group just observing the process speaks up and says, "Dr. Rodriguez, I respect everything you bring to the table, but as Ann said, we have to work towards a solution, so please come with some ideas, thank you." Just as she finished speaking a younger man knocks on the door; he doesn't have the security clearance to enter the room. Rashad walked to the door and opens it, the man is an intern at HETI and has been sent to the room by another technician. He says, "Excuse me sir, but Brian asked me to tell you he needed to speak to you immediately." Rashad walks with the intern and enters the separate monitoring room. On the screen is nonsense; it looked like a couple of lines then some numbers then lines. Where there was normally a message, there was a mystery.

Rashad asks Brain to come with him so they could get everything turned on in the meeting room. Once there Rashad says, "Ok everyone, we need to put the meeting on hold. We have a new message, but it's not like anything we have seen before."Brian and Rashad turned all the large screened TV's on, and the images appeared on the screens.

Mia steps up and says, "Well, what do we have here?"

Ann said, "I have no idea."

Mia steps away from the group of people that were all in several separate discussions and calls Gabriel; Gabriel answers the phone. Mia says, "Gabriel, can you come to the meeting room? We have something on the screen that makes no sense."

Gabriel says, "Sure thing, I am on my way."

Jordan walks into his home; it is quiet, he looks upstairs and can see the blue light of their television in their room. Before he walked up, he stepped into the kitchen and brought out a bottle of whiskey he had just bought. It has been several years since he has drunk any alcohol, but it has become a regular occurrence since he has lost his son. He poured himself a double shot and downed it; he poured another and drank that as well. He poured a third glass but then added some ice to it and walked into his office. He slid the gun he had just purchased out from behind his jacket and started to put it in his drawer when suddenly the light comes on. Jasmine stands in the doorway with her eyes wide and focused on the gun. He starts to stammer and give some excuses. He says, "Jasmine, it is just for protection."

She says, "Bullshit, I know what that piece is for, and I want in."

Jordan says, "What? Baby, I have to do this, you are the best thing Michele has for the future. You know if I do this, I am gone, forever, even if I survive."

Jasmine says, "Ok, what can I do to help then?"

Jordan says, "Nope, you can't know anything, you need plausible deniability, so we never had this conversation."

Jasmine walks up and stands in front of him. For the first time since they had lost Jordan, she looks into his eyes, she reaches for him, Jordan takes her into his arms, and they hug each other. They hold each other for a long time. Jordan pulls back a little and brings his lips to hers and kisses her deeply; they separate, and Jordan puts the gun into a safe he had, shuts the lights off, and they go upstairs holding hands with the anticipation of a night of lovemaking they had not had in a long time.

Faizan came out of his bedroom and went to the dinner table; his mother had just announced to him and his father that dinner was ready. After a few minutes Faizan says, "So, I wanted to talk to you both about something one of my friends approached me about."

His father says, "What is that?"

Faizan says, "Well a few of my friends are taking a trip across a few of the states, and they asked me if I wanted to go. I would love to do it if you both say it is ok."

His father asks, "Well, where are you going? How are you paying for it?"

Faizan says, "I have about a thousand dollars saved up, and we plan on camping instead of hotels. There are some theme parks they want to go to; one is in Ohio, another is in Indiana, and they are talking about going to Chicago as well."

His father looks at his mother then back at him and says, "You know what, I say yes, you should go, you are young only once."

Faizan says, "Thank you so much; I will keep in touch as we travel. We will leave this Saturday, so in three days."

His mother tears up and starts clearing the table, Faizan stands and steps up to her and says, "Mother, you know I will be back, I love you."

∞

It is early in the west wing, and the President of the United States, Sarah, is waking up next to her husband, Tim. They are both jet-lagged from the flight from China. She quietly gets up from the bed and creeps into the bathroom. She had too much to do and couldn't afford to sleep in today. She calls the kitchen and asks for some coffee, something she rarely did. Normally she would get it herself, but she needed to wake up and get things going. Today was going to be a big day. She was going to call the U.N. and all the nation's leaders today and personally ask them to attend a meeting that would have an everlasting effect on the world as we know it. She steps out of the shower and dries off. After she is dressed and ready to face the day, she sits at the small antique desk that is in the room. Her cup of coffee had been waiting for her after her shower and a bagel with cream cheese. They knew her well, what great people they are, she thought to herself. She opened her laptop and opened the document she had created on the plane ride home. It was a list of the one hundred and ninety-five countries she would be calling today. She was reviewing it and searching for some information online for some of the leaders she had not met yet.

At about seven thirty Tim woke up and saw his wife working on the computer, already showered, dressed and munching on a bagel and drinking coffee. Sarah could tell Tim was awake; she looked over at him and said good morning. Tim said, "Good morning beautiful, how long have you been up?"

Sarah said, "I got up at about six o'clock."

Tim walked over and kissed his wife on the cheek and left to shower. Sarah turned back to her computer, she saved her document and told Tim she was going to her office, meaning the oval office. She traditionally used it for official work, and she wanted to get started on her calls. Once in her office, a few of her aids came in and discussed a few of the issues at hand. She asked one to relay a message to the Secretary of State. She said, "Tell her that I want to review our response on the Canadian stance as it relates to their new water tax policy."

Once her aid left, Sarah turned to her phone on her desk. Her first call would be to the Secretary-General of the United Nations, Aldo Muller. The phone rang, and a young woman answered, Sarah stated who she was and asked to speak to Aldo. The call was transferred, and Aldo answered. Sarah said, "Hello Aldo, this is Sarah. I was wondering if you have a few minutes to talk."

He said, "Absolutely Madam President, what can I do for you?"

Sarah said, "Well, I can't go into details, but I need to call an unusual emergency session, only I want to invite all nations, not just the members."

Aldo says, "Madam that is almost two hundred nations and highly unusual."

Sarah responds, "I completely understand, but it is what I feel I need to do."

"Very well, Madam, I will put calls into the members that we will be having a session on Monday, does that work for you?"

Sarah replies, "Yes it does, thank you so very much."

They hang up, and she begins making her calls. She decides to make the tougher calls first. So, first was North Korea. The call went about as expected; he was cold and short, but she made the offer for them to attend and they said they would consider it. Next was Iran, then Cuba and they all went about the same way, cold and short, but she could at least say she offered. Her true intention was for them to attend and she sincerely hoped they did. This was too big for them not to be involved. She worked all morning making calls, working through translators and waiting for leaders to come to the phone as it was different times of the day and night around the world. She took a break for lunch and ate with Tim. They had a nice lunch, and it was just what she needed. Tim was always a calming presence for her and provided the energy she needed to keep her grounded.

After lunch, she went back to the office to continue her calls. Finally, at about 6:00 PM she got off the phone with the prime minister of England. She felt good about their responses, but she had been vague so the actual meeting would be a different story.

Gabriel walks into the meeting room and looks at the screen. He is as confused as everyone else. Gabriel says, "Hello everyone, what have we got here?"

Mia says, "Brian alerted us that he had a message and Rashad pulled it up on the monitors in this room; we have some of the smartest people in the world here Gabriel, and we are at a loss, but this is just initial thoughts."

Rashad is sitting in front of one of the monitors with a keyboard at his fingertips. His fingers are flying around the keys. He backs the feed up to before the message changes and sees what they've seen for a while...the first message all the way to the most recent one, then a blank screen, and finally the new message.

Mia is behind Rashad along with the majority of people that had been attending the meeting. She turns around and says, "Ok everyone, I think we will adjourn the meeting for today; you are more than welcome to stick around though. If you leave, we will meet back here tomorrow at eight o'clock AM." Nobody moved, everyone stayed where they were so Mia said, "Ok if everyone is sticking around, let's break out into groups. Some stay here and some go to our message room where Brian is. Let start spitballing some ideas right now."

Everyone turns and starts talking to each other, and finally a couple of groups form with some staying and some leaving to go to the new message room. Mia sits next to Gabriel with Rashad not far away. Gabriel leans towards Mia and says, "Ok, tell me what you think, you're the smartest person in this place, so, if you have no idea, it is going to be a while before we figure this one out."

Mia says, "Ok, so let's take a look again at this."They sit in front of the monitor and look at the image again. "Let's focus on the word in the corner; please magnify it. I am pretty sure I know what that says. בהשראה Ok, I am pretty sure that says "inspired", let me run it through the translator." Mia types the characters, and the word inspired comes up. Now they were even more perplexed, Mia says, "Ok, I think we know how the messaging works, we know that there is more in the message, so maybe we need to wait until more information comes through before we know what we have here."

Gabriel says, "Sounds like a good plan to me. Mia, please let me know if anything else comes through."

Mia says, "I will."

Gabe leaves and calls Rai; she answers. Gabe says, "Hey baby, I am on my way home. I will swing by and pick you up to go meet Pastor Gary Manns; I figured we could stop for some dinner before we meet him at six thirty."

Rai says, "Sounds great baby, what do you think he will say? We haven't known him that long; do you think he will agree to marry us?"

Gabe says, "I get the sense that he will. I should be home soon; I'll see you then, I Love You."

Rai responds, "I Love you too."

∞

Young Ra-il had been called to meet with several high-ranking officials. He was at a table when suddenly the doors open and the Supreme leader of North Korea enters the room. Everyone stood and bowed deeply. He sat down, and he motioned for everyone else to sit. He said, "The President of the United States has contacted me. I have been invited to sit at the table of all other countries for a big announcement from the Americans. I intend to be present at this meeting, but we have to speed up operation Chollima."

Everyone sits while Young Ra-ill spoke and said, "Not a problem Great Supreme Leader. My team and I have been very successful in completing all assigned tasks. We are ready to move the cargo into place."

The Supreme Leader simply says, "Very good, complete the task. I want it all moved in now, and I want it done in a week."

Young Ra-ill swallowed hard. He knew it was a near impossible task, but he said, "Not a problem, Great Leader. I will have it done by then." The Supreme Leader didn't respond, he just got up and walked out with his guards moving with him.

After getting off the phone with Zou Hailian, Huan Ji calls the President of the Chinese Academy of Science and says, "Wei Yuand a, The President of the United States just left, I need you to meet me at my residence immediately."

Wei Yuand a says, "Yes Chairman Huan Ji, Right away."

Huan Ji hangs up his phone, and he walks into the sitting room where his wife is and says, "I like her, I like her a lot, but I am very disappointed we didn't find this first. Now, I will be standing at her side, but she should be standing at my side!"He takes a drink of his tea when there is a knock at their door. The housemaid answers the door, and Wei Yuand a was there. Huan Ji walked across the room and said, "Thank you for coming so quickly, I need to speak to you, please sit down. Now, what I am about to tell you is extremely sensitive and I must ask you not to repeat what I am about to tell you. Soon, the President of the United States will convene a meeting at the United Nations. At this meeting, she will announce that they have detected a message from another planet. They have decoded and translated the messages. Essentially, these messages prove the existence of Jesus. First, I must tell you; I am extremely disappointed that we did not follow up on the signal we detected. If this were a different time or I not a kind and gentle leader, I would have had you killed. However, I am not going to do that. I want you to gather a team of people to go to America and learn all that they know. They have offered to have us come and examine their data."

Wei Yuand a stands then bows and begins an apology that almost sounds like a cry. When his apology is done, he says, "I will not fail you," and then leaves the room.

Gabe pulls up to their home and Rai walks out the front door, she gets into his car, and he kisses her. They drive to their favorite little place to eat, Lola's Kitchen. They order and while waiting, Gabe says, "So, I want to get baptized and I need to let you know I am going to break slightly with my commitment of silence regarding the messages today when we meet with Pastor Manns. I feel I need to talk to him about what is going on with the messages because I have so many questions."

Rai says, "Do you think that's a good idea?"

Gabe says, "No but it's what my gut is telling me to do."

Rai said, "Ok, I will always have your back baby." He reached over and squeezes her hand. Once they finish their meal, they drive to the church and walk in. Once inside, they walk to Pastor Manns' office. He is there at his desk, he looks up, and a warm smile spreads across his face as they enter. He is genuinely happy to see them. He stands and shakes their hands and says, "Come in, come in, have a seat. Ok, what can I do for you fine folks today?"

Gabe says, "Well sir, I haven't had a chance to give you much background on us, but Rai and I have known each other since college and were married pretty young, and after college, we pursued our careers. We were pulled in different directions and felt we should split up and follow our dreams. That was over twenty years ago, and we have always stayed close. Obviously we have a daughter together but, honestly, I think we never fell out of love with each other. She is the only woman I will ever love for the rest of my life." Tears were welling up in Rai's eyes as he spoke. She knew all of this but to hear it professed to someone else was drilling deep into her heart. Gabe continues, "Also, I have found Christ, and with him in my life, it seems to have made our love even deeper, it is almost like we have a new love, a new found love."

Gary says, "What a nice story, Jesus has a way of doing that, He is love, and once He is in your life, your perspective changes."

Gabe says, "We would like to remarry, and we would like for you to preside over the ceremony."

Gary says, "I would be honored! When are you thinking of getting married?"

"As soon as possible, maybe in the next two weeks?" Gabe responds.

Gary says, "I can look at my schedule and let you know when I am free. Do you want to use the church?"

Gabe says, "Actually there is a park we would like to use, so once you let us know a date we will reserve the gazebo." Gabe continues, "Also before we get married, I would like it if you could baptize me."

Gary says with a huge warm smile, "Absolutely!"

Gabe says, "But, Gary, there is something else that I need to talk to you about."

Gary looks at Gabe and says, "What is it?"

Gabe says, "Gary, what I am going to tell you is top secret and if you don't want me to go any further I won't."

Gary says, "Ok, is it going to get me killed?"

Gabe says, "No, as a matter of fact, I don't think it is going to be top secret much longer."

Gary says, "Ok, but, just so you know, I treat our conversations almost like a lawyers client/privilege; what we talk about stays between us."

Gabe says, "Ok, well, prepare yourself, Pastor Manns, because you're going to think I am crazy. A few months ago, my team at the The Space Network (T.S.N.) received a signal. We have been able to decode this message; it was, in fact, a message from another world."

Gary says, "Um, ok."

Gabe continues, "This message was decoded, and It was in an ancient form of Hebrew."

Gary says, "Wait, what? That is crazy! You have been hacked,Gabriel."

Gabe says, "Gary, I have the best minds in the world working on this, we have performed every possible test and have confirmed these are indeed messages from another world and they are communicating in Hebrew. The next thing I am going to tell you will shock you as well, Gary, we have received several messages, and after they were decoded and translated, they were all telling us they knew the Messiah, the all mighty Jesus."

Gary again looks at Gabe and says, "You are sure?"

Gabe says, "Yes, one hundred percent sure, Gary, there is a world five light years from us that knows Jesus."

Gary, immediately knowing what this meant, fell to his knees, He cried out, "Oh Jesus, My God, I am not worthy, I am so full of sin, I try to live the way you want us to, but I can still feel the sin in me. Please help me to be the man you want me to be. Lord Jesus, I Love you, guide me, and tell me what you want from me."

Then, a voice spoke to him, he had always thought he was talking to God, but this, this was different. He felt almost like he was dreaming, but he was not. The voice said, "My son, know you are loved, I feel your love as well, I want you to tell the world about my word, there will be a need soon for a spiritual leader to lead everyone to me, you will be that person."

Gary looked up and said, "God, surely you can find someone that is better than me to deliver your children."

The voice said, "I know what I can do, I have chosen you, your love is pure, now do as I ask, you will know when it is time to deliver my message, be with Gabriel and it will be revealed."

Gabe and Rai were standing close to him and had watched him talking to God. Gary stood, looked at Gabe and said, "Gabriel,

God just spoke to me, He told me I was to be with you and that I am to deliver His message of Love."

Gabe was confused, but Rai spoke up and said, "God will tell us what to do and when to do it." The three of them hugged, and Gabe said he would be in touch when he thought he was supposed to be, and Gary said, "Likewise."

Chapter 9

Sarah is on Air Force One, looking over her notes and continuing to refine her speech. This had to be the speech of her lifetime. She was about to change the course of the world, and It had to be perfect. Tim was beside her reading a book; he looked up at his wife as she worked so hard on her speech. He admired her, and he was as in love with her now as he had been all those years ago when they were just kids. He had always thought she was brilliant and now the whole world got to benefit from all of those beautiful brains of hers, then he thought, hmm, her heart too, she has an amazing heart, and that is something few people possess, an amazing heart to go with the magnificent brain to temper her decisions. Yep, he thought, the world was lucky that she was the leader of the free world at this point. Sarah looked up and saw him staring, and she said, "What honey?" Tim says, "Oh, I just love you, my beautiful wife."

She smiled and said, "I love you too," and she faced her laptop again.

∞

Wei Yuand a is on a flight from Beijing to Washington D.C. with a crew of 10 scientists that were at the top in their fields. They were making their approach to the airport. Looking out the window, he could see the capitol and all the other familiar landmarks he had seen in pictures and videos. He had very strict orders to gain as much information that he could during his stay in the United States. Wei Yuand a was slightly disappointed; he felt the buildings in China were much more colorful than these buildings. The flight lands and he and his team of scientist disembark the plane and make their way through customs. Once they have recovered their luggage, they are met by a driver who takes them to meet with Ben at his office. Wei Yuand a can speak enough English to communicate well enough to get by. They are driven to their hotel; the driver tells them that Ben will be meeting them for dinner at the restaurant at the hotel at 7:00 later that evening.

Finally, Ben meets them outside the restaurant, and they have a good meal and fair conversation. They all agree that they will meet Ben at his office the next morning to discuss all the events up to this point. They will then be boarding a flight for California to tour the facilities and review all their data.

The next morning, Ben welcomes the team from China to his office. Everyone is in a meeting room, and Ben begins about an hour-long discussion about protocols, stand ards, data evaluation and analysis. Once done they have lunch, and they are off to the airport. After their flight to Los Angeles and their drive to Barstow, they were exhausted. They checked into their hotel and got a good night's sleep. At eight o'clock AM a black passenger van with dark tinted windows was waiting for them in front of their hotel. The driver was a government employee and looked almost silly. He had on a black suit, white shirt, thin black tie and dark sunglasses. He simply asked them their names and checked them off his list. He then told them to get into the van, and they were off.

They arrived at the TSN site where they were to meet with Gabriel and Mia as well as their team. Gabriel and Mia met them all in the conference room for some small talk, and a light breakfast of danishes, pastries, bagels, coffee and tea. Gabriel finally stood up and began talking to the group. He said, "Hello everyone and welcome to the TSN. I know you all have spent some time in D.C. and Ben brought you all up to speed on everything." Gabriel had to pause because most of the Chinese scientists spoke poor English, so they had an interpreter translating what he said. "We continue to get new messages and are currently trying to figure out the last message. So, I don't want to put you through a bunch of boring talks; let's head to the message room, and I will introduce you all to our team. I have instructed my team to answer any and all questions you have."

Then, Gabriel walks over to another table picks up a large binder and gives it to Wei Yuand a. This is all our data. It contains all the messages to date. Wei Yuand a thanks him and takes the binder. They then all leave the room and walk to the message room. After introducing them to his team, the Chinese team fans out and begin talking to different people at different stations. Gabriel and Mia sit down with Wei Yuand a and show him the most recent message. He looks at it for a while and asks them if they have the newest version of XLTZ SLAYER program; they did, so they pull the program up. Wei Yuand a works on the program; he also pulls out a memory stick and asks them if he can upload an update to increase the function of the program. He is then able to move the raw data into the program. He starts manipulating the data and lets the program work. It is close to lunch time, so they take a break and enjoy a meal together. Wei Yuand a breaks away and pulls out his phone; he makes a call directly to Huan Ji, as he was instructed to do. He says, "Sir, Yes, I have uploaded the tracking program, but sir, I must tell you, I don't feel like they are hiding anything. They have given me complete access to all of their files, and they gave a binder to me full of all of the data. Also, sir, I must tell you, everything I see here tells me that this is real. They have run every possible test to ensure this is a legitimate message from where they say it comes from." Huan Ji says, "You are sure?" He says, "I am uploading an update to a program that they have but have not used it to run their data through. The program might give us a little more information within the data, but yes, I think it is real; you should support the American President." Huan Ji says, "Very well, I just arrived for the meeting and am meeting with Madam President soon; well done Wei Yuand a."

∞

Sarah and Tim arrive at their hotel in St. Moritz, Switzerland, which was traditionally the secret venue of the Club annual meeting that used to be held years ago and is the perfect place to hold this meeting. Upon arrival, she contacts Huan Ji and requests a meeting. Huan Ji says he will meet her in the conference room provided by the resort. Sara tells Tim she is meeting with Huan Ji and she leaves after kissing him on the cheek. Huan Ji and Sarah arrive at the conference room at the same time. Both are glad to see each other. Initially, they shake hands but then Sarah closes the gap and gives an unusual hug to Huan Ji. They enter the room and sit down. Sarah says, "Huan Ji, I am so glad to see you and want to thank you for meeting with me before the Multi-Lateral U.N. address. I wanted to ask you if you will stand with me for this speech."

Huan Ji says, "Sarah, I must say, that I have been very skeptical of this whole thing, I am ready to stand with you first as a friend, I would do it no matter what evidence there is for your claims. However, I have heard from my people that are currently visiting your facility in California, and they confirm that everything is legitimate. I honestly don't know how to feel about it. That Jesus is real, what does that do to all the different societies in the world? There are so many wars predicated on the fact that each feels their religion is the correct one. Jesus Christ makes all of those conflicts null and void."

Sarah says, "That is correct, I am telling this to the world because they deserve to know, they can do with it as they will, but I don't have the right to keep it to myself."

Huan Ji says, "Very well, I will be at your side during your speech."

Sarah is so relieved. But then says, "Huan Ji, I must tell you, this is going to be an unusual speech, I only ask that you keep an open mind and support me through the whole speech."

Huan Ji says, "That is not a problem." The two shake hands again and say their farewells until the next day.

∞

It is Thursday morning; the time is nine forty-five and Sarah and Huan Ji stand outside the main conference hall room. They can hear the leaders from all around the world talking, some heated, some laughing. Sarah was informed that every leader she had invited was in attendance. A U.N. assistant walks out and asks them to come in and take their seat on the stage. As they did this, slowly the room became quieter. Huan Ji and Sarah walk up the steps to the stage, and they take their seats. After a minute, Aldo Muller walks out from the back of the stage; there was a series of very tall, blue curtains, and they swayed as he pushed them aside. Aldo approaches the microphone holding up a pair of headphones and says, "Ladies and Gentlemen if you haven't already done it, would you please put your headphones that were assigned to you on, they are an automatic translator, and you will know what is said in real time."

After about a minute, he begins again. "First, Welcome to this, the first meeting of every nation that exists in the world. I was contacted a few weeks ago by Madam President of the United States and agreed to assist her in setting this meeting up and to be honest; even I do not know why we are here, so without any further ado, I give you Madam President of the UnitedStates.

Sarah stood and walked up and shook Aldo's hand and thanked him, Huan Ji did the same and then stood next to her. She thanked everyone for taking time out of their extremely busy schedules to attend this meeting and she says, "You might be wondering why President Huan Ji is with me. I will tell you why, Over the years, there have been tensions between our countries, but I submit to you that, that is all in the past. Also, what I am about to tell you, is going to be unbelievable, and I needed someone to have an independent view, so he has sent people to the United States to confirm what I am about to tell you. Before I go any further, I ask that everyone keep an open mind and that you please stay for the whole time I am speaking. Before I go any further, I want to start with something very unusual, but you will understand why I have chosen to speak to this in just a bit. I want to start with the Sermon on the Mount delivered by Jesus of Nazareth." Sarah opens her binder that contains her speech, she adjusts the microphone and begins speaking,

"Now when Jesus saw the crowds, he went up on a mountainside and sat down. His disciples came to him, and he began to teach them. He said: "Blessed are the poor in spirit, for theirs is the kingdom of heaven. Blessed are those who mourn, for they will be comforted. Blessed are the meek, for they will inherit the earth. Blessed are those who hunger and thirst for righteousness, for they will be filled. Blessed are the merciful, for they will be shown mercy. Blessed are the pure in heart, for they will see God. Blessed are the peacemakers, for they will be called children of God. Blessed are those who are persecuted because of righteousness, for theirs is the kingdom of heaven. Blessed are you when people insult you, persecute you and falsely say all kinds of evil against you because of me.

Rejoice and be glad, because great is your reward in heaven, for, in the same way, they persecuted the prophets who were before you; Salt and Light, you are the salt of the earth. But if the salt loses its saltiness, how can it be made salty again? It is no longer good for anything, except to be thrown out and trampled underfoot. You are the light of the world. A town built on a hill cannot be hidden. Neither do people light a lamp and put it under a bowl. Instead, they put it on its stand, and it gives light to everyone in the house. In the same way, let your light shine before others, that they may see your good deeds and glorify your Father in heaven.

The Fulfillment of the Law, do not think that I have come to abolish the Law or the Prophets; I have not come to abolish them but to fulfill them. For truly I tell you until heaven and earth disappear, not the smallest letter, not the least stroke of a pen, will by any means disappear from the Law until everything is accomplished. Therefore, anyone who sets aside one of the least of these commands and teaches others accordingly will be called least in the kingdom of heaven, but whoever practices and teaches these commands will be called great in the kingdom of heaven. For I tell you that unless your righteousness surpasses that of the Pharisees and the teachers of the law, you will certainly not enter the kingdom of heaven.

Murder, "You have heard that it was said to the people long ago, 'You shall not murder, and anyone who murders will be subject to judgment. But I tell you that anyone who is angry with a brother or sister will be subject to judgment. Again, anyone who says to a brother or sister, 'Raca,' is answerable to the court. And anyone who says, 'You fool!' will be in danger of the fire of hell. Therefore, if you are offering your gift at the altar remember that your brother or sister has something against you leave your gift there in front of the altar. First, go and be reconciled to them; then come and offer your gift. Settle matters quickly with your adversary who is taking you to court. Do it while you are still together on the way, or your adversary may hand you over to the judge, and the judge may hand you over to the officer, and you may be thrown into prison. Truly I tell you, you will not get out until you have paid the last penny.

Adultery, you have heard that it was said, 'You shall not commit adultery. But I tell you that anyone who looks at a woman lustfully has already committed adultery with her in his heart. If your right eye causes you to stumble, gouge it out and throw it away. It is better for you to lose one part of your body than for your whole body to be thrown into hell. And if your right-hand causes you to stumble, cut it off and throw it away. It is better for you to lose one part of your body than for your whole body to go into hell.

Divorce, it has been said, 'Anyone who divorces his wife must give her a certificate of divorce. But I tell you that anyone who divorces his wife, except for sexual immorality, makes her the victim of adultery, and anyone who marries a divorced woman commits adultery. Oaths, again, you have heard that it was said to the people long ago, 'Do not break your oath but fulfill to the Lord the vows you have made. But I tell you, do not swear an oath at all: either by heaven, for it is God's throne; or by the earth, for it is his footstool; or by Jerusalem, for it is the city of the Great King. And do not swear by your head, for you cannot make even one hair white or black. All you need to say is simply 'Yes' or 'No'; anything beyond this comes from the evil one.

Eye for Eye, You have heard that it was said, 'Eye for eye, and a tooth for a tooth. But I tell you, do not resist an evil person. If anyone slaps you on the right cheek, turn to them the other cheek also. And if anyone wants to sue you and take your shirt, hand over your coat as well. If anyone forces you to go one mile, go with them two miles. Give to the one who asks you, and do not turn away from the one who wants to borrow from you.

Love for Enemies, You have heard that it was said, 'Love your neighbor and hate your enemy. But I tell you, love your enemies and pray for those who persecute you, that you may be children of your Father in heaven. He causes his sun to rise on the evil and the good and sends rain on the righteous and the unrighteous. If you love those who love you, what reward will you get? Are not even the tax collectors doing that? And if you greet only your own people, what are you doing more than others? Do not even pagans do that? Be perfect, therefore, as your heavenly Father is perfect. Giving to the Needy, Be careful not to practice your righteousness in front of others to be seen by them. If you do, you will have no reward from your Father in heaven. So when you give to the needy, do not announce it with trumpets, as the hypocrites do in the synagogues and on the streets, to be honored by others. Truly I tell you, they have received their reward in full. But when you give to the needy, do not let your left hand know what your right hand is doing, so that your giving may be in secret. Then your Father, who sees what is done in secret, will reward you.

Prayer, And when you pray, do not be like the hypocrites, for they love to pray standing in the synagogues and on the street corners to be seen by others. Truly I tell you, they have received their reward in full. But when you pray, go into your room, close the door and pray to your Father, who is unseen. Then your Father, who sees what is done in secret, will reward you. And when you pray, do not keep on babbling like pagans, for they think they will be heard because of their many words. Do not be like them, for your Father knows what you need before you ask him. This, then, is how you should pray: 'Our Father in heaven, hallowed be your name, your kingdom come, your will be done, on earth as it is in heaven. Give us today our daily bread. And forgive us our debts, as we also have forgiven our debtors. And lead us not into temptation, but deliver us from the evil one. For if you forgive other people when they sin against you, your heavenly Father will also forgive you. But if you do not forgive others their sins, your Father will not forgive your sins.

Fasting , when you fast, do not look somber as the hypocrites do, for they disfigure their faces to show others they are fasting. Truly I tell you, they have received their reward in full. But when you fast, put oil on your head and wash your face, so that it will not be obvious to others that you are fasting, but only to your Father, who is unseen; and your Father, who sees what is done in secret, will reward you.

Treasures in Heaven, do not store up for yourselves treasures on earth, where moths and vermin destroy, and where thieves break in and steal. But store up for yourselves treasures in heaven, where moths and vermin do not destroy, and where thieves do not break in and steal. For where your treasure is, there your heart will be also. The eye is the lamp of the body. If your eyes are healthy, your whole body will be full of light. But if your eyes are unhealthy, your whole body will be full of darkness. If then the light within you is darkness, how great is that darkness! No one can serve two masters. Either you will hate the one and love the other, or you will be devoted to the one and despise the other. You cannot serve both God and money.

Do Not Worry. Therefore I tell you, do not worry about your life, what you will eat or drink; or about your body, what you will wear. Is not life more than food, and the body more than clothes? Look at the birds of the air; they do not sow or reap or store away in barns, and yet your heavenly Father feeds them. Are you not much more valuable than they? Can anyone of you by worrying add a single hour to your life¹? And why do you worry about clothes? See how the flowers of the field grow. They do not labor or spin. Yet I tell you that not even Solomon in all His splendor was dressed like one of these. If that is how God clothes the grass of the field, which is here today and tomorrow is thrown into the fire, will he not much more clothe you-you of little faith? So do not worry, saying, 'What shall we eat?' or 'What shall we drink?' or 'What shall we wear?' For the pagans run after all these things, and your heavenly Father knows that you need them. But seek first his kingdom and his righteousness, and all these, things will be given to you as well. Therefore, do not worry about tomorrow, for tomorrow will worry about itself. Each day has enough trouble of its own.

Judging Others, Do not judge, or you too will be judged. For in the same way you judge others, you will be judged, and with the measure you use, it will be measured to you. Why do you look at the speck of sawdust in your brother's eye and pay no attention to the plank in your own eye? How can you say to your brother, 'Let me take the speck out of your eye,' when all the time there is a plank in your own eye? You hypocrite, first take the plank out of your own eye, and then you will see clearly to remove the speck from your brother's eye. Do not give dogs what is sacred; do not throw your pearls to pigs. If you do, they may trample them under their feet, and turn and tear you to pieces.

Ask, Seek, Knock, Ask and it will be given to you; seek and you will find; knock and the doors will be opened to you. For everyone who asks receives; the one who seeks finds; and to the one who knocks, the door will be opened. Which of you, if your son asks for bread, will give him a stone? Or if he asks for a fish, will give him a snake? If you, then, though you are evil, know how to give good gifts to your children, how much more will your Father in heaven give good gifts to those who ask him!

So in everything, do to others what you would have them do to you, for this sums up the Law and the Prophets. The Narrow and Wide Gates, Enter through the narrow gate. For wide is the gate and broad is the road that leads to destruction, and many enter through it. But small is the gate and narrow the road that leads to life, and only a few find it.

True and False Prophets, Watch out for false prophets. They come to you in sheep's clothing, but inwardly they are ferocious wolves. By their fruit, you will recognize them. Do people pick grapes from thornbushes or figs from thistles? Likewise, every good tree bears good fruit, but a bad tree bears bad fruit. A good tree cannot bear bad fruit, and a bad tree cannot bear good fruit. Every tree that does not bear good fruit is cut down and thrown into the fire. Thus, by their fruit, you will recognize them.

True and False Disciples, Not everyone who says to me, 'Lord, Lord,' will enter the kingdom of heaven, but only the one who does the will of my Father who is in heaven. Many will say to me on that day, 'Lord, Lord, did we not prophesy in your name and in your name drive out demons and in your name perform many miracles?' Then I will tell them plainly, I never knew you, away from me, you evildoers!

The Wise and Foolish Builders, Therefore everyone who hears these words of mine and puts them into practice is like a wise man who built his house on the rock. The rain came down, the streams rose, and the winds blew and beat against that house, yet it did not fall, because it had its foundation on the rock. But everyone who hears these words of mine and does not put them into practice is like a foolish man who built his house on sand. The rain came down, the streams rose, and the winds blew and beat against that house, and it fell with a great crash.

When Jesus had finished saying these things, the crowds were amazed at his teaching, because he taught as one who had authority, and not as their teachers of the law (NIV®)."

Chapter 10

Sarah stepped away from the microphone and took a long drink of water; she then walks back up to the microphone and said, "These are the laws of God, remember them. Why I told them to you just now will become apparent. Today, we stand as one world, a race, of humans. We stand together on a precipice. Once we step off, there is no going back." she pauses long enough to let anyone who wishes to leave, to do so but no one does. Then she continues, "About six months ago our teams at TASA, HETI, and the TSN detected a signal from deep space. My people have spoken to several of your scientists, and we know that many of you have detected this signal as well. However, we were able to detect that signal, decode it and translate it. We have run many diagnostic tests on this signal. We also upgraded our systems to run independently, meaning we needed to eliminate the possibility of outside interference or hacking. I have also asked Huan Ji, to send a team of his top scientist to our facility to confirm our findings; I will ask him to come up and speak in just a moment," as she turns towards him, she says, "I want to thank Huan Ji for all he has done on this endeavor."

Huan Ji nods and says, "Our pleasure Madam President."

Sarah continues, "Ladies and Gentlemen, leaders of the world, what I am about to tell you will seem unbelievable, it is probably the most incredible finding this world has ever encountered...even today, as I am about to tell you this, I can hardly believe it myself. As I said, about six months ago, we encountered the initial signal; we were able to decode it and translate it. I must tell you first, that we had to translate it from an ancient Hebrew language." It took a few seconds for all the translations to take place, but as they did, the place erupted into a loud whisper. People were talking to each other, waving their hands as if they were insulted. Sarah began speaking again and asked for everyone to please quiet down if they could. Sarah continues, "I know it sounds unbelievable, that is what I said before I started. Once we translated it, the message was something I was not prepared for; you will not be prepared for it either. The message was Mashiach or translated, 'Messiah'." Again, after a short pause, the entire hall erupted; people were yelling and shouting at her. She knew this was going to happen; it was a lot for anyone to take in.

Sarah had stepped away from the microphone to gather herself and drink some water; she stepped back up to the microphone and started asking everyone to please take their seats and to calm down. After a minute the place was quiet again. She continued, "We have received many messages since then. I will release all of our data, and you will see all of the messages yourself, but I must tell you the most significant one we have received out of them all, and that is Yeshua or Jesus." Again, the place erupted but beyond anything like before. People were genuinely upset. It was too much for some people to accept. Sarah stepped back and her security detail, who had been nervous the whole time, stepped in and surrounded her. Leaders of other countries were acting like an angry mob, shouting at her and shaking their fists at her. Finally, a voice spreads over the room; it has an accent, a male voice, finally. People looked towards the microphone, and they could see Huan Ji there, calmly asking for their attention. He raised his headphones in the air over his head and said, "Everyone, please, put your headphones back on."

After everyone calmed down and were seated again, he spoke,

"Thank you, everyone, please, know that my reaction to this news was exactly like yours. Madam President Sarah and I have become unlikely friends, and she flew to Beijing to discuss this with me. After my initial reaction, like yours, I listened to what she had to say, and I began to accept it. Also, my team of scientists, who flew to the United States, has been given complete and total access to all of their equipment and data. I was informed by my leader there that everything is as they say it is. They have even given us all their data and the means to decode and translate the signal ourselves in the future. So, I am here to tell you that what she is saying is, in fact, true. There is a planet that is about five light-years from us, and they know who Jesus is, and they call him Messiah. Where we go from here is up to us all."

Huan Ji bows and steps away and as he does so, Sarah walks up and hugs him and thanks him emphatically. She then walks back up to the microphone and says, "Next, I want to read an excerpt from a speech given by the 14th Dalai Lama of Tibet titled A Human Approach to World Peace. By far the greatest single danger facing humankind - in fact, all living beings on our planet - is the threat of nuclear destruction. I need not elaborate on this danger, but I would like to appeal to all the leaders of the nuclear powers who literally hold the future of the world in their hands.Also, to the scientists and technicians who continue to create these awesome weapons of destruction, and to all the people at large who are in a position to influence their leaders: I appeal to them to exercise their sanity and begin to work at dismantling and destroying all nuclear weapons. We know that in the event of a nuclear war there will be no victors because there will be no survivors! Is it not frightening to contemplate such inhuman and heartless destruction? And, is it not logical that we should remove the cause for our own destruction when we know the cause and have both the time and the means to do so? Often we cannot overcome our problems because we either do not know the cause, or, if we understand it, do not have the means to remove it. This is not the case with the nuclear threat. I can tell you that I am ready to enter into those talks with anyone at anytime. I thank each and every one of you for attending this meeting today. I will be making available to everyone all of our data and the means to decode and translate the signals yourselves. One last thing, I intend to release this information to the public upon my return to the United States."

As she and Huan Ji leave the stage, he pulls her aside and says, "Sarah, why did you recite the excerpt from the Dalai Lama?"

Sarah says, "Well, I felt that I now know that the Prince of Peace is real. I have always thought that the presence of our nuclear arsenals are a massive threat to the world and that, although it was a bit premature to talk about it as it relates to the information I just presented, I had every leader in the world under one roof, and I might never get a chance to at least nudge the beginning of a worldwide peace process."

Huan Ji simply says, "Ah, brilliant, well done my friend, well done."

∞

Faizan arrived in Pakistan and had been in training for about a month. He had made friends and was learning so much about the Koran. Karimah was giving Faizan a portion of his meal for the evening. That was one thing he had not anticipated…there was little food available, and for the most part, they ate once a day. He had never really known hunger until now. So he was very thankful for the food she had given him. Omer Abad and Karimah had taken the young man into their home and Omer had grown very fond of him. He had such a hunger for knowledge about the Koran and wanted to know more about Mohamed. It was clear Faizan loved Allah as much as he himself did. Omer was sitting next to Faizan; he asked Faizan to pray over the food. A year ago Faizan would have been too embarrassed to do that, but he had learned so much about prayer from Omer that he was eager to thank Allah for the food in front of him. Normally this was done silently, but Omer was testing Faizan and wanted to see if he remembered the proper prayer for a meal. Faizan began, "Oh Allah! Bless the food You have provided us and save us from the punishment of the hellfire, In the name of Allah."

Omer said, "Well done, how is your training progressing in the field?"

Faizan said, "I think it is going great, there is so much to know. The weapons knowledge alone is immense, but I am getting it. Running the mock drills is a lot of fun too. All of the year's running track and playing soccer have made me the fastest in my group."

Omer says, "Yes, so I am told, you are doing well Faizan, I am pleased with your progress in just a month. Usually it takes many months to get a new student to the stage you are at in just a month. Tonight I want to sit down with you and start reviewing the plan for which you are being trained."

Faizan was extremely excited to hear this, he said, "Oh that sounds great!"

Just then Omer's two children came running in, and both tried to jump into Faizan's lap. The two had become very attached to him in the month he had been staying there. Faizan felt like he had two new siblings now, he hugged them both, and they sat down to eat. Faizan took his plate into the kitchen and thanked Karimah for the delicious meal. She said, "You are welcome."

Karimah had tried for the first week or so to not get close to Faizan; she knew why he was there, but eventually, his cheerful attitude and love for her family won her over, and she too thought of him as a son in her family. Omer called him into the sitting room, where he was spreading maps and blueprints all over a table. Omer says to Faizan, "What I am about to tell you is in the strictest of confidence. If you tell anyone what I am about to tell

117

you, I will kill you myself, and you will not enter heaven. You will be dishonored, and Allah will not accept your unclean soul."

Faizan says, "Never sir, I would never do that."

Omer says, "I know, but I had to tell you that. Come on over and let's get started. First, you must know that this is the largest strike on any one target that we or anyone else has made on a target. Our target is the Capitol of the United States. We have over 200 operatives in the states as we speak, with another one hundred set to move in when I say. It is a multi-pronged attack like the world has never seen. Your role, though son, is the most important one of all. You will be the one to take down the actual capitol building with a miniature nuclear device. We will have small distractions all around the capitol that will block access for emergency responders; we have two small planes to fly in to distract attention from you. We will be blocking the 14th Street Bridge, all exits for interstates 395 and 695; we will block Constitution Avenue at 4thStreet NW and 2nd street NE and all four drives leading into the Capitol. All you will need to do is walk into the visitor's entrance and press a button. If you do, Allah will be so pleased with you. You will have a special place in heaven with your seven virgins. Soon you will be ready, and then we will move you back to the United States."

Faizan had just about every emotion that existed running through his body. He was scared as hell, not because he was afraid to do it, he just wanted to get his role perfect, and he was excited to learn everything he needed to. The only thing he felt bad about was his parents. He knew they would be broken hearted, but he was doing what he knew was right. The United States had such a history of putting their nose where it didn't belong. The capitalism of the country made them worship money and not Allah. They needed to learn the ways of Islam.

∞

Gabe and Rai are looking over some resorts for their honeymoon. Rai says, "Yep, as close to the ocean as we can get. I want to be right on the beach." Gabe is scrolling over some possible options when Rai's phone rings, she answers it; it's Hayden. Rai says, "Hello?"

Hayden says, "Meet me at the hospital, Sophie passed out, and we are on our way there now."

Rai says, "On our way."

She hangs up, and Gabe asks, "What is going on?"

Rai just says, "Get in the car and drive to the hospital, Hayden is on his way there with Sophie…she passed out."

Two years before the signal is detected Sean Fillmore is building a large house. Sean is an ex-marine who had spent five years in a secret assignment assisting a large covert operation. When he got out, he had seen and done some things that sent him spiraling down a long and maddening road fraught with terrifying memories. He barely kept his sanity together. He was in and out of therapy, drank too much and had anger issues. After about a year of being out of the service, he was still living with his parents.

One night he was in a restless sleep, he was never one to remember his dreams, but this is one he would remember for sure. A voice spoke to him as clear as if he were awake; it said, "Sean, I am here to give you an opportunity, you are a unique individual, much like me, together we can rule the world, and I will sit on my rightful throne instead of the one they call God."

Sean asked, "Who are you?"

The voice said, "I think you already know, but if I must lower myself to bring you over, then let me introduce myself, I am the most beautiful of all angels, the one who was cast out, I am Lucifer the mighty Seraphim of heaven."

Sean was immediately drawn to this individual, and he told Lucifer he would be his right hand. Lucifer said, "Very well, I will first provide you with the resources needed to begin the contrivance, and at the right time I will explain more of my plan."

The next morning all was normal, but he could remember his dream as if it had really happened. Then, that evening an officer came to his door and informed him that his mother and father were killed in a car accident. Oddly, it didn't affect him that much. He had loved them, but these days, he felt very little. The things he did in his past made him numb to everything.

After their funeral, he was to attend the reading of their will. He knew they had some money so he thought he might get a few thousand dollars, but the lawyer announced that in fact, he was to receive their full estate and the balance in all of their accounts as well as their stocks and bonds. The lawyer said, "Once everything is cashed out, you will receive 9.6 million dollars." Sean was shocked, he had no idea they had that kind of money. Then, he remembered what he was told in his dream and for a moment he was terrified, but the feeling quickly passed because now he knew this was his path and he would do whatever Lucifer wanted him to do.

After a few months, everything was transferred to his own accounts, and he decided to move. He was told by Lucifer to live a fair distance from everyone; he had always wanted to live in Colorado. He simply looked at a map and felt he was being told to move to Crested Butte, Colorado. He drove out and started looking for the perfect property. After a few weeks of looking, he finally found what Lucifer wanted. Each night when he slept, Lucifer would talk to him and explain more to him. Lucifer would also tell him why God was inferior to him and how God told him he was the greatest of angels. Lucifer told him to build his home off of Journeys End road about a mile outside of town.

Before construction started, he was given a design in his sleep for a massive underground wine cellar with one-foot thick concrete walls and a concrete roof over the cellar. While he was building his home, he decided to get a job. It wasn't because he needed the money; it was to meet people, namely women. Sean was about six foot four inches and extremely fit, he was a rugged and handsome white man with a short haircut and a beard that he kept neatly trimmed. The most remarkable things about him were his arms and shoulders; they were immense, measuring about twenty-two inches around. He was always working out, so he decided to become a personal trainer and later a ski instructor. For the most part, Sean appeared to be a normal guy doing normal things. He went on some dates but never got super close to anyone. Eventually, his house was finished, and he moved in, he was very happy with it. When someone would enter his home, it was a quaint, cozy, comfortable home. It had five bedrooms and six bathrooms, an entertainment room and a huge kitchen. It was an open plan so the living room, dining room and kitchen were all one massive space. When you walked in through the front door you could see all the way through the rooms. Instead of a wall on the opposite side of the house, there was nothing but glass. You could see a beautiful mountain with incredible pine trees lining a lake. It was breathtaking the first time you saw it. But, then there was the basement, which appeared to be a fairly normal basement, however, if you moved a large bookcase that was on a series of hinges, you would find a door. This door leads to a staircase which led to the "Wine cellar." In fact, the wine cellar had twenty small rooms with doors on them. If someone were to scream, there would be no way anyone could hear them. Sean tested this by playing extremely loud music in this area and standing in his kitchen to listen for the music; he could not hear the music at all. So, it was time to begin the plan set forth by his Dark Lord.

Before Sean had designed the house, Sean was sleeping and Lucifer spoke to Sean, he said, "I need you to sacrifice for me, I need the sacrifice of innocent blood."

Sean said, "Like a virgin you mean?"

Lucifer said, "No, even they might not be so innocent, I need true innocents."

Sean began to understand, he needed children. As if he had said this, but he had not, Lucifer said, "No, MORE innocent!"

Sean said, "You need the blood of a baby?"

Lucifer said, "No, babies. One every month, it is up to you to figure out how to get them." That is how Sean had come up with the design of his home. He would lure young women to his beautiful home, start a romantic relationship and once they trusted him, he would trap them and lock them in the rooms downstairs. He would get them pregnant and he would have his sacrifices.

∞

Rai and Gabe are at the hospital with Sophie and Hayden. Gabe says, "So, just low blood sugar?"

Sophie says, "Yep, Doc says I need to eat better, he is gonna run some tests but thinks I should be out in an hour?"

Just then Gabe's phone rings, he says, "Hello?"

Mia says, "Gabriel, we have another message coming in."

He says, "Ok, I'll be there in just a bit." He hangs up and says, "Baby, I need to go to work for a bit, are you going to be ok?"

Sophie says, "Yes dad, I will be fine." He kisses her and Rai and shakes Hayden's hand and thanks him for everything he has done.

Gabriel arrives at the TSN message room, he walks in and says hello to everyone. Mia says, "Ok, we are just sending it through the newly updated program that Wei Yuand a uploaded and should get the translated version of the message soon."

Gabriel says to Mia, "So while we are waiting, I wanted to find out how Ann, Robert, Rashad and the rest of the team are doing with solving our issue of long-distance communication."

Mia said, "Well, there has not been a lot of progress, we are getting some help from the Chinese now, and they have some good theories but, it still seems like this stuff is still out of our reach."

Gabriel said, "That's understand able, and I am glad we are getting help from them." Just then Mia's computer started producing results from the last message. It was more of the perplexing message they had gotten before. After the decoding and translating was done the message had more of what looked like a drawing and some more words that read, "we build this according to…"that was it.

Gabriel was frustrated because he knew there was more to the message, they just couldn't receive it. This was evidenced by the ability of the Chinese to extract more out of the other messages they had received before. One thing was clear now though; they were receiving instructions on how to build something, they just didn't know what. Gabriel reported his findings thus far to Dan and Dan to Ben. Ben then calls Sarah; Sarah answers the phone, "Hello?" It was about three AM where she was; she had delivered her speech the evening before and was still in St. Moritz, Switzerland.

Ben says, "Madam President, I wanted to update you on our continued signals at the TSN."

Sarah says, "Ok, what is going on there?"

Ben says, "Madam, we have gotten two messages that are clearly connected, and it seems they are sending us instruction on how to build something."

Sarah says, "Very interesting; it looks like I might have to go to Congress and ask for some funding then?"

Ben says, "I think so."

Sarah says, "Ok, and Ben, just a heads up, I am in Switzerland and I have just convened a meeting with the leaders from around the entire world and I have told them everything we know, I will be holding a press conference once I return to the U.S. and explaining to the American people what we know."

Ben was shocked but simply said, "Very well Madam President."

They hung up and Sarah thought to herself, this is going to change the world as we know it, be it for the better or for worse, but it will never be the same again. She lies back down next to Tim, his arm is behind her, and he pulls her closer and says, "Is everything alright?"

Sarah says, "Yes honey, go back to sleep." Sarah thinks to herself; I am so lucky to have this man in my life, he is so patient and loving, what would I do without him.

Chapter 11

The Supreme leader of North Korea had just left Switzerland and was on his flight back to his home. He was concerned about what he had been told by the American President. His concern was that his hold over his people was dependent on their belief that he was equal to a God. If this information got to his people, it would destroy his hold on them. He had to make sure there was no way that they would ever get this information. He also needed to ensure that they stockpiled as many nukes as they could because if the world destroys their arsenals, North Korea would have the only nukes on the planet and would be the most powerful nation on Earth. Once he lands, he immediately calls a meeting with his heads of state.

Young Ra-il is busy in the newly constructed facility when he is requested to come to the surface. Once he arrives, he is greeted by a helicopter and told he was to attend a meeting with the Supreme Leader. Young Ra-il did as he was told, but he was nervous. You never know what the whims of the leader were. When he arrived at the building where the meeting was being held he went inside. He was met by several heads of state. He did not understand, why would he be present at a meeting with this level of authority? He sat with the others, nobody spoke, they all just waited. Finally, the Leader walked in and sat down. The Leader said, "I went to the meeting held primarily by the Americans."He spoke about some crazy speech where the President spoke about Jesus and that it was time for the removal of all nuclear devices. Young Ra-il was uneasy; he had no idea what the Leader was going to ask of them. The Leader said, "I do not plan on doing any such thing." Applause erupted in the room, which made the Leader smile. "We will speed up our operation and increase our warheads as well!"

∞

Abarron was working many hours, but Liala knew there was nothing she could do to assist him. This was God's directive; Abarron was known to have the clearest connection of anyone to God's words since the fall. Back then, everyone could talk to God, but since the fall very few could, but none as clear as Abarron. She entered the room he worked in. She thought to herself, so strange, this room. No one had seen anything like it. It was as if Abarron had just built it out of nothing and these machines had never been seen. Liala said, "Husband, dinner is served, will you be coming soon? I would love for you to say a blessing over the food."

Abarron was startled by her voice, he had been working all day, he was compelled to send more information through the device. He could hear God tell him, he needed to rest, and his family was important as well, so he turned and stood, he looked at his beautiful wife and reached for her, he wrapped his arms around her and said, "Yes my wife, I will come with you now. I am so thankful for you my love. I know I have been so busy with this work but God has just spoken to me and reminded me of the gift he gave me in you and our children. So, I am blessed, and I would love to come say the blessing over the food with my family." Before they left, he turned and ran through his routine for sending a message; after the final switch was turned, he left with his wife.

∞

Faizan walked off the plane and into the terminal. He walked to baggage claim, grabbed his bag and walked outside. His parents were waiting for him at the curbside pickup, his mother got out and hugged him, and his father was unusually happy and shook his hand and gave him a half hug at the same time. Faizan was not used to this; his father was usually very unemotional. They were both genuinely happy to see him. They started asking a bunch of questions, but Faizan had lied to his parents about where he had been all summer, so he just said, "I am pretty tired, can we talk about all of that later?" His parents stopped asking questions, and they continued their way home. Once he was home, he went to his room. It was nice, yet strange to be back in the USA. It was his home but after what he had been through, the knowledge he had now and knowing his objective, he was conflicted yet determined to be successful in carrying out his orders. He had been given exact directions while in training. He had practiced every step, every procedure that he would carry out leading up to his final actions and now, when he was alone, he mentally repeated his part over and over. He could mentally visualize it because they had built and replicated everything they needed to for their training. It was very exciting when they trained. The roads were blocked, different people had different roles, and then he was to walk into the visitor area and simply press a button. As he lay in bed with his eyes closed, you would assume he was asleep, but he wasn't, he was going over the plan over and over again. His mother knocked, but Faizan was concentrating so much he never heard her. It wasn't until she was in his room and shaking him that he opened his eyes. She told him dinner was ready. Faizan said, "Ok mother, I will be down in a minute." She left, and Faizan got up, stretched and went downstairs. One thing he had learned in Pakistan was that food was taken for granted in America. It was not just about money, but there were some things that you literally could not get. For example, when he was in training, if he wanted to go buy a watermelon, it was not available, you could not get it, but in the USA he could buy a watermelon any time he wanted to. Right now, however, he was truly hungry and could not wait to have some of his Mother's Chicken Pad Thai.

∞

Sarah was waiting for Ben to show up for a brief meeting about what had transpired at the summit. She decided to call the Prime Minister of Canada in the meantime. Sarah said, "Prime Minister, hello, I wanted to call and thank you for coming to the summit in Switzerland last week, but also, I wanted to discuss this water tax you are planning to impose on your water exports. I would love to talk to you about some reasons why that might not be the best approach; would it be possible for you and me to get together and discuss this further? Very well, sir, I will have my assistant work with your people to set something up, thank you."

Ben finally arrived and entered her office, they shook hands, and she invited him to sit. Sarah said, "Thank you for coming on such short notice. As I said on the phone, I just got back from Switzerland, I met with every leader from every country and revealed what we know. I am about to go to the American people and tell them the same thing. Here is what I am looking for - I would really like a pastor with me when I do this. However, I don't want a stereotypical TV evangelist or some super well-known pastor seeking fame and trying to make more money. Can you help me with this?"

Ben said, "Sure thing, I actually might have just the guy for you but will need to talk to Gabriel."

Sarah says, "Gabriel, from the TSN?"

Ben said, "Yes, I remember having a conversation with him not too long ago about a pastor he had met and how calm and pure of heart he was. Gabriel is getting remarried to his now ex-wife, and this pastor is marrying them. I will call Gabriel and have a conversation about this pastor."

Sarah said, "Very good; I am just looking for someone who can answer potential biblical questions that I cannot answer."

Ben said, "I will let you know what he says as soon as I talk to him." Sarah thanked him, and Ben left her office.

Gabriel walked out of his office and found Mia in the message room and says, "Mia, can I see you in my office?"

Mia says, "Sure, just let me finish filing this data, and I will be right there."

Gabriel was back in his office, and Mia knocked. Gabriel told her to come in. Mia says, "Hey Gabriel, what's up?"

Gabriel said, "I got a call from Dan today; they want to move part of the operation to Cape Canaveral, Florida."

Mia says, "What? Why do they want to do that and what part?"

Gabriel said, "They want the development of the communication device sent out there. Ben said they want the team that would actually be building a device to be part of the development."

Mia said, "Ok, and who is going to head that up?"

Gabriel said, "Dan is leaving that up to me, so the question is, do you want to relocate out there or do I promote Robert?"

Mia sat for a moment then said, "I can't, Gabriel, I have a family. I am needed here anyhow. If Robert is gone, I will need to fill his role at least for a while."

Gabriel said, "Ok, I figured you would say that but wanted to give you first dibs on it."

Mia got up and said, "Thank you for the chance; should I tell Robert you want to see him?"

Gabriel said, "Please do."

Mia left Gabriel's office and found Robert and told him he needed to see Gabriel in his office. Robert made his way to Gabriel's office and knocked. Gabriel told him to come in. Robert says, "Mia told me you wanted to see me?"

Gabriel said, "Yes, have a seat, I wanted to tell you first that we are very pleased with your work here at the TSN. I got a call today from Dan - we are moving the development of the communication device to Cape Canaveral, Florida and we need someone to head that team up. I would like you to take that position, Robert."

Robert was surprised and very excited. He was a single man with no family here in California, and this sounded exciting. Robert said, "Oh, that would be great sir!"

Gabriel said, "So you accept?"

Robert said, "Yes sir!"

Robert stood, and they shook hands. Gabriel said, "Plan on being there in a month; I will have HR go over your compensation with you." Robert started to walk out but then turned and said, "Thank you very much, sir."

∞

Later that evening.

"Daddy, you have to understand, sometimes this happens. It is just a setback is all."

Gabe says, "So you're saying you just got results from that hospital visit when you fainted? Why did it take so long?"

Sophie says, "They re-ran all of the tests to be sure. It has not only come back, but it has spread to my bladder as well. I begin treatment right away."

Rai and Hayden are both there as well. Sophie and Hayden had come to Gabe and Rai's house to break the news. Gabe reaches for her and hugs her, she is stiff this time, and half-heartedly hugs him back. Gabe lets her go and sits down and asks everyone to join him and holds hands so they could pray over Sophie. Sophie pulls away and says, "Dad, no, not this time. It's not gonna help, and I am having my doubts about God right now."

Gabe says, "Ok baby, but look, God is one hundred percent real, and I will be praying for you."

Sophie and Hayden hug them goodbye and leave. Rai and Gabe are left reeling from the news, they walk out to the patio, the sun is just setting, and it is another beautiful sunset. Rai says, "Why, Gabe? Why does God do things like this?"

"I am honestly not sure, but Pastor Manns tells me God always has a plan. Sometimes bad things happen for a reason; we just don't know that reason."

Rai gets up and says, "I am going to have some wine, would you like a glass?"

Gabe says, "Sure thank you, love."

Gabe looks out at the setting sun again, he closes his eyes and begins to pray. With a soft cry in his voice, he says, "God, why, I know you know why, but I need to know why. Please don't take my precious daughter, and if there is something to come of this, please God, show me soon. It is in your Son's precious name Jesus that I pray, Amen."

Rai is standing there waiting, she hands him his wine, she simply sits beside him, and they cuddle up together and watch the sunset in silence. Rai leans over says, "I love you, Gabe."

∞

Sean is talking to Tracey, a new client. He is coaching her on her form on the bench curls she is doing with some free weights. Tracey who is a tall, shapely, blonde woman in her early to mid-twenties, asks, "Why free weights?"

131

Sean answers, "It forces all parts of your arm muscles to work, where a machine does some of the work for you, like instead of you stabilizing the weight, the machine does that for you, so you get more of a benefit from it."

Tracey says, "That makes a lot of sense." She says, "You are pretty good at this -do you want to get a drink after this?"

Sean says. "Sure, what do you have in mind?"

Tracey says, "There is a little Irish pub not too far away."

Sean says, "Sounds good."

∞

Gabriel is working in his office when Bobbi tells him Ben Williams from Washington D.C. is on the line for him. Gabriel picks up the phone and says, "Hello sir, what can I do for you?"

Ben says, "Hello Gabriel, how is everything going there?"

Gabriel says, "Everything is going well, we continue to get signals, it's an enormous amount of information, and we are working as you know with a team from China and now, we have a team from Israel with us."

Ben says, "Very good…listen, the project is not really why I called. I have a strange request; I have been told that you have been talking to a pastor there as of late."

Gabriel, feeling kind of exposed, says, "Yes sir, I have, why do ask about that?"

Ben says, "To be honest, Madam President was asking me for a recommendation for a pastor to help her with a press conference she is planning. I was talking to Dan, and he told me you had been talking to a pastor and that he was going to marry you and your fiancé as well."

Gabriel said, "That is correct, I am getting remarried to my ex-wife next weekend."

Ben said, "Ok, do you think he would be willing to help out with this?"

Gabriel says, "I don't know, but I can talk to him about it."

Ben says, "That would be great; once you do, please call me back and let me know what he says."

Gabriel says, "I will call you tomorrow, I am going to see him tonight, so I will talk to him then."

Ben says, "Great, thank you."

Gabriel says, "No problem, goodbye."

Ben says, "Goodbye.

∞

Wei Yuand a is working with Mia and Robert on compiling the most recent massages. Robert says, "Ok, we have gotten sixty-three different messages that seem to be connected to each other; the amount of data we are getting has filled almost all of our data storage. We need to figure this out, and we need to increase our data storage."

Wei Yuand a says, "Please consider just connecting to the cloud; the amount of storage available there is almost unlimited,"

Mia says, "No way, we can't chance someone infiltrating what we are doing, and It will open us up for criticism down the road."

Robert says, "I will talk to Gabriel about finding a way to increase our storage."

Wei Yuand a says, "Ok, so let's get back to the task at hand. I see some connections between messages, but I wonder if we need to create a program to run all the messages through to see what connections there are. Perhaps there is something there that the human eye isn't catching."

Mia says, "Ok, let's get the programming team up here, and we can tell them what we are looking for."

Just as they finish talking the computer indicated there is yet another new message coming in and Robert says, "Make that sixty-four."

∞

Jordan and Jasmine woke up in each other's arms, something that had not happened in a long time. Even before they had lost Jordan, they had been together a long time, and the routine of life happened, and they had become distant. While they still loved each other, they were not intimate very often, but even if they were, once they were finished there was no closeness afterward. But last night had been different, it was passionate and raw, and then they were wrapped up in each other and fell into a deep sleep afterward. Today, Jordan had taken the day off, he would be studying the patterns of his foe or as he liked to think of him, his prey. He got ready as did Jasmine; then they had their breakfast together with Michelle. There was some talk about school and some issues she was having with her grades; she traditionally brought home good grades but watching her brother get shot right in front of her had taken its toll on her. Jordan was surprised when she said she wanted to go to school as soon as she did. It was time for Jordan to take her to school so they each said goodbye to Jasmine with Jordan giving her a deep kiss. Michelle said, "Holy cow guys, get a room!"

After they left Jasmine felt a tiny, tiny bit of normalcy in her life for the first time since her son had been killed. She turned the television and coffee pot off and left her house. Jordan had dropped Michelle off and made his way to the police station. He stayed about a half a block away. It was about eight o'clock AM and the shifts would be changing; he knew the officer worked the day shift since the incident, so he sat in his car drinking his coffee, waiting to get a glimpse of the scum bag who murdered his son. Jordan had known he would get angry when he saw him, so he left his gun at home. He knew he would not be able to control himself when he laid eyes on him. So, he sat, when finally, the man walked across the street dressed in his uniform. He walked with another officer, a younger female. This complicated things; he must have taken on a partner. Jordan had no desire to kill randomly or unnecessarily, so he would have to do this when he was off duty or in route to his home. He would have to tail him and see where he lived this evening as well.

∞

Sean and Tracey were at the pub where she had suggested having a drink; he was drinking a light beer, it was just to appear "normal" to her; normally he didn't drink. He worked very hard to keep his body in perfect shape. Since he was in high school, he had taken a lot of pride in being in great shape, and the military had helped him perfect his body. Sean said to Tracey, "Yep, in the military for a long time. I lost my parents about a year ago and decided I didn't want to stay where all the memories were, so I literally pulled out a map, closed my eyes and pointed…this is where my finger landed."

Tracey said, "Wow, you poor thing! You pretty much just lost your parents? How, if I may ask?"

Sean says, "Car accident. I was living with them at the time. I was trying to get my crap together from everything I did in the service when an officer came to my door and informed me, they had been in a head-on collision and were killed on impact."

Tracey said, "Oh Sean, I am so sorry."

Sean said, "Thank you. Look I should probably get home, but was wondering if maybe you wanted to have dinner tomorrow night?"

Tracey said, "That would be great, what time?"

Sean said, "How does six o'clock sound?"

She said, "Great, should I meet you somewhere?"

Sean said, "Would you like me to pick you up?"

Tracey said, "Sure, I will text you my address."

They left, and Sean found himself essentially praying, but praying to the dark one that was giving him his new purpose. He could have sworn he heard Lucifer reply as if he were in the car next to him. Maybe he was going crazy, but the voice said, "No, I am here with you, I am always with you, I see what you are doing with this young lady, and it is perfect. I have chosen well in you. I have such great plans for us, but I need those innocent souls before we can move forward with it all."

Sean said, "I will do your bidding my Lord."

Lucifer was pleased with this title, Lord, it was his true title so, yes, I am his Lord and I will be the Lord to many people in the future. Lucifer said to him, "Proceed as planned, oh and well done, Sean."

Sean drove home and went to the little workout room he had designed when they built the house. He worked out with massive amounts of weight with many repetitions. After he was done with his workout, he went down to the future "wives" rooms; he was still perfecting them. He wanted them to be comfortable while they were there so he was putting beds in and furniture that would make them comfortable as well as stocking them with things they would need. Once he was done with that, he showered and went to bed, where he and Lucifer would talk all night while he slept. This night Lucifer revealed to him that the years of leadership he had displayed in the service would soon be a benefit to them both. He would be a leader of leaders, a world leader at his side. Sean was so excited for this opportunity and was determined to execute the Dark one's commands to the very letter. As the morning approached, Sean would always wake up well rested but would remember everything he and Lucifer had discussed all night. He had much to do and was excited about his future.

∞

Gabe and Rai are in Gary Mann's office again; they are talking about the wedding plans and Gabe's Baptism. Gary says, "So, I will meet you at Lake Jodie around eleven o'clock and baptize you. Then we will meet back here in Barstow at four o'clock for a five o'clock wedding. Correct?"

Gabe says, "Yes, do you think that is doable?"

Gary said, "Yes I think it is very doable."

Gabe said, "Great; also, Gary, I need to talk to you about something else."

Gary said, "Ok, what is that Gabe?"

Gabe said, "Well, remember our conversation about the signal?"

Gary said, "Remember? How could I forget?"

Gabe said, "Ok, so, I got a call from D.C. this morning and the president of the United States needs a Pastor for a press conference she is going to be holding soon and somehow, you have been presented as a possible person to help with this event - how would you feel about doing this?"

Gary was quiet for a bit and was about to say no way but then remembered the conversation he had with God, and he said, "Why me? Why not some famous or well-known man of God?"

Gabe said, "Gary, she doesn't want someone who has an ulterior motive. She doesn't want someone there to try to boost their congregation or make money; she needs someone to help her make the case for Christ."

Suddenly Gary was so aware of the fact that this was God at work. He was amazed at how clear God had spoken to him, and now it was happening just like he said it would. So, he looked at Gabe and said, "Gabe, you won't believe this, but God told me this was going to happen; I had a long discourse with God about how I was not the man to do this, but God told me this would happen so I will listen to him, I will do it."

Gabe said, "Excellent, I will be calling Ben in the morning and informing him that you will do it. I am sure they will want you to come out and discuss things with the staff there and perhaps the President herself."

Gary said, "Ok, my only commitment this week is marrying you two."

Gabe said, "Ok, shall I give them the church number or your cell number?"

Gary said, "Give them my cell phone number please, I don't need the front desk getting that call. That will raise a lot of eyebrows around here." Gabe and Rai left, and Gary sat in his chair in his office and prayed to God, giving him praise and thanking him for having faith in him.

Chapter 12

Lee Suk-Park was continuing to put the finishing touches on the installation facility, although they had already begun accepting inventory as fast as they could move it down. Even though he had been part of the team overseeing the building of the facility, it was still impressive to see them lower these massive missiles down from the surface on the extremely capable lifting system. It was essentially an elevator that moved the missiles from the top of the mountain all the way to the center where they would be holding the bulk of their arsenal. He had heard some strange rumors about why they were doing this; he normally didn't listen to rumors, and these were very strange, so he decided just to keep doing his job - after all, that is how he got where he was today. He just kept his head down and did his work; he had seen too many people get too involved in discussions that had nothing to do with them and then they would disappear. So, that is what he would do now, just do his job and do it well.

Lee Suk-Park could hear the massive door to the facility opening, and In walked Song Mi-hang. She seemed to be in a hurry and agitated. Once she walked across the huge room to where he was working, she said, "Lee Suk-Park, we need to talk immediately."

Lee Suk-Park was already bowing when she approached, so he stood and said: "Yes, Great Assistant."

Song Mi-hang said, "It has come to my attention that there is a very high likelihood that we will be going into battle shortly and that we should be ready to deploy any and all armament at our disposal, should we get the signal."

Lee Suk-Park was shocked and frightened at the same time. He thought to himself, what was going on and how had he gotten himself into this predicament? Lee Suk-Park's reply, however, was simple he just said, "Yes great assistant."

Song Mi-hang then asked to see his progress on the work he had been doing the last nine hours. After reviewing everything, she said, "Very well, continue; it is almost dinner time, you may break then, but then I need you to work until this equipment is installed and running."

Lee Suk-Park just bowed and said, "Thank you, Great Assistant," and then she left. He stood for a moment, but then he got back to work like nothing had ever happened. Meanwhile, in Pyongyang, there was something very unusual happening: Young Ra-il was recounting a dream he had the night before to his sister. He said, "It was like the voice was right there with me in my room, only we weren't in my room."

His sister asked, "Where were you then?"

Young Ra-il said, "I don't remember, but I do remember everything he said to me."

His sister said, "Ok, and that was what?"

Young Ra-il recounted his conversation with this person. "He said that it was very important to move forward with the current operation and complete it as soon as possible and that North Korea was about to come into power, but there would be a new figure to help guide our nation into the new era."

Mia sat in her office when Bobbi called her to inform her that the programmer was here to meet with her. Mia said, "Great, I will come up and meet him."

Bobbi said, "Her." Mia said, "Excuse me, her?" Bobbi said, "Yes, it's a her."

Mia said, "Oh, ok, I will be there in a second."

Mia made her way to the front office area, and she saw a dark-haired woman in her mid-thirties dressed in a skirt and conservative blouse. Mia approached her and said, "Hello, I am Mia, the Deputy Director her at the TSN."

The woman said, "Hello, I am Virginia Rhodes, I am a computer programmer with the CIA and was instructed to report here."

Mia said, "Very well, follow me please."

The two women walked through the facility with Mia pointing out important aspects she would need to know about. Once they arrived at the messaging room, Mia went through the routine of clearing herself through the security measures. Once they gained access and entered the room, Virginia was noticeably curious about what this room was used for. Mia introduced Robert and then said, "So, have a seat and we will get you up to date on what we are dealing with here but first, what have you been told about what we are doing?"

Virginia said, "Nothing madam."

Mia said, "Ok, well, here is the short story. We have gotten a series of signals from a planet that is about five light years from Earth. We have been successful in deciphering and then translating these messages until the most recent ones. Actually let me rephrase that, we feel like we aren't doing it efficiently and would like to see if we, or actually, you can design a program that connects the most recent series of messages because we are convinced that they are connected, but we can't seem to piece them together."

Virginia sat for a moment and then said, "Very well, show me what you've got so far."

Mia looked at Robert with a slightly surprised look on her face and then said, "Let's go over to this computer and Robert can run you through what we have done so far and the challenging series we have gotten recently. I am going to run up to Gabriel's office for a few minutes, but then I will be back down."

∞

Sean had just pulled out of his long driveway at his home to pick Tracey up at her house. He had twenty minutes to get there, so he was in no rush. As he drove, the now familiar voice spoke to him. Lucifer said to him, "Sean, do not rush this, you need to take your time and gain her confidence."

Sean said, "Yes Lord, I understand." And then he was silent again. Sean had gotten used to this now. Sometimes he would have long conversations with Lucifer and other times it was just a few words, but he trusted what he said so he remained patient the whole time. Sean pulled up to Tracey's house, a small place with almost no yard. He walked up to her door and knocked. Tracey answered the door and Sean was taken by how beautiful she was. Sean said, "Hello, you look amazing, Tracey."

She said, "Oh thank you, Sean, so do you."

They got into the car and drove to the restaurant with more conversation about his past and a little about her. She was a graduate of the University of Colorado Boulder (UCB) with an MBA in Business from the Leeds School of Business, an offshoot of UCB. She was in the area to start a restaurant; she had start-up money from her father and was looking at properties currently. Tracey was saying, "There is a building coming available next month; it is in a great location and has the potential to be converted to a nice restaurant. It also has great parking and an awesome view. Lastly, it is on the exit side of the Crested Butte Resort, and I would get lots of overflow from their restaurants in the season as well."

Sean said, "Wow, that all sounds great!"

They arrived at the restaurant, and Sean hurried around to her side and opened her door. Tracey said, "I thought chivalry was dead."

Sean said, "Not while I am alive it's not."

Sean was taking her to the Place, one of the high-end restaurants in Crested Butte. Tracey remarked, "Wow, I've not been here yet, I hear it's really good but really expensive."

Sean said, "Yes, it is a great place; I've been here a few times since I have moved here."

Tracey made a note of this, not that she was a shallow gold digger but any man she might have a future with had to measure up to her father's standards and at six foot four inches, his massive arms and his ability to eat at a place like this, Sean could be a potential suitor for her. They walked to the restaurant's entrance where he again held the door open for her. They walked up to the host and Sean said, "Reservation for two, Fillmore."

The host said, "Ah yes, I have you right here, follow me please."

After being seated Sean ordered a bottle of their finest red wine; he then ordered for them both. After about an hour of great food and conversation the meal was wrapping up, Sean said, "I can take you home after this if you would like, Tracey."

Tracey said, "I was hoping we could go back to your place."

Sean said, "That would be fine."

After Sean paid for their meal, they drove back to his home. As they turned into his driveway, Tracey was clearly shocked and impressed. As they entered his home, Tracey says, "Sean, this is a great place!"

Sean said, "Thank you, I designed it myself with the help of an architect."

Sean poured a few drinks, and they had a great night of conversation, yet Sean never even tried to kiss her. Around ten o'clock Sean told Tracey he would drive her home, which he did. When they got to her house, Sean walked her to her door and leaned in to hug her but she pulled his face to hers and kissed him. Sean kissed her back, he pulled her closer, and they kissed again only longer and deeper. This was stirring many feelings in Sean that he had not let out in years. He began to squeeze her to him and kiss her harder, but Tracey pulled away a bit saying, "Sean you're hurting me a little."

Sean released her and said, "I'm so sorry Tracey, sometimes I don't know my own strength and it has been a long time since I have felt a woman's touch."

She said, "It's ok, just go easy."

Sean gave her one more kiss and then told her good night. Sean was driving home when Lucifer said, "Very good, although you almost screwed it all up, you have to control yourself at least for now. There will be a time and a place for you to release your passions in the future, but until then self-control is the key. You have to gain their confidence until you have their guard lowered and they are in just the right place; then you can do whatever you want to with them."

∞

Sarah is in the Oval Office with a few of her Aids and Marvin Steelman, her Chief of Staff. She says, "I will need all forms of media alerted including all social media, any cable stations and print." They write her instructions down and wait for her to continue. She says, "Also I need this Pastor - who is out in California, his name is Gary Manns - contacted and flown out here to meet me, and I want him treated very well. Put him in the best hotel in the area; give him a perdiem of a few hundred dollars a day and a driver."

They write this down as well and wait for more instructions. She continues, "Please contact the top producers and directors of television to help us produce the most effective news release in history. Also, contact Gabriel Dane of the TSN; I want to do this at his facility."

With that, she thanked them and told them she was done. Then the aids left the oval office. Marvin remained because he had some concerns. Marvin said, "Madam President, may I have a word?"

Sarah said, "By all means Marvin, what is on your mind?"

Marvin said, "I respect you, and will always follow through on what you want me to, but are you sure about this?"

She said, "Yes, I am one hundred percent sure, why do you ask?"

He said, "Well, I mean think about what you are about to do. You are about to tell the American people that there are aliens on another world that know who Jesus is,"

Sarah said, "I am totally aware of what I am going to do, and I understand how crazy it sounds and that there could be unexpected consequences as well."

He said, "Very well Madam, I will oversee your requests of the aids."

Sarah said, "Thank you, Marvin, I appreciate your concern."

∞

Faizan had spent a week at his parents' home when he got a call from Qadeer. He said, "You are to proceed with act 1." That was all he said and hung up. Faizan knew that act 1 was code for a preliminary practice run. He was to get on a train and go to Washington D.C. to practice his route and then go into the visitor's area for the White House. He told his parents he would be gone for a day on Friday and that he was meeting friends there and doing some sightseeing. They seemed un-phased by this; he was after all an adult about to leave the nest, and he figured they had gotten used to this reality.

On Friday he made his way to the train and boarded. As he rode, he seemed to be looking at the world differently; soon, he wouldn't be living in this world. It was the first time he really thought about this, the things he would miss. But he told himself that he was doing God's work and he had been chosen for this. What he didn't see initially finally caught his eye. A few seats away from him he could see that a girl was looking at him; as he turned, she looked down at her phone. He was able to get a good long look at her. She had long, jet black hair that seemed to shine like silk; it was the most beautiful hair he had ever seen. Her skin was an olive color but very clear, not a blemish that he could see. He could tell she was Middle Eastern, maybe Iranian? He continued his study of this beautiful girl; her hands were slender with nice painted nails but not a bright color, just well kept. Then she looked at him, and he thought, my God, I have never seen such beautiful eyes. They were shaped with a slight slant and were a perfect dark chocolate brown. He realized he had been staring into her eyes and he looked away quickly. Then, to his horror, she got up and walked towards him. She approached him and said, "Hello my name is Anahita, what is your name?"

He stood and said, "My name is Faizan Baqri."

As he reached out his hand, she reached out and grabbed it and they shook hands, but it was like electricity had just run through him - he was mesmerized by this girl. She said, "Where are you headed?"

He said, "I am doing some sightseeing in D.C."

Anahita said, "Oh, really? I live in D.C. what do you want to see?"

Faizan said, "The white house."

She said, "Well, I have the day off, I could show you around."

He said, "That would be great!" Realizing how emphatic he had just spoken, he calmed himself and repeated, "That would be great."

They sat down together, and he asked, "Are you from D.C.?"

She said, "Actually I was born in New York, New York but my father's work brought us here. He is a lobbyist. Where do you live?"

He said, "I was born in Bethesda, Maryland. My parents are from Pakistan."

She said, "My parents are from Iran, but they both moved here as children so you would never know." She said, "We have to get off at the next stop and change trains."

Eventually, they made their way to their final stop. Faizan was paying attention to everything he had been instructed to, like where the police were and what traffic was like at that time of day. They walked together; as they turned the corner he says, "The Capitol."He was not expecting to feel anything when he saw it, but he was oddly in awe of it. He then struggled to get his head back on straight, and he told himself, these are capitalist pigs, this country must fall. He then stopped in his tracks and looked at Anahita and said, "Wait, so your father works in the capitol?"

She said, "Yes, that's right, why?"

He snapped out of his thought and said, "No reason, I was just asking." He said, "Hey would you like to get some lunch?"

She said, "Sure, that'd be great. What are you hungry for?" She said, "I don't eat meat, but I can usually find something anywhere I go."

He said, "This is your city, so you pick."

They found a mobile food truck that she said served great tacos, so they got some food and found a bench and sat down. Faizan finally could look at this amazing girl again; he found himself studying her features - she was possibly the most beautiful girl he had ever seen. Then he found himself saying to her, "Anahita, I have to tell you, that you are the most beautiful girl I have ever seen."

She looked at him and was slightly embarrassed, but she said: "Thank you."

Faizan then said, "Can I ask how old you are?"

She said, "I am eighteen, and you?"

He said, "I am eighteen as well. I am going to university at the end of the summer."

She said, "Me too, where are you going?"

He said, "George Washington University."

She said, "What, really, come on, seriously?"

He said, "Yes, why?"

She said, "Oh well that is where I am going too! I am hoping to get involved in some of the research they are doing with Orangutans at the Zoo."

Faizan was shocked by this information, and then he thought to himself, am I being tested? Was this beautiful girl put in my path to distract me from my path? He started to get up and say his goodbyes, but then he looked into her eyes and saw how excited she was that they were going to the same school...those eyes, he thought I can't just walk away from her, so he was resolved not to leave this girl but still accomplish his part in the plan.

Gabriel, Rai, Sophie, and Hayden were all on the edge of Lake Jodi, a lake a short drive outside of Barstow. Gabe was in a pair of swim trunks and a t-shirt. With them was Pastor Gary Manns. He too was in swim trunks and t-shirt. He asked Gabe, "Are you ready?"

Gabe said, "Yes, I am ready."

The two of them walked out to about waist deep water, and Gary walked him through what he would be doing. Gary said, "I will have my right hand on the back of your neck and my left hand on your left wrist, you will hold your nose with your right hand and grab your right wrist with your left hand. I will ask you a question, you will answer, then I will dunk you backward and then raise you back up, do you understand all of that?"

Gabe said, "Yes, I understand."

Gary then says, "Ok, position your hands as I told you to. This is Gabriel Dane; he comes today to be baptized into Christ. Please repeat after me the words of the Good Confession. I believe that Jesus is the Christ, the Son of the Living God, my Lord, and my Savior."

Gabe says, "I believe that Jesus is the Christ, the Son of the Living God, my Lord, and my Savior."

Gary then says, "Gabriel, I now baptize you in the Name of the Father, and of the Son, and of the Holy Spirit, for the forgiveness of your sins, and the gift of the Holy Spirit."

Gary tilted Gabriel back into the water then brought him back up. Gary said, "Congratulations brother."

They walked back up to the shore and Rai hugged him, he kissed her, dried off a little then walked off by himself and found a fallen tree in the shade, he sat and began to pray. "Father, I am so thankful for this gift, I am thankful for everything that you have given me, I know I owe everything to you, it is all yours anyway. I will try my absolute best to live the way Jesus wants me to live. I love you, God. It is in your Son's name Jesus, that I pray, Amen."

∞

Omer walked into a large room with about a dozen men; all of them were having conversations as they were all brothers in a war against the infidels in America. Once everyone saw Omer, they all stopped talking. Omer said, "It is good to see you all. Please, everyone have a seat so we can get to work." Finally, once they all had sat down, Omer stated, "I trust everyone has completed their tasks?" Everyone signaled that they had completed their assignments. He said, "Very good; now, I want to introduce everyone to a new brother in the cause. Actually, he has been working privately for me to get ready for the grand event." A man walked into the room, he was a tall man with a dark beard and wore glasses. Omer stood and said, "Let me introduce Amir Muhammad. He has many credentials and has been working in the Pakistani Nuclear program for the last fifteen years. Today, I am going to have him reveal what he has achieved for us in our cause. I give you, Amir."

After a short round of applause, Amir said, "Thank you, it has been an honor to have played a role in this mission. Today I am presenting to you a device that is the size of a shoebox but the power of the first bomb to hit Hiroshima. It can be detonated manually by the operative or remotely." The group was shocked and very pleased, everyone stood and gave him another loud round of applause. He said, "Thank you."

Omer stood up and said, "Thank you, brother Amir. Now Qadeer, tell me how our operative is doing."

Qadeer stood and said, "We have chosen a fine brother in Faizan; he did amazingly well in training and is now making his initial practice run in Washington D.C."

∞

Sean is working deep in the sub-levels of his immaculate home. His expectation for this work, just like everything he executed, every detail is perfection. He knew he would be holding these women against their will but that didn't mean they had to be treated poorly, or that they shouldn't have a nice place to sleep, so each of the rooms had a nice queen size bed, a shower, and toilet, along with a small kitchenette stocked with food and drinks. He checks his phone and sees it is getting close to five o'clock; he only has an hour to get ready for dinner and go pick Tracey up for dinner. So, he stops what he is doing and rushes upstairs to get ready and then he leaves.

He picks Tracey up, and they have a nice meal then head back to Sean's home. Tonight, Sean had plans of taking their relationship to the next level. They are having drinks and listening to music, when Sean says, "Hey, would you like to watch a movie?"

Tracey says, "Sure, but something funny."

Sean says, "Ok, we can find something on one of the pay channels or I think I have a few of the old DVD's upstairs."

She says, "What do you have?"

"Well, I have some really old Jerry Lewis movies and a bunch of Three Stooges, oh and one of my favorites, Young Frankenstein."

Tracey says, "Well let's watch those then; I've never seen any."

He says, "I have to go upstairs, so I'll be back in a bit. I have to find them."

For a few minutes, Tracey sat listening to music, but she got bored and decided to look around his house; she had not explored his amazing home. She looked around the kitchen; then she found his weight room. She was not super shocked to find this room. Continuing, she found a door with steps going down. At first she thought, I shouldn't go down here, but her curiosity got the best of her, and she found a light and continued down the stairs. She found your average basement but then saw another open door with a light on beyond it. When she opened the door a little more she saw another set of stairs going down even further; this is when her gut was telling her just to turn around and go back upstairs, but she was also inherently curious, so she kept going. Once at the bottom of the stairs, there was a long narrow hallway with doors leading off of it. It looked much like a hallway you would see at a hotel. She walked a little further until she came to the first door; she put her hand on the door handle and turned it - it turned, and she pushed the door open to reveal a strange scene in front of her. A nicely decorated room with all the amenities a person would need, she entered the room.

Sean, meanwhile, was looking for the movie they were going to watch; he opened a closet and found the box with the DVDs in it. He found the movie and returned the box. He headed downstairs but didn't see Tracey; he assumed she was in the restroom, but after a few minutes she didn't come out, so he called for her and told her the movie was ready to be started. Still, she didn't come out or even reply. Sean knocked on the bathroom door, and the door opened, she was not in the bathroom, so he started looking around and immediately remembered he was in a rush to get ready for their date and he had not secured the door to the stairs going to the rooms below. Immediately he headed for the basement; when he got there, he found the door open and the light on. Damn it, he thought to himself. He rushed down the stairs and just as he had remembered, the next door was wide open, and the light was on. He crossed the room and went down the stairs; he could see that the first room was open; this is where he found Tracey.

As he entered the room, she spun around and pulled back a little as he walked in. Sean says, "What are you doing down here?"

She said, "I am sorry Sean, I started looking around and just made my way down here; cool room, what is it for?"

Sean could tell that she was nervous, and she had an idea what this room was for, but she was trying to play it off like this was no big deal. Sean sighed and said, "Tracey, you weren't supposed to come down here, you weren't supposed to see this room for at least a few weeks."

She said, "Wait, what do you mean?"

With that question, Sean simply stepped backward out of the room, closed the heavy metal door and slid the two massive bolts across, locking it. She ran forward and tried to open the door, she screamed and pounded on it. She even kicked it, but the door was never going to open; she was not going to get through that door unless Sean wanted her to. He walked upstairs and closed all the doors behind him. He could not hear her even though he was sure she was screaming in her room. In the quiet house he could hear Lucifer say to him, "And so, it has started."

Chapter 13

Annbella, Omer, Mia, and Robert were all huddled around the computer monitor with Virginia sitting in front of the computer. Virginia says, "What I did was I took the existing program you were using along with the Chinese upgrade, and I essentially tore it apart. I gave it more dimension and the ability to multitask. The only problem is, I have maxed out your memory so will need a significant upgrade. However, it will operate with the amount of memory you have right now, but when you start downloading data, you will not have room for it."

Mia says, "Robert, can you look into upgrading our memory and I will get the funding approved."

Robert says, "I will look into it."

They all turn their attention back to what Virginia is doing; as they watch, they see each of the sixty-four messages appear on the screen. She drags her mouse up to the top of the screen, and she clicks a simple start. After she does this, they watch as the pages begin to move around, some come together and stay, but some do not and continue to move around the screen. Eventually, a picture begins to form, along with a few messages within and around the pictures. Some of the words stay where they were, but some do not, they move to different areas. Finally, after about a half hour, the program stopped, and they all looked on in amazement. It was clear that what they were receiving was directions on how to build something - what it was, was not clear, but it was something huge and complicated.

Gabriel walks in and says hello and then asks, "How is everything going here?"

Mia says, "Gabriel, it is going fantastic. Virginia has been able to create a very user-friendly program that will enable us to compile our already decoded and translated messages."

Gabriel says, "That is fantastic, great job Virginia. So what messages have you compiled thus far?"

Mia says, "Well, the ones that didn't seem to make sense to us once we sent them through the first program."

Gabriel says, "Hmm, what if you sent the other messages through this program?"

Robert says, "Crap, why didn't I think of that!"

Mia says, "Well, it won't hurt anything so we can start that right away."

Robert asks Virginia to let him sit down so he could pull up the other messages. Once they are pulled up, he moves to let Virginia sit back down and run them through the new program. She opens the program back up, and the newly configured messages are on the monitor. She is about to close the page to start the same process with the old messages when Mia yells, "Wait! I see something; there, in the top right corner…it looks like two pages have been brought together to form a word."

Virginia zooms in on the area, and there is a word that she is not familiar with, but Mia is. She sees the word "ta'ane". Mia goes over to a different desk and pulls out a sheet of paper. She writes, Anita and Ana, these are present and past tenses of the Hebrew word answer but this word, it is the future tense of the word "answer" or "you will answer."

Mia gets up and walks back to the group who has been watching her as she wrote. She sets the paper down, and Gabriel reads it allowed, "You will answer? What does that mean?"

Robert shouts, "That's it, they want us to respond to their message!"

Gabriel says, "And how do we do that?"

Robert says, "They are showing us how! All of the data we have been receiving are directions or a blueprint to some kind of device to use to communicate back to them with!"

Jordan calls Jasmine; she says, "Hey babe, what's going on?"

Jordan says, "I've been tailing him all day. It has been hard to keep up with them when they get a call, but I can usually find them if I lose sight of them."

Jasmine says, "So, when he gets off of work, then what are you going to do?"

He says, "I want to know where he lives, I want to see his family. I want to see what I can take from him."

Jasmine says, "Wait, what do you mean, take from him?"

Jordan says, "I am not sure yet, I am keeping my options open."

Jasmine says, "Babe, I am all about an eye for an eye but, not going after his family if that is what you are thinking."

He says, "I will just see what happens, but not tonight, I am just getting an idea of where he lives tonight."

She says, "Ok, Bye, I love you."

He says, "Bye babe, I love you too."

She says, "Oh and babe, don't forget you have a daughter still."

He says, "I know."

After another hour of driving, they finally drove back to the police station. Knowing they would be awhile filling out reports, Jordan decided to drive to his house and grab a snack before they are finished with their shift. As he finishes eating, he uses the restroom, and then as he was walking through his house, he walked into his office and grabbed the gun he had purchased. He wasn't sure why he took it, but he was now on his way back to the station, with his gun.

As he pulled up, he waited about ten minutes, and the punk officer walked out, got in his vehicle and drove off with Jordan following him. Jordan was a little confused because the car was making odd turns, then he pulled into a grocery store. The guy got out of his car and walked into the store. Jordan was waiting for him to come out when he sees the guy walking right up to his car, he knocks on his window, and Jordan rolls his window down. What the cop didn't see was the gun that Jordan had pulled out of his center console and was pointing right at him. Just as the man said, "Can I help you?" Jordan raised the gun and said, you need to get into the car.

The man walked around and got into the passenger seat; it was then that he recognized the man with the gun. Jordan had some zip ties that he put on his wrists, and then he fastened him to a piece of metal under the seat. He was stuck. Jordan drove away and headed to the only place he could think of - home. Once there, he opened the garage and drove in and closed the door. Luckily no one was home. He called Michelle and told her to go to her friend's house, and he would pick her up later. Then he walked the cop into the kitchen and tied him to a chair. Eventually, Jasmine came home, she walked in and surveyed the situation and said what the hell is going on."

Jordan said, "Change of plans, at least for now."

Jasmine says, "What's this white boy's name?"

The man says, "I'm Logan, Logan Philips and yes, I am the one who killed your son. I understand what you all are doing - hell, I'd probably do the same thing,"

Jasmine says, "This is not what I agreed to."

Jordan says, "I know but, like I said, there's been a change of plans. He spotted me and got a bit of a drop on me, but I saw him coming, too many people around, so I pulled the gun out and told him to get in the car and here we are."

She says, "Now what?"

Jordan says, "I need to move him out of here. I'm gonna call one of my boys from back in the day; they'll have a place I can take him. He pulls his phone out and makes a call, He says, "Jamall, hey, yea. We all good man, but look I need a place to lay low for a while, no questions though man. Uh huh, yep, red top mountain, nothin closer? Ok man, look I appreciate it brother, keep your head up man." Jordan says, "Ok, I got a place, get up, we are going."

Jasmine says, "And what am I supposed to do?"

He says, "Go get Michelle."

Jordan grabs Logan by the arm and guides him out to the garage where they get into the car and leave.

∞

Rai and Sophie are in a travel trailer that is parked in the parking lot of the park where Rai and Gabe will be re-married. Sophie is helping Rai get on her dress. A modest, slim, white dress with a length that is just past her knees. The neckline is cut just low enough to show slight cleavage under a small amount of lace. The sleeves come down to her elbows, and there is lace on the bottom edge of the dress as well. She wears a light golden chain around her neck with a small golden cross as well. She has on white pantyhose and white shoes with a small heel on them. The white dress against her tan skin was striking; she was beautiful, to say the least.

Gabe had gotten ready at home and was driving to the park to remarry the woman with whom he would share the rest of his life. On his drive, he found himself talking to God, he thanked him for putting Rai in his life all those years ago and keeping her in his life. He said, aloud, "I don't know what I would do without her, and I can only thank you, God, for keeping us in each other's life and guiding us back into a relationship with you at the center."

He was driving up to the parking area where he saw Hayden standing beside his car. Gabe got out and said hello to Hayden and shook his hand. They began walking to the area where he and Rai would be exchanging their vows. As they came up the path the gazebo came into view, Hayden and Sophie had come up earlier and done some minor decorations on it, Gabe remarked, "Wow, this looks great."

They walked up, and Pastor Gary Manns was there with his bible open, and he was reading from it. As they walk up, and Gary says, "Hello!"

Gabe and Hayden each say hello and shake his hand. Gabe, for the sake of conversation, says, "What are you reading there, sir?"

Gary says, "Well, actually, with all of this talk, I have been digging into Revelations."

Hayden looks at Gabe with a deep questioning look and says, "What talk?"

Gabe says, "I'll talk to you later about it."

Gary gets the hint and stops talking about it. Just then Sophie walks up to the gazebo and says, "Hello, everyone, I was just making sure everyone was here; I will go tell Mom we are ready."

She walks away and about five minutes later with no music Rai walks slowly up the path to the gazebo with Sophie's arm through hers. Gabe watches her walk up; her beauty absolutely dumbfounds him. How could he deserve such an amazing and beautiful bride? She walks up the steps, and he takes his hand, he wants nothing more than to grab her and kiss her deeply, but instead, they each face the pastor. Gary says, "We have come together today in the presence of God to witness the joining of Gabriel and Rai in Holy Matrimony. This is a special time of celebration that they will long remember, and because of this, they are thankful you are here to share their joy. From the dawn of human history, it has been customary for the family to place its seal of approval upon the union of two persons in marriage. If these solemn vows that they are about to make are kept faithfully, God will bless their marriage. Gracious God, before whom we stand, look with favor upon this man and this woman who desire to make their vows before you and this gathering of family and friends. We are grateful for their families, which have reared them to maturity; and for the church, which has nurtured them in the faith. May they experience your presence as they pledge their lives, one to another, and may they ever walk the pleasant paths of righteousness, this we pray through Christ our Lord. There is a skill to marriage, as there is to any activity in which people engage. This art requires that we pay thoughtfulness to the little things as well as the big ones that are part of the closeness of matrimony. Develop the capacity to forgive and forget and heal quarrels as they happen. Say, 'I love you' and speak words of appreciation often. Do not come to take each other for granted and demonstrate your gratitude in thoughtful ways. Never grow too old to hold hands. Do not expect perfection of each other; perfection is only for God. Make your search for the good and the beautiful a common search. A good marriage evolves when two separate souls face life's pleasures and sadness in harmony, not in unison."

Gary then asks for the rings so he can bless them; he then gives Gabriel's ring to Rai and Rai's ring to Gabriel. He then asks Gabriel to repeat after him. He says, "I promise to be your lover, companion, and friend, your partner in parenthood, your ally in conflict, your greatest fan, and your best friend. Your comrade in adventure, your student and your teacher, your consolation in disappointment, your accomplice in mischief, your strength in your need - and vulnerable to you in my own -and most of all, your associate in the search for enlightenment. You may place the ring on her left hand."

He then asks Rai to repeat after him. "I promise to be your lover, companion, and friend, your partner in parenthood, your ally in conflict, your greatest fan, and your best friend. Your comrade in adventure, your student and your teacher, your consolation in disappointment, your accomplice in mischief, your strength in your need and vulnerable to you in my own, and most of all, your associate in the search for enlightenment." Gary asks Rai to place the ring on Gabriel's finger. He then tells Gabriel, "You may kiss your bride." Gabe pulls her to him, and they kiss deeply. Once they separate Gary says, "I pronounce you husband and wife."

After everyone congratulates them, Gabe and Rai step aside, and Hayden steps up to Sophie, and he says, "Sophie, you are the love of my life, the one I want to spend the rest of my days with and I want that to start now." He knelt down on one knee and continued, "I know you have said yes to marrying me, but will you marry me now?"

Sophie is shocked; she looks at Gabe and Rai and says, "You knew about this?" They both nod yes. She turns to Hayden and says, "Yes, yes I will." They embrace for a moment then Gary asks them to face him, they repeat the ceremony and end with a kiss and Gary pronounces them husband and wife.

Everyone hugs and after some conversations and pictures they commence to clean the place up. Then Gabe said to Gary, "Are you still able to join us for dinner?"

Gary says, "Yes, but then I have to go home, pack and catch the red-eye to D.C. to go meet with the President."

∞

Sean walks into a room he had only been in a couple of times since he moved into the house. In front of him are twelve different television screens mounted to the wall. There is a table with a computer; he reaches down and turns on the computer. After a few seconds, the computer is on, and the television screens are as well. He opens a program on the computer where each of the rooms appears. He clicks on the box that has Tracey on it, and she appears on one of the television screens on the wall. He then clicks

161

on a microphone icon and speaks to her. He says, "Tracey, I can see you now."

She says, "Screw you!"

Sean says, "Look; I didn't want to do this, I was told to."

She says, "Told to, by who?"

He says, "That is not important right now, and even if I told you, you wouldn't believe me."

Quickly, Tracey composes herself, and she says, "Sean, why don't you try me, I will remain open-minded."

For a second Sean thought about opening up to her but quickly focuses back on the task at hand. He says, "Look, all you need to know is that I will not harm you as long as you do what I tell you to do and that you have everything you need to live comfortably."

Sean turns the microphone off and leans back in the chair. He then hears the voice that he considers a friend now, Lucifer whispers, "Now, you need to start now." Sean knows what he meant, and he answers, "Now, why now?" Lucifer says, "She is ripe right now, she will conceive tonight."

Sean stands and paces around the room; could he do this, take a woman against her will? He then hears Lucifer scream, "Now!"

Sean stops and goes to the computer again, he turns the microphone on and says, "Tracey, I need you to do something. You cannot ask questions and you must do exactly what I say. I do not want to harm you, so please follow these directions. I am going to come to your door, I will open the small door in the center of the door, and you will turn around and place your hands through that opening, do you understand?"

Tracey wants to scream, hell no! Instead, she simply says yes. Sean makes his way to the lower levels of his home and walks up to her door, he opens the small opening and waits for her to place her hands through it. Once they are out, he places zip ties around them to secure them. He says, "Very good, now go sit on the bed."

He bends down to watch her walk away, and once she is seated, he opens the door. He then says, "As I said, I am only doing what I am told, so know that I have never done anything like this, but I am going to need you to turn around and bend over the bed."

Tracey knew this was probably coming; there was nothing she could do. Even if she stood and rushed towards him to try to knock him down, he was a mountain of a man; he could do whatever he wanted, so, she stood, turned around and bent over as he asked. At first, Sean had trouble getting ready for the act, but eventually, he was able to, it was painful, but she didn't make a sound; once it was over, she just stood, sat down and he walked out of the room. Once the door was closed, he told her to put her hands through the door, and he would remove the ties. She did as he asked, and he closed and locked the door and left. Once she was alone, she lay down on the bed and buried her face and cried quietly. She just kept saying, "why, why?"

∞

Gary was on his flight to Washington D.C. trying to sleep; he found himself praying to God, asking for courage and wisdom. He said, "God, you know I will do what you ask, but are you sure I am the one for this job?" He opened his eyes and grabbed his bible; he looked up a verse he remembered and read, Joshua 1:3-9 I promise you what I promised Moses: "Wherever you set foot, you will be on land I have given you ... No one will be able to stand against you as long as you live. For I will be with you as I was with Moses. I will not fail you or abandon you. Be strong and courageous, for you are the one who will lead these people to possess all the land I swore to their ancestors I would give them. Be strong and very courageous, study this book of Instruction continually. Meditate on it day and night so you will be sure to obey everything written in it. Only then will you prosper and succeed in all you do. This is my command—be strong and courageous! Do not be afraid or discouraged. For the Lord, your God is with you wherever you go. (NIV®)" He thought "God, is great," he then leaned back in his seat and fell asleep.

Sara is in her office waiting for her Aid to transfer a call to her, her phone rang, and she picked it up saying, "Hello Gabriel, I trust all is well with you?"

Gabriel said, "Madam President, hello, yes all is great, I just got remarried to Rai."

She said, "Oh, that is fantastic…should I let you go?"

He said, "No Madam, what can I do for you?"

She said, "Well, I won't be long. I am planning a press conference to release our information to the public next week, probably Wednesday. I would like it if you could be there to help me explain to the world everything we know."

Gabriel said, "Absolutely, that is not a problem."

She said, "Fantastic, I will have my aids set everything up. Thank you, Gabriel.

He answered, "Thank you…goodbye Madam President."

∞

Gary arrives at the White House having been picked up at his hotel by a driver in a limo. He had never experienced anything like this; he was just a small-town pastor. He got out of the limo and is greeted by a couple of young people who seemingly had been expecting him. The young black lady who introduced herself as Shareese tells him to follow her, with the young man following them. They enter the building where they are screened for weapons by security, then move through the building until they come to a closed door with two large men dressed in suits standing on each side of the door. The young lady shows them her ID, then one of the men turns and knocks on the door and opens it. There, seated at her desk in the Oval Office is Madam President who stands and greets them as warmly as someone would if they were working in some small southern dinner in North Carolina. He was already impressed by this woman, she was so disarming and genuinely sweet, but he could also tell there was a hidden strength that simmered somewhere underneath the charm. They sat, and Sara said, "Pastor Manns, I want first to clear the air here, what has Gabriel told you so far about why you are here?"

He says, "Well, honestly, he spoke to me about a signal that the United States had received and the importance of these messages you've received and that you needed some guidance on theology for your address."

She said, "So he told you the nature of the messages?"

He said, "Yes he did."

She said, "Ok, I wanted to make sure you were up to speed on everything, but before we go any further, I need you to sign this non-disclosure agreement. Do you have a problem with this?"

He said, "No not at all."

After he briefly reads the agreement, he signs and dates it, and then Shareese walks across the room and takes the document and leaves the room, leaving them alone for the first time. Sara motions for him to take a seat on one of the chairs away from her desk. He sits in the chair with Sara sitting on the small couch across from him. She says, "May I call you Gary?"

He says, "By all means Madam."

She says, "Please, call me Sara when we are alone. Gary, I need to be honest here, I am frankly terrified about what I am planning here. I am worried about what the ramification of this information is going to have on our country as well as the international community."

He says, "I understand, do you feel led to do this?"

She says, "One hundred percent, it is as if I am in actual communication with God as it relates to this message."

He says, "Then you must do it, but remember that God does not want you to worry. In Luke 12:25 He says, "And which of you by being anxious can add a single hour to his span of life (NIV®)?"

She knew right away that Gary was exactly who she needed by her side for this task. She says, "Gary, I am sorry for taking up your Saturday, but how much of the next couple of days do you have available to help me with this message?"

He says, "I am at your disposal, so as much time as you need. I will need to make a few arrangements at my house and the church."

"Very well, I want to have this wrapped up by Monday and plan on delivering it Wednesday, so how about we get some lunch then we can spend the afternoon working on it?"

He says, "That sounds great."

They both get up and leave the office, then go to the dining room and take a seat. An older white lady probably in her early seventies comes to the table and says hello to them both, Sara says, "How are you doing Stella? How is that grandson of yours doing?"

Stella said, "I am doing well madam, and he is doing great, he is studying like crazy for the spelling bee, he is such a smart kid."

Sara says, "That is great!"

Just then, Tim walks in, and Sara introduces Tim to Gary. Then, Tim takes a seat next to his wife. Stella says, "What can I get for you all?"

Sara asks for some tomato soup and a grilled cheese sandwich, Tim asks for a Caesar salad, and Gary asks for a turkey and swiss cheese on wheat. Gary continues to be impressed by this lady; it would be so easy to let the power of the presidency inflate your ego but not Sara, she was as warm and polite as some mom on an old television show. He was encouraged by this; he felt that if anyone could handle the task at hand, she could.

Chapter 14

Sean is in the little coffee shop in town eating a bran muffin and drinking a black coffee; there was a young lady that he had seen in here a few times and thought she could be next for his project, he was hoping she would stop in today. He was just about to leave when she walked in. She ordered a breakfast sandwich and an iced coffee, then took a seat. She had long almost jet- black hair, the more he looked at her he began to realize she was Native American or at least mostly Native American. She was about five feet six inches with beautiful dark brown eyes. She was listening to music on her phone with earbuds in her ears; he did notice her looking at him when he would look away. Finally, he knew Lucifer would get angry if he didn't continue to acquire objectives for the project. He got up and introduced himself. He said, "Hello, I am Sean, I noticed you and wanted to say hello and tell you how beautiful you are,"

The girl looked up, took her earbuds out and said, "That's nice." Sean stood there for a few more seconds then turned to walk away, then she said, "I am sorry, I just hate getting hit on, I didn't mean to be rude."

Sean turned back around and said, "No I am sorry, I shouldn't have just walked up and said that. I am sorry for interrupting you."

He turned and walked out of the shop; she sat there for a few more seconds, then grabbed her stuff and left as well, she caught up to Sean and said, "Hey, hold up!"

Sean stopped and turned around; he said, "Yes?"

She said, "Emma, my name is Emma Begay, it is nice to meet you, Sean."

As she said this, she realized just how big this guy was; she had to look up at a sharp angle to meet his eyes. They found a bench and sat down; he asked where she was from. She said, "Right here, born and raised."

He said, "Wow, I haven't met anyone from here yet, seems like most people are transplants. Say, Emma, I know this is pretty forward of me, but would you care to join me for dinner tonight?"

She said, "Sure, what time and where and I will meet you there."

He said, "How is Seven o'clock at the Place?"

She was surprised and said, "Are you sure? That place is expensive; I've never eaten there."

He says, "Yes, I am sure, they know me pretty well there." He shakes her hand, and they go their separate ways. She had just a little bit of an odd feeling but, ah, the Place, she would at least get a good meal out of the deal.

Sean was driving home when Lucifer said, "She is going to be a difficult one, you might need to move fast with her."

Sean said, "She is skeptical, but I can get her secured. She was interested in the restaurant, I just have to get her home, and I will move on her right away. Now that I have done it once I have a little more confidence."

Lucifer said, "Sean, soon you will be ready for an even bigger role in my plan."

Sean said, "Oh, like what?"

Lucifer says, "In due time, in due time, but you need to speed the plan up, things are happening that will change everything on this world."

Sean thought to himself, this world, what does that mean?

∞

Jordan is driving up to a cabin with the Logan in the trunk; he had taped him up very well with duct tape so he couldn't signal anyone that he was there. Jordan had come down from the adrenalin from all the events of the day and was becoming exhausted. He had to stop for gas, but he had to be very quick. He knew that the cop would try to escape or try to get help. He had to be smart about where he stopped and how he positioned his vehicle. He found a station that was relatively slow, so he decided to stop in there and get a little gas to make it the rest of the way to the cabin. Jordan turned the radio on to some local talk show and turned it up just enough to drown out any noise Logan might try to make. Jordan got out, slid his card and started pumping. As soon as he started, a car pulled up on the other side of the pump. Jordan thought to himself, "Of course you had to decide to stop there, six other pumps and you just had to pick this one." A tall, thin forty-something white man got out and said hello to Jordan as he walked to his pump to start pumping gas. He said to Jordan, "Where ya headed?"

"Oh just a few more miles; I've got a cabin up here."

The other guy says, "Oh, so do we."

Meanwhile, Jordan is sure that Logan is going to start kicking and screaming; he had to be able to hear this conversation. But to his surprise, Jordan was able to fill the tank, tell the guy goodbye and get back in the car with no issues. He was relieved and just wanted to get to where he was going. After about thirty minutes of driving, he came upon the place his homey let him use. It was small but perfect for what he needed. It was dark, and he couldn't see any other lights around, so he felt like they were isolated here. He pulled his gun out and opened the trunk; he told the cop to get out and walk into the cabin. The cop did so with no problems. Jordan thought to himself, why is he so agreeable? Once they were inside, he told him to sit in a chair that was by a table; he then tied and taped him until he was sure he couldn't escape.

Jordan wasn't sure what he was going to do with him yet except he did know he would make him pay.

∞

Dan has flown to D.C. to meet with Ben to discuss the direction the messages have taken. Dan walks up to a desk with a lady sitting in her chair working on a computer. She looks up and says, "May I help you?"

He says, "Yes, I am here to see Ben, he is expecting me."

She says, "You can have a seat, I will let him know you are here." She calls and tells him Dan is there to see him.

About a minute later Ben walks through a door and says, "Dan, it is great to see you again. Come on back to my office."

They walk by the lady at the desk, Ben thanking her as they leave. Walking back to his office, they stop at a break room. Ben pours himself a cup of coffee, black and offers some to Dan. Dan takes a cup of black coffee as well. Once in Ben's office, Ben says to Dan, "So tell me what brings you all the way to D.C.?"

Dan says, "Well, we've had some development on the messages. As you know, we had an outside consultant come in and develop a program to help us with the new messages. They were not making sense to anyone on the team. Well, they've taken the program the Chinese gave us and reworked it, and now we can make sense of it all."

Ben leans back and thinks for a moment, then he says, "Ok, what is the message telling us?"

Dan says, "It is less of a message and more like directions."

Ben has a slight questioning look on his face, he says, "Directions for what?"

Dan says, "Ben, the team is convinced that the messages are directions to build a device to help us communicate back to the ones that have been sending us the messages."

Ben says, "Hmm, ok, what do you mean directions?"

Dan says, "Actually, it's more like a combination of directions and blueprints."

Ben says, "That's incredible Dan, do you have all of the directions to build it?"

Dan says, "No not yet, they have what they think is around half of the information they need, but we are not sure about that. They keep getting more data, processing it and adding it to the rest of the arrangement."

Ben then says, "Ok, not to be a jerk...and I'll admit that it is incredible...I mean the whole thing is incredible, but couldn't you have just called me and told me all of this?"

Dan said, "Yes, but I am not done. I need to ask you to find the money to build this thing. It has some pretty crazy technology, some of which we don't fully understand, but it's going to cost a lot of money."

Ben thought for a moment, then said, "Do you have any idea how much I should ask for?"

Dan said, "I would start with 20 Billion."

Ben sat up hard and said, "What! I can't ask for that kind of money. We will have to go to Congress for it."

Dan then said, "Or the United Nations."

Ben relaxed a little and said, "That is an intriguing suggestion, I mean, why should we foot the bill for something the whole world has a vested interest in?"

Dan said, "That's kind of what I was thinking."

Ben stood and said, "Ok, I will see if the president is available to meet with us this afternoon...do you want to go grab some lunch?"

Dan said, "Sure, sounds like a great idea."

After Ben set up the meeting, the two of them left for lunch with plans to meet with the president at 2:00 PM that afternoon.

∞

Faizan is in his room at his parent's home where he continues to rehearse the plan over and over. He is following orders and laying low. The most positive thing that has been happening is that he has talked to Anahita every day since they had met. He has learned a lot about her, and she is going to come to his parent's house this evening and then they will be going out for some dinner. He was becoming very fond of her even though he knew it was not a good idea. But he couldn't help himself, she was without a doubt the most beautiful girl he had ever seen, and their conversations were so deep and thought-provoking. The two of them would talk on video on their phones for hours sometimes. So, he figured for the little time he had left that he would enjoy this young lady's company until he got the call to enact his orders.

∞

Gabe and Rai are sitting on the beach in San Diego on their short, weekend-long honeymoon. Gabe says, "Man I needed this, I haven't had a chance just to stop and relax with everything going on."

Rai says, "I can imagine babe, what a whirlwind of events. It is all so unimaginable but here we are, with knowledge of another world in the universe that has intelligent life on it…which is just crazy when you think about it."

Gabe says, "I know, and that is what I mean, I haven't stopped and truly wrapped my brain around that. Anyhow, I am just glad I am with you, here, now. I love you so much, my beautiful wife."

Rai said, "I love you too babe."

After a few hours of relaxing time on the beach, they decided to head back to the hotel to get ready for dinner. Once they got back, Gabe had left his phone on the charger in the room, he decided to check for messages, and there was one from Mia, a text message saying, "Gabriel, we need to talk soon, we have run all of the old messages through the newest version of the program Virginia set up for us. You need to have all the information in the messages sent to us. Thanks."

He thought, I better call her, but then, he heard his wife say, "Are you going to join me in the shower?" The old Gabriel would have called Mia, but he didn't want to mess this up, his wife was the priority, Mia could wait. He put the phone down and walked into the bathroom.

∞

Gary has been working with the President all weekend and was fully aware of everything she was going to say. He was shocked to find out that she had already told every leader in the world about the messages and had given them all the coordinates to find the messages as well as offering the programs that had been developed to decode and translate the messages. He also found out that not only would he be present for the press event she was planning but Gabriel would be there as well as other top members of scientific fields that have been working on this project, but the most surprising thing was that the President of China Huan Ji would be present. He was very pleased with what they had written; it had taken many hours but what they had to say to the citizens of the United States as well as to the citizens of the world, would change everything they knew to be true. Sara had offered to fly him home on Monday and then back on Wednesday for the press event, but Gary did not relish the idea of flying all the way back to California only to turn around a day and a half later to fly back to D.C., so he had decided to stay until the press event. He figured he would take in some of the touristy things; he might not get another chance to see the capitol again. So, he figured he would take advantage of the time he had left on this cool sunny Monday afternoon. He looked at some of the pamphlets in the hotel and decided to take the train to see the Washington Monument first, then maybe the Lincoln Memorial.

∞

Dan and Ben are waiting outside the Oval Office to speak to the president. Finally Marvin Steelman opens the door and says, "The President will see you now."

They enter the office, and Sara walked around her desk shaking their hand and saying hello to them both. They sit across from her as she sits at her desk. She says, "What can I help you with today?"

Ben says, "First, thank you for meeting us on such short notice. Dan flew out to meet with me to give me an update and I felt we needed to elevate this information to you as well as figure out next steps."

Sara says, "Ok, what is it we need to discuss?"

Ben asks Dan to start the discussion. Dan says, "Madam President, some time ago, we started receiving a message that was unlike the other messages. We were running them through the new program given to us from the Chinese, but it was not making sense, so we had an outside consultant from the CIA, she is a computer programmer for them. Her name is Virginia Rhodes. Gabriel brought her in and showed her everything they had and the challenges they were having. She took the program given to us by the Chinese and reworked it and came up with a solution to their problems. They started sending all the new messages through the new program and what they figured out was quite remarkable, Madam. What the messages contain are directions on building a device to be able to reply to them or communicate back to them."

Sara was enthralled with the information and couldn't believe what she was hearing. She says, "So, you are telling me, we will be able to talk with these beings in real time?"

Dan says, "We think so Madam, we have about what we think is half of the data we need to build the device."

Ben says, "But, the problem is, Madam President…is money. It is going to be very expensive to build the device based on what we have so far."

Sara says, "Ok, how much are we talking about here?"

Dan says, "We should start with 20 billion."

Sara doesn't reply right away, she thinks for a minute then says, "Well, I could go to Congress for the money."

Ben speaks up and says, "Madam, Dan had an interesting idea…what if we go to the UN for the Money?"

Again, she doesn't answer right away, then she says, "I don't think I like that idea. We would be at the mercy of the UN; I would rather us have control of this device. I will find the money somewhere else. I will be reducing some of the military spendings so I might be able to justify diverting some of that money to the building of the device. Where would you build it?"

Ben says, "Well, back when we were going to try and design and build our own device, we were going to build it in Cocoa Beach, Florida. I think we would like to stick with that. We have a lot of fabrication ability there."

She says, "Makes sense…sounds good to me. Ok, let me find the money and I will contact you, Ben, when I have it."

Ben and Dan stand, Ben says, "Thank you so much Madam President."

She wishes them luck and thanks them for the work they are doing. Dan and Ben are outside of the Oval Office, and both let out an audible sigh of relief. Ben says, "Well, that went great, now I know why she is the President of the United States, what an incredible mind she has."

Dan says, "Ok, thank you so much for everything, Ben. I am going to head to the airport and find a flight back to California."

They shake hands and part ways outside.

∞

Logan has no feeling in his hands; he has been tied up in the chair for at least twenty-four hours. All Jordan has given him is one drink of water, and that was because he begged for it. Jordan only caved in because he wanted to shut Logan up. When Jordan had given him some water, he didn't replace the tape over his mouth, but he stayed silent so he wouldn't bring attention to this fact. Eventually, Jordan spoke to him and said, "I think it is getting close to that time, I have done enough thinking about this and I am ready to do it.

Logan said, "Ok, that is fine."He closed his eyes and began praying, he remembered a verse from 2 Timothy 4:7-8"I have fought the good fight, I have finished the race, I have kept the faith. Henceforth there is laid up for me the crown of righteousness, which the Lord, the righteous judge, will award to me on that Day, and not only to me but also to all who have loved his appearing (NIV®)."

Jordan listened to his rambling and said, "Are you ready to meet your maker then?"

Logan said, "If it is my time, then I am ready to meet Jesus."

Jordan pulled the gun out, raised it to Logan's head, put his finger on the trigger but then stopped and lowered the gun, then he said, "You believe all the crap man?"

Logan said, "With all of my heart and soul."

Jordan said, "Man, ain't no way there is a God. Too much bad crap has happened to me for that to be true."

Logan just said, "There is a reason for everything God does. I have no idea why he put your son in that car when I was there, but he did, and if I could take it all back, or do it over again, I might do things differently. However, we are trained to respond a certain way, and I did exactly as I was trained to do, but I wish your son were alive today sir, I truly do. I also understand what you are doing right now and why, so I am ready."

Jordan raised the gun, closed his eyes and pulled the trigger.

∞

Gabe and Rai were driving back from the coast and had gotten a call that Sophie was sick, and that Hayden was taking her to the hospital as they spoke. Gabe said, "We are almost home, we will change and meet you there."

Once home, they quickly showered, got dressed and headed to the hospital. This time Sophie was really sick, probably the sickest they'd seen her. Gabe spoke to Hayden; probably a little more sternly than he planned, he said, "What the hell happened Hayden?"

Hayden said, "She was sick yesterday, and I tried to get her to let me take her to the hospital, but she insisted she was going to be ok...then this morning she was a little better. I got some water in her and some fruit, but then it was downhill from there. I am sorry guys; I am trying hard to do my best here."

Rai said, "Hayden, it is ok...you are doing your best, and we are thankful that you are in her life."

Gabe said, "I am sorry for being so forceful a minute ago. I know you're doing all you can."

Rai then asked, "What did the doctor say?"

Hayden responded, "Nothing yet, they've only taken vitals, the doctor has not been in yet."

Gabe said, "Ok, coffee anyone? I am going to go grab a cup."

Both said no, and Gabe left for the cafeteria. His cell phone rang, and he saw it was Bobbi. Gabe answered, and she said,

"Gabriel, I just wanted to touch base before you head to D.C., will you be in the office tomorrow before your flight?"

He said, "As of right now, that is the plan, but we are at the hospital with Sophie right now, so it depends on what the doctor says…if it is bad, I might not even be going."

Bobbi says, "Oh God Gabriel, I am so sorry. I will say a prayer for all of you.Please let me know if I can do anything for you."

Gabriel said, "Thank you Bobbi." and then hung up his phone. He grabbed two coffees; he knew when he got back Rai would smell his and wish she had gotten some.

When he got back to Sophie's room, she was awake but very weak. He kissed her on the cheek and said, "Hi honey."

She said, "Hi daddy how was your honeymoon?"

He said, "It was fantastic."

Just then the doctor walked in and surveyed the room; he said, "Hello everyone, can I just ask you all to back away for a minute while I examine Sophie?"

They did as they were asked and waited. After about twenty minutes, the doctor invited them to step back up and told all of them that Sophie was in late stages of her cancer and that they would need to get more aggressive with their treatment. Gabe was crushed; he wanted to be angry at someone but then calmed down and began to pray. He prayed to himself at first then, after the doctor left, he prayed over Sophie and everyone in the room. He knew that God had a plan and he had to accept that. After an hour of talking to Sophie, they decided to head home, and that Gabe would go ahead and fly to D.C. for the press conference.

Chapter 15

Sean and Emma were finishing up dinner with plans to go out for a drink before calling it a night. Sean knew how to be extremely charming, all he had to do was turn it on a little. That, along with his physique, is why he was able to charm many ladies. Emma was no exception; he was able to size her up as a bit of a partier. She just wanted to have fun, so Sean acted the part and was able to convince her to go out after dinner. They found a night club with loud music. They went in and danced a little, then they left there and found a smaller pub where they were able to talk a bit easier. Sean was a big guy and could handle a lot of alcohol, but Emma was very small and was trying to keep up with him. By about one o'clock in the morning, she was almost to the point of blacking out. Sean paid their bill with a hefty tip, with a look to the bartender as if to say, you didn't see me here. He helped Emma to his car and drove her to his home where he carried her all the way down to the lower level of his home. Once inside, he figured Lucifer was going to yell at him to take her now, so he did the same thing with her that he had done with Tracey. It was easier this time, and once he finished, he moved her back up onto the bed and left her there, locking the large door behind him.

The next morning, he decided to check on the two women via his camera system. He turned their microphones on; both were cursing him, with Emma though, she had no clue what had happened. She was pissed one minute, then crying the next. Lucifer had commended Sean for all his actions. He was proud of himself. Then, he could hear Lucifer saying, "Don't get comfortable, we still have a lot of rooms to fill."

∞

Gabriel walks into the hotel; he has flown to D.C., and he sees Dan and Ben walking through the lobby, he yells for them to hold up. Dan sees him and waits for him to catch up with them. Gabriel says, "Hey guys, it is great to see you both."

Dan and Ben each shake his hand. Dan says, "How was your flight?"

Gabriel says, "It was ok, I need to check in still, want to meet in the bar in thirty minutes?"

Dan says, "Sure, sounds good, we will see you then."

Gabriel checked in and went up to his room; he couldn't get Sophie out of his head. His one daughter, he loved her so much, then as if not by thought, but by the will of God, he fell to his knees. He heard a voice as clear as if the speaker was in the room with him. It said, "Gabriel, my child, know that when I take Sophie, she is not gone, she is but a spirit, in heaven, you can still talk to her, you will see her again. I am not saying when I will take her, but someday she will come home, everything is according to my plan child. I ask that you have faith and love her."

Gabriel said, "God, I trust in you, I am but human and have such a hard time understanding your ways, I will, however, have faith in you. Take her when it is her time, I understand everything happens according to your plan Lord. God, thank you for everything you have blessed me with, and if you take her soon, thank you for the time I have had with her. I love you, Lord."

The voice of God then told him that He loved him as well, then he said, "Gabriel, you have important work to do, I trust you with the others to deliver my message."

Gabriel opened his eyes; he was now on his hands and knees with tears running down his face. He had not been conscious of the fact that he was crying. He looked at his watch, and he had been there for thirty minutes. He felt like he had just run a marathon. Exhausted, he stood and washed his face and straightened his clothes out, then he left his room. He needed to get downstairs to meet with Ben and Dan. Tomorrow was the big day, and the three of them needed to make sure their message was consistent, and they needed to figure out who would talk about each aspect of the events. As the elevator opened, Gary was there waiting to go up. Gabriel said, "Gary, so great to see you."

Gary said, "It is great to see you as well, how was your honeymoon?"

He said, "It was great, hey I am meeting with Dan and Ben at the bar, would you care to join us?"

Gary said, "Sure, I would love to."

So, they walked to the bar that was located in the hotel and found Dan and Ben. The four men talked about the events that had taken place over the past year and who should talk about what. After a few hours they each felt comfortable with their roles in the press conference. Just as they were about to leave, they could see a large group of men walking through the hall. Gabriel caught a glimpse of who he was sure was the President of China, Huan Ji. Gabriel thought, "Why in blazes would he be here?"

Sara was now in the press briefing room; she was talking to the producer, Liam McLean whom she had brought on to make this the best news conference possible. Sara said, "Liam, I need a very large screen behind me. I have some visuals that I need to display."

Liam said, "No problem."

Sara said, "I also need to know how you want everyone arranged. I will have Huan Ji, Gabriel, Dan, Ben and Gary here with me."

Liam said, "Very well, we will have you and Huan Ji at the forefront and the others behind you. I will do a lapel microphone on each of them for questions. Do you have the thumb drive with the presentation on it?"

Sara gave him the drive then said she needed to make a call and that she would be back. Sara first went to the residence and spoke to Tim. She said, "Hey love, are you almost ready to join me in the briefing room? I want to review everything with you; I trust your opinion above anyone else's."

Tim says, "I sure am babe, just putting my shoes on and I am ready."

She says, "I love that suit on you, the grey jacket and red tie looks amazing."

While he was finishing up, Sara was informed that Dan, Ben, Gabriel, and Gary were all waiting to meet with her, so on their way back to the briefing room she met them and had them follow her. Sara had Liam review everything with them; they did a practice run with Sara going over her speech and running through her presentation. They then had Gary come forward and offer his remarks as the spiritual representative for the president. Once that was finished Liam had a list of questions that were likely to get asked and had each individual come forward and answer the question. Everything ran smoothly, Sara was feeling good about everything. It was about six o'clock, so she and the group with her went up to the dining room to have dinner. Then they would be back around seven thirty for final preparations for the briefing at eight o'clock.

Sara had planned ahead to have dinner with this group, so everything was ready when they arrived. It was a delicious meal with great conversation. The mood was very upbeat; Sara was excited to move forward with this endeavor, she hated secrets and didn't like keeping this from the American people. Just as they were finishing dinner, Marvin entered the room and told Sara that Huan Jihad arrived. Sara excused herself and told them that Tim would escort them back to the briefing room. Sara greeted Huan Ji with a hug and thanked him for coming. They then started walking to the briefing room and arrived just after the others in the group had arrived. Sara said, "Liam, let me introduce you to the President of China, Huan Ji. Huan Ji, Liam will review everything with you, we go on air in less than thirty minutes. Remember that this is not just on network television, but on all available platforms including all social media, we will be seen all over the world, live."

At five minutes to air everyone was positioned in front of the cameras. Liam had to move a few folks so not to have anyone covered up during the speech. He had placed black tape on the floor, so each person knew where to stand, Liam heard prompt for one minute until air, so he moved off to the side. He had done everything he could to make this go perfectly, all he could do now is sit back and let the President do her job.

∞

Someone counted off five, four, three, two, one. The center red light on the camera turned on, and Sara began speaking. Sara said, "Ladies and Gentlemen, citizens of the United States and citizens of the world, today will mark a change for us as a human race. So much has happened over the last year that I personally felt it was time for you all to know what we are faced with. Let me begin with a statement by C.S. Lewis in his book published as the book Mere Christianity. C.S. Lewis said, "I am trying here to prevent anyone saying the really foolish thing that people often say about Him: I'm ready to accept Jesus as a great moral teacher, but I don't accept his claim to be God. That is the one thing we must not say. A man who was merely a man and said the sort of things Jesus said would not be a great moral teacher. He would either be a lunatic — on the level with the man who says he is a poached egg — or else he would be the Devil of Hell. You must make your choice. Either this man was, and is, the Son of God, or else a madman or something worse. You can shut him up for a fool, you can spit at him and kill him as a demon, or you can fall at his feet and call him Lord and God, but let us not come with any patronizing nonsense about his being a great human teacher. He has not left that open to us. He did not intend to. Now it seems to me obvious that He was neither a lunatic nor a fiend: and consequently, however strange or terrifying or unlikely it may seem, I have to accept the view that He was and is God (C.S. Lewis Copyright ©)."

Sara continued, "You might be asking yourselves, why is the president of the United States of America speaking to us about such an odd subject? I stand here in front of you all to tell you that about eleven months ago, we had a team of scientists from the The Space Network, or TSN, intercept a message that was unlike anything any of them had ever seen before. After some time, they were able to slowly decode and decipher it; then eventually, they were able to translate it, as well as pinpoint the location and origin of the messages. Before I proceed, I need all of you to prepare yourselves for what I am about to tell you. I can tell you that we are one hundred percent confident in our findings here, We have had every professional organization at our disposal review, examine and cross-check every piece of data in our possession as well as all of our protocols, we even brought the Chinese in to review everything. This evening I am here to tell you all that we have received messages from another world. This planet is located close to Proxima Centauri."

The press core gasped, with low murmurs of discussions happening. Sara continued, "We have received hundreds of messages from them, and now have a very efficient program that deciphers and translates the messages. I need to prepare you for the even more incredible part of the news I have for you today.

These messages have been sent to us in an ancient form of Hebrew, the raw data we received was the most difficult thing to deal with, but once we deciphered and decoded it, the rest was a matter of translating it from the almost unspoken Hebrew to English. The next thing I need to tell you will be doubted, scrutinized, reviewed and even rejected, but I have a responsibility as your leader to tell you everything. The original message, after it was deciphered and translated was Messiah, as well as other similar messages and then followed by the word, Jesus."

Someone yelled, "What, no way."

Other comments were shouted out as well. "Yes, citizens of earth, we have a civilized community of beings who live about five light years away from our world that know, follow and love Jesus. I have already met with every leader of every nation. We met in Switzerland in a secret location, and I revealed everything I just told you along with coordinates for the signal and all of our programs to help decode, decipher and translate everything as well as our data. I wanted to be transparent, because this, I believe, changes the world as we know it. Once everyone can process and accept this information, your heart will belong to Jesus, and it will change how we all live together. I am in beginning talks with Congress to propose that we as a nation begin a drastic reduction in our nuclear arms and then I will have unilateral talks with all nations who possess them to reduce their arms as well, and eventually, eliminate them all together; my goal is world peace."

Huan Ji stepped forward and said, "I want to first thank Madam President Sara Murphy for trusting me to assist with this event and for having a vision that we hope leads to world peace. My people have examined everything she has talked about here today, and it is, in fact, all true. We have taken all the information back to our country and continue to monitor all messages on our

186

own. Thank you, and I look forward to playing any role she sees fit for us to fill."

Sara thanks Huan Ji, then says, "Now, I would like to have Pastor Gary Manns come forward and say a few things and then we will have our experts available for questions."

Gary walked forward and said, "Thank you Madam President, what we have learned is the most remarkable thing since Jesus was born here on earth. But to learn that God sent his Son to another world, I assume for the same reason, is incredible, to say the least. When the President asked me to speak here today, I had many internal conversations with myself, and with God. I was truly struggling with what to say. Should I spend many hours typing out some long speech to deliver the message of Jesus? And then God spoke to me, just as clear as if he were in the room with me. So, today I am compelled to tell you that of all the things I have learned in the 30 plus years of studying the word of God, the two most important things you must know are found in Matthew 22:36-40 it reads, 'Teacher, what is the most important commandment in the Law?" Jesus answered: Love the Lord your God with all your heart, soul, and mind. This is the first and most important commandment. The second most important commandment is like this one. And it is, "Love others as much as you love yourself (NIV®)." All the Laws of Moses and the Books of the Prophets are based on these two commandments." Moving forward in the future, as we learn more about the beings that sent these messages and decisions need to be made as it relates to the information we are getting, I have been asked to advise Madam President on these matters." Gary said thank you and stepped back.

Sara stepped back up and said, "Thank you, Gary, we will take questions now. I would like to ask my panel of experts to come forward. Let me introduce Gabriel Dane the Director of the TSN, Dan Henry the Director and CEO of HETI and Ben Williams our

TASA Administrator. My press secretary, Imala Anderson, will field the questions."

Immediately, hands shot up with everyone yelling at the same time, Imala asked everyone to calm down then she called on a young lady to her far right. She stood and said, "Are we able to communicate back to them?"

Gabriel stepped up and said, "We have a team of scientists and engineers who have been tasked with coming up with a way to do just that. After many ideas, we still did not have any clear direction for moving forward with any way to communicate back to them. A few weeks ago we started getting a different type of signal, and after a new program was written with the help of a computer programmer from the CIA, we were able to reconfigure the data and make sense of what they were trying to tell us. We finally understood that what they were sending us was essentially a blueprint to build exactly what we needed to reply to them. We are still receiving data for the blueprints; once the stream of data ends, we will begin the task of moving forward with building it."

Gabriel stepped back, and all the hands shot up again with reporters yelling questions. Imala stepped up and asked politely, "Please everyone, we will try to get everyone's questions, so please wait until you are called on then ask your question, thank you."

She then motioned to the center, an older man stood and said, "Why are you using the Chinese to be your measure of transparency?"

Sara stepped back up and said, "This was done at my request. First, I knew that they are the global leaders for writing computer code, and we would benefit from their involvement. I also knew that if the government of China, who are skeptics of the west and one of the most anti-religious nations in the world, were convinced, that the world would see that our claim would have more validity to it."

Sara stepped back; the next reporter was a small, young, white man. He stood and said, "So, are little green men going to try and invade our planet?"

Ben stepped up and said, "No, as scientists, we know that this world is about five light years away. That would mean that they would have to travel at the speed of light to get to us, but, if you took any basic science classes in school, you would know that matter cannot travel at the speed of light because it takes on more mass as it speeds up, thus needing more power and speed. However, radio waves do travel close to the speed of light, so if we sent a message now, it would take a little more than five years for them to receive it. We have been sending messages to them through our normal means of communication; our goal is to be able to communicate in close to real time. In closing, we are confident that we will not be meeting these beings."

The questions went on for about another forty-five minutes, then Sara stepped back up and said, "Ladies and gentlemen, thank you for your time. I will be giving you, the American people, updates on our progress as I have information available to me. Before I close, I would invite everyone to read Jesus' Sermon on the Mount. It gave me great insight on how I should live my life in a way that pleases Jesus. So, for tonight, again, I thank you for your time, God bless you, and God bless the United States of America."

∞

Omer is in his home and calls Qadeer; He tells him that it is time to set the plan in motion. He is to contact all the operatives in the United States and begin to complete their assignments. Qadeer says, "Yes sir, I will be accessing the account to transfer the agreed upon money for the families of all of the martyrs."

Omer said, "Very well."

Qadeer hung up the phone and began his calls; the way it worked was each one of his contacts also had contacts, and those contact had contacts. Once everyone was contacted, over two hundred people would be put into motion to pull this event off. Once he called his last contact, he had one more call to make; he dialed it, and Faizan said, "Hello?"

Qadeer said, "My young friend, it is time, tomorrow at ten o'clock AM."

Faizan simply said, "Ok."

He hung up the phone and walked downstairs; his father had just turned the news on, he walked into the kitchen where he could smell dinner cooking. His mother was humming a sweet song as she cut some cucumbers to put into the yogurt for the naan bread. He grabbed a glass for some water, kissed his mother on the cheek and went back into the living room and sat with his father. He noticed his father was not reclined in his chair comfortably but was instead, sitting up and was on the edge of his seat. His father yelled for his mother to come into the living room. She came into the room and sat down; the president was on the television - Faizan noticed that he was getting a ton of notifications on his phone as well. This was broadcasted on every social media application he had. What could be this important? They watched the President give her speech as well as the Pastor and then they listened to all the questions and the answers. Then it was over, and just like that, everything he and his family believed in, was now not true. Faizan thought to himself, "Now what? What do I do?"

He and his parents were sitting in disbelief; all were absolutely without words. Fear was creeping into their very beings, would God cast them out? Would he forgive them? Finally, Faizan's father spoke, he said, "Ok, I think we should eat, then I will start researching this myself. Perhaps we should plan to find a church and learn all we can."

While cleaning up dishes from dinner, Faizan's phone rang, he excused himself and went outside to take the call. He said, "Hello?"

Omer said, "My friend, it is me."

Faizan said, "Oh, it is an honor to speak to you, sir."

Omer said, "The honor is mine, my friend, I just saw what you just saw, and it is a lie young Faizan, we must follow the plan the one true God Allah has planned out for us. I heard him as clear as day; every detail was given to me by him. The plan is a go, are you?"

Faizan hesitated at first, and then he cleared his throat and said, "Yes sir."

After they hung up, he immediately called Anahita. He said, "Hey, did you see it?"

She said, "Yes, yes I did, my whole family is in shock."

He said, "Mine too."

She said, "What do you think, what are you gonna do?"

He said, "My father is going to do some research, and he wants us to go to a church service this weekend."

She said, "That sounds like a pretty good plan."

He said, "I really need to see you, I miss you, can we meet?"

She said, "Sure, we can meet half-way, there is a Starbucks on Connecticut Avenue by the school. Does that work?"

Trying not to sound like a child about to open his birthday gift, he said, "Yes that works great, Seven o'clock?"

She said, "See you then."

He went back inside and told his parents he was going out. He went upstairs and cleaned up a bit, then left to catch a train south.

Chapter 16

Jordan opened his eyes; nothing had happened. The gun never went off. Jordan examined the gun, it was loaded and not jammed. He walked back up to Logan and pointed the gun at his head again. Logan was at peace with God, and ready to go, so he just sat there with his eyes closed, deep in prayer, unflinching and said, "Jordan, God loves you and so do I."

Jordan's phone rang, he saw that it was Jasmine, so he answered it. He said, "Hello."

She said, "Jordan, what have you done?"

He said, "Nothing, the gun didn't go off."

She said, "Ok, I am sending you a link and you need to watch it right away."

He said slowly, "Um, ok."

Once they hung up, he received the link and opened it. It was a video, so he started it. On the video he saw the President giving a speech. He turned the volume up and he listened, silently. Logan could hear what the video was saying as well. As it went on, Jordan leaned against a wall, and then slid down until he was sitting on the floor, not a great distance from Logan. He watched the speech she gave and then the pastor; he then shut it off. He sat on the floor, thinking about his entire life, all the crap he had been through, the obstacles he and Jasmine had overcome. Now, Jesus? Jesus is real? He lost it, everything hit him, like a sweeping wave of emotions that he could not control. He lay on the floor and began to cry. He cried like a newborn infant after taking its first breath, he couldn't control it.

For about ten minutes Jordan cried off and on, thinking about all he had and all he had lost yet the things he had were still things to be thankful for. He had a beautiful wife that he loved today as much as he did when he first fell in love with her and his beautiful daughter Michelle; she has such a great future ahead of her. Then it hit him like clouds clearing from the sun, what he was about to do would keep him from ever seeing her grow into a woman, start a career and a family. He stood up, walked to the counter, grabbed a knife, and walked up to Logan and cut him free. He said, "Go, get out." Logan didn't move. Jordan said, "You can go, get out of here." Logan just sat not moving. Jordan said, "What are you doing? You need to leave."

Logan finally spoke, he said, "Jordan, I need to tell you something, when you pulled the trigger, I was deep in prayer, I was asking God to stop the bullet, stop the gun. Something, anything, you see, I am in no hurry to go to heaven, I have much to do here on earth first, and I have a wife and kids. If God decided it was my time, I was ready, but I was praying that he would stop it. My prayer was answered, Jordan, I meant what I said, God loves you, and so do I."

Jordan was ashamed of what he had done; he could see that this man had not intended to kill his son. Jordan stood and extended his hand and said, "I am so sorry Logan."

Logan stood and pulled Jordan in and hugged him. Jordan said, "I am ready to face the consequences for my actions now Logan."

After a moment, Logan said, "It never happened."

Jordan said, "What?"

Logan said, "Jordan, I told you before, I probably would have done the same thing if I were in your position."

Jordan said, "I don't know what to say."

Logan said, "You don't have to say anything. Do me a favor though."

Jordan said, "Anything, what do you need?"
Logan said, "Food, a beer and a ride home."
Jordan gave a faint laugh and said, "Done."
They got into the car and headed back to the city.

∞

Young Ra-il was in a room with a group of officers including Song Mi-hyang, Lee Suk-park, and some other higher-ranking officials. They were sitting as they had before waiting for the Dear Leader. After about thirty minutes of sitting in a silent room, he walked in. No one dared look in his direction; most looked at the floor in a slight bow in their seat. He sat down and said, "Ok, everyone look at me, I need your attention. Today much has changed; the United States and the rest of the world are talking about world peace and eliminating their nuclear weapons. Do you see now? I am Supreme; I know things before they happen, you are lucky to be in my presence today. We will prepare for a war like this world has never seen and in the end, we will be the leaders of it. Then we will create true peace in the world; continue to stockpile our arsenal of weapons." He stood and left quickly. Everyone was left in a state of confusion, what else had happened? With no outside contact, they would never know.

∞

Sean was working at a frenetic pace, looking for women. He now had four in his care and working on his fifth. He had confirmed pregnancy on three of the women and Lucifer was pleased with him. Sean was currently dating a woman named Cathy. She was a tall, buxom, beautiful brunet. At almost thirty years old, she was a little on the older side for his purpose but still able to conceive according to his Lord. This woman was very intelligent and was proving to be a bit of a challenge for him; Lucifer told him to be patient and that the opportunity would present itself eventually. She had refused to let him pick her up, they always met at their agreed upon location, and she had not agreed to go home with him either. Tonight, however, she was going to come over and let him cook her dinner. He knew he had to get this right, so he spent much of the day preparing the meal. He had stocked the bar as well. He knew he had to get her to lower her guard; then he would simply overpower her and take her down to join the rest of the ladies.

For dinner, he was making Lentil-Barley Burgers with Fiery Fruit with a Roasted Asparagus and Tomato Penne Salad with Goat Cheese, and for dessert, he made a Raw Cashew Cheesecake. He had cooked most of the afternoon and around four o'clock decided he would first feed the women downstairs, then he would get cleaned up for dinner and wait for her arrival at around six o'clock. He took their dinner down to them and talked with each one; he asked if they needed anything and as always told them that as long as they didn't cause any trouble that nothing bad would happen to them. At around five o'clock he headed upstairs to get ready for dinner then around six o'clock Cathy arrived. Sean welcomed her in, then took her coat and told her to make herself comfortable. Cathy was rather impressed, and she told him as much. She was a lawyer in the small town, so she did ok for herself but not this well. They sat for about fifteen minutes then Sean asked her if she was ready to eat. They moved to the table, and Sean brought her plate to her. Cathy said, "Oh my you went all out for me. It is so nice of you to make a vegan meal for me."

He said, "It was my pleasure."

After their meal, he brought the dessert out and told her what he had put in it. She was thoroughly impressed with Sean, but she had been in an abusive relationship just before meeting Sean, so she was very cautious, yet Sean was beginning to make her feel comfortable. She said, "What do you have to drink in this place?"

He said, "You name it, I probably have it."

She said, "Vodka martini please."

He said, "Coming right up."

They moved to the deck outside, it was an unseasonably mild evening, and he had a magnificent view of the sunset behind the mountains. Cathy found herself relaxing more and more, and the Vodka was flowing, the next thing she knew, she was in bed with Sean, and they were becoming intimate. Sean gave her yet another drink, and that was the last thing she remembered. The next morning, she woke up in a different room, it was not Sean's bed. She was horribly hung over and needed some water. She got up and saw a sink and some glasses. She poured herself some water and took and long quenching drink. Then she set out to find Sean, she went to the door and tried to turn the handle, but it wouldn't budge. She tried again with the same result, she yelled for Sean. Sean didn't reply. However, she did hear someone. It was a female voice, she put her ear to the door, and she could hear other women. They said, "It is no use, you are stuck like us."

Cathy said, "Us? How many of you are there?"

The voice said, "You are number five."

She sat on the bed and assessed her situation. Cursing herself, "How could I be so stupid?" She heard Sean's voice in another room, then a different room, and then on the speaker he spoke to her. He said, "Cathy, I am sorry; please know that I am only following orders. As long as you do what I ask, I will not hurt you."

She said, "Hey Sean, go screw yourself." For the first time, she realized the severity of her situation. She had not told anyone where she was going or who with. She was alone with a crazy man, and she had no idea why he had done this. With tears in her eyes, she swore that she would get out of this place and Sean would pay for what he had done.

∞

Robert was on a flight to Orlando to begin his transition to running the design and build out of the device. Mia calculated that there were just a few more messages necessary, and the device's design would be complete. They had enough to start the project, and the President wanted to move forward with building it as soon as possible. She had moved some of the funding from the defense budget to the device project, so Robert had a budget of fifty billion dollars under the oversight of Gabriel Dane.

Robert landed and gathered his luggage and was met outside the airport by a military vehicle. He got in, and they headed to the coast. The driver was a US Army private -her name was Bridget Walker, Sara wanted elevated security for the leadership team for this project, so she had asked the Pentagon to provide the personnel for this detail. Bridget asked how the flight was and how the move was going so far. Robert said," Flight was good, and the movers are supposed to arrive in three days." It was Robert's first time in Florida. He was so used to the desert, to see the lush greenery all around him was very different.

They arrived at the coast, and the director of the facility met him. Robert had made a note of how easy it was to talk to Bridget; they had a lot of good conversation on the way from Orlando to Cocoa Beach. They had hit some traffic on the Bee Line, so it added some time to their trip. He also noted the girl next door beauty she had as well. Robert said, "So, Bridget, will you be driving me on a regular basis?"

She said, "I follow orders, and since there are three of us driving you all around, you have a one in three chance of seeing me."

Robert said, "Great, I like my odds, I'll see you around, Thank you." She drove away with a simple nod.

∞

Faizan got off the train and found the Starbucks after a short walk. As he was about to enter, he could see Anahita sitting at a booth, looking at her phone as she waited for him. He had not seen her in person for some time, he stopped there and looked at her, she truly was one of the most beautiful girls he had ever seen. The light from the phone was causing a bit of a glint in her eyes, she had a slight smile, her lips were just the right size and she wore a subtle shade of lipstick but it was perfect for her.Just as he was about to enter, she looked in his direction, and she smiled but not just with her mouth, it was a smile that came from every part of her face and her oh-so-beautiful eyes. It was a smile that seemed to light the room up, and he thought to himself, she is smiling because of me, never in my life has anyone smiled like this just for me. He went inside and rushed to her, she met him as she stood, and they embraced. As soon as they made contact, the world disappeared, no other person existed but for the two of them. There was no kiss, no words, there was just a melting of two people into each other. Finally, they parted and sat down, only not across from each other but beside each other. They held hands, faced each other and Faizan said, "I missed you Anahita."

She said, "I missed you, too."

Faizan said, "I am supposed to go do something tomorrow, and I might not see you again, I might not come back." As he said this, he could see the utter destruction of her heart; she went from a bright smiling happy girl to a broken soul in a matter of seconds.

She pulled her hands away, and said, "Why Faizan, why would you do this? I thought you cared for me."

He said, "I do, I do care for you, I am in love with you Anahita."

As she grabbed his hands again, she said, "Oh, Faizan, I love you too. But if that is the case, why are you leaving?"

He said, "I can't explain that to you. I am sworn to secrecy. Just know, that I love you and if I had met you before this whole thing came about then things would be different, but I have sworn an oath to Allah, and there would be no honor if I don't follow through."

She said, "Faizan, did you not see the President speak? There is no Allah, or not in the sense we have known; there is Allah or God but to be with God, we must accept Jesus as our Lord and savior."

He said, "My friend called me and told me it was a lie."

She said, "Well, I believe it, and I am going to a Christian church this weekend, and I am going to accept Jesus into my heart."

Faizan was so confused; he didn't know what to think, what to feel. He felt like he should still follow through with the plan. He said, "Anahita, can we just be with each other right now? Can I just hold you, I want to feel your hands, your face, I want to smell your hair, I just want us to be here in this moment right now."

She said, "Yes, we can do that, we can be here in this moment that will last forever in our minds and our hearts." She moved towards the wall and lay back a bit, and he lay back on her with her arms wrapped around him and his arms twisted in hers and their hands clasped together. She kissed his cheek, and a tiny tear rolled down Faizan's face. He thought, if only…

∞

Gabe is back in California, sitting at his daughter's bedside in the hospital. He calls Gary who has stayed in D.C. to assist Sara in the calls and backlash they knew would come after the press event.

He explains the situation with Sophie and asks him to pray for her right now, with Rai and Hayden in the room. He puts the phone on speaker, Gary says, "Heavenly Father, You are intimately aware of the Struggle that Sophie is experiencing, You know her pain and her despair. You know the desire of her heart to be healed of this illness. I ask now for Your healing touch; I know that You are able and that just like Bible times, You can heal her. I also understand that You will choose what is best for her. I pray that through this trial, she will draw closer to you, that You will be her comfort and strength. I pray that ultimately, whatever happens, You will be glorified through all of us. I pray this in Jesus' name, Amen."

Gabe took the phone off of speaker and said, "Thank you, Gary, It is not looking good for her." Gabe started to cry but stopped himself and said, "Good luck out there in D.C.; we are all blessed to have you there on the front lines during these times."

Gary said, "Thanks Gabriel, and remember, prayers can be answered, pray with all of your heart. God doesn't answer every prayer, but He does answer prayers."

Gabe said, "Thank you, my friend, Goodbye."

Gary said, "Goodbye." Gabe sat and took his daughter's hand, laid his forehead on her and began a silent prayer - and he prayed with all his heart.

∞

"Victoria," she said, "my name is Victoria."

Sean said, "It is very nice to meet you."

She had been a waitress at the Place, but he had never actually been served by her. He knew he wanted her to be the last of the 12 women. He needed to be careful that he was not seen with her so there would not be a connection with him and her disappearance. Instead of talking to her at the restaurant he had followed her one evening after she got out of work. Luckily, she stopped at the grocery store, so he planned an accidental meeting. It was a pretty silly plan, but he "accidentally" bumped his cart into hers. From there, he mentioned seeing her at the restaurant.

After about five minutes of Sean spreading the charm on as thick as he could, she said, "It was great to meet you, but I need to get going."

They went their separate ways after he checked out, he made sure to bump into her again. He said, "Hey, I know this is crazy, since we just met, but, I don't know a lot of people in the area and was wondering if you would have dinner with me tonight."

She said, "Oh, I am not so sure about that, I mean I just met you, in a store."

He says, "I know, but at some point, you have to throw caution to the wind and go for it, you only go around once, live and let live, you know, all of those sayings."

Victoria was slightly amused, but she was still getting a funny feeling about this guy. He says, "I'll tell you what, you pick the place, we meet there, then leave by yourself. Everything will be in the public that way."

She thought about it, then she says, "Ok, let's meet at the Italian place on highway 58."

He says, "It's a deal, six o'clock?"

She says, "Ok, See you then."

Sean was taking his cart back to the store that was in a strip mall. After he put it back, he passed a small restaurant and could see that everyone in the place was gathered around a television. He went in and walked up and said, "What's going on?" A few people glanced at him, but no one responded to him. He started focusing on what was going on. It was President Sara Murphy, she was talking about something, but he could barely hear her. He moved up, pushing people out of the way. His size gave him the latitude to do such things; people never challenged him. He was finally able to hear her. She was saying, "This evening I am here to tell you all, that we have received messages from another world. This planet is located close to Proxima Centauri." The press core gasped, with low murmurs of discussions happening. She continued, "We have received dozens of messages from them, and now have a very efficient program that deciphers and translates the messages. I need to prepare you for the even more incredible part of the news I have for you today. These messages are being sent to us in an ancient form of Hebrew, the raw data we received was the most difficult thing to deal with, but once we deciphered and decoded it, the rest was a matter of translating it from the almost unspoken Hebrew to English. The next thing I need to tell you will be doubted, scrutinized, reviewed and even rejected, but I have a responsibility as your leader to tell you everything. The original message, after it was deciphered and translated was Messiah, as well as other similar messages and then followed by the word, Jesus."

Sean stood straight, turned and left, he drove home and turned the news on to find the news anchors pouring over everything she had said. This was no surprise to Sean; he assumed that if Lucifer was talking to him and was real that Jesus and God were as well. Just as he turned the television off, he received a call; it was a blocked number, but that very familiar voice told him to answer it. The voice on the line had a very thick Asian accent; she said, "I am here with the Supreme Leader of North Korea. He says the two of you have a mutual acquaintance and that he was instructed to contact you for the next steps in his plan."

∞

Robert is on site where they will be building the device; as he walks into the meeting room he says, "Good morning everyone." They all say good morning in return. Then Robert says, "Today is everyone's first day on this job. You have all been hand chosen for the role you will play in accomplishing this task. I know you have been told everything we do here is top secret, and you've signed nondisclosure agreements, but I am going to say this again, everything we do here does not leave this facility. Not because we want to hide what we are doing from the public, but because we don't want ill-intentioned people to try to disrupt what we are doing. Now, as I understand it, we just got what we think is the last of the designs for the device. Mia at the TSN tells me they've not received any new messages for more than seventy-two hours. So, let's get started on turning these designs into reality."

∞

Faizan wakes up early, he sits up and initially thinks about the girl he is in love with, then reality sets in and the realization that this is his last day on earth creeps into his brain. He thinks, "What have I done, why is this girl in my life now?" Then a thought flitters through his brain, what if this is a test...to see if I am worthy of my place in heaven. He had a new resolve; he was going to do it.

He got out of bed and took a shower; he got ready like he always would. He walked down the stairs and said good morning to his parents and had breakfast with them. He cleaned up after himself and then told them both that he loved them, he kissed his mom on the cheek and, as he was leaving, turned to look at them again, they both smiled at him, he turned and left. He walked to the bus that would then take him to the train he needed to board. He was instructed to walk into the burger place once he got off the train. While on the train, Anahita called him, but he did not answer it. He knew he was not strong enough to hear her voice and not want to go back to her.

The ride was uneventful, and he got off the train and walked into the fast food restaurant he was instructed to go to. He saw a man make eye contact with him; he started to walk towards him, but the man shook his head as if to tell him to stop. The man then took his backpack off and set it on a chair. He then left and made eye contact again with Faizan, then the bag. Faizan walked over to the bag, picked it up and left with it on his back. It was about nine thirty AM now; everything would start in thirty minutes. There would be carnage the likes of which this city, hell, this country has ever seen; it will make 9/11 look small. He continued his walk to the White House; he made good time, so he stopped and sat on a bench. He was thinking about all his training and what he had to do. He was thinking about ascending to heaven and seeing Allah. He was praying and practicing everything, over and over, focused on this one thing he would do. He would be remembered forever. All in Islam would know his name.

Then, just like that, her face appeared in his mind. He opened his eyes and said, no, I cannot think about her. He had about eight minutes now; it was time for him to start his walk into the visitor's area of the White House. There was a series of doors that allowed people to enter the visitor's area; he stopped just outside and stood for a moment. There were a series of events that were to happen that cued him to go inside and push the button before the guards knew what hit them. He waited there and then he heard it. Way off in the distance, he heard a car accident, then another and another. He heard sirens going off everywhere; he could hear other smaller explosions going off miles away. He saw jets flying over, and heard a helicopter hovering somewhere close by. He was waiting for his final cue which was a plane crashing in front of the white house, but it was not happening. Had the jets he saw fly over him stopped the plane from making it this far? He was waiting, hoping maybe he would get a call, but nothing happened. It was very loud with all of the sirens going off; he pulled his phone out to make a call to see what he should do, just then he got a call with a blocked number; he answered it, and the voice said, "Go, go in now."

Faizan turned around to enter the building, he walked in, put his thumb on the button that was sewn into the strap. Just as he did, he saw her in his mind's eye, the most beautiful girl he had ever seen, he saw her smile, he could remember every detail of her face, every curve that made her so beautiful. He could see the shiny black hairs that hung down in front of her face, her beautiful lips and perfect teeth, but the smile, it was what made her so beautiful. It was a smile that was a window into her soul, and It could make everything else that was ugly in this world, disappear. Also, he had thought a lot about the press event and the news that Jesus, the son of God was real; he was beginning to have doubts about everything he had known to be true. Faizan had been completely ignored when he walked in. So much was going on all around the city that it made people forget what their jobs were. He thought to himself, I could walk all the way into the building, but, instead, he took his thumb off of the button, he turned around and walked out of the building, but before he did, he took the bag off and told an older officer that he had found the bag, he handed the bag to him and left. He called Anahita and said, "I love you, where are you?"

∞

Huan Ji and Sara are in the Oval Office. Sara says, "When are you meeting with the Prime Minister of Italy?"

He says, "In two days, then I fly to Iran."

She says, "It is remarkable that they are even entertaining the idea of giving up their arsenal."

He says, "Well, he said he would meet with me. I am not holding my breath though."

She said, "I had some intelligence come into this office. We have tracked a phone call from North Korea to here in the United States, Colorado to be exact. We are trying to pinpoint the exact location, but something is not right about it."

Huan Ji said, "I will put more of my people on surveillance of North Korea."

She said, "Ok, that would be great, thank you. Are you making any progress with India and Pakistan?"

He says, "I am optimistic, I have had several positive conversations with both leaders. How is Israel responding to you?"

She says, "Not great, oddly enough. They worry about Iran, and their recent increased activity in building more warheads, which makes your discussions with the Iranians even more important."

He says, "I will do my best. And Russia?"

Sara says, "Hardly any contact, they are being very difficult."

He says, "Shall I make a call?"

She says, "It is worth a try I suppose."

He says, "Very well, I will set up a call with him tomorrow."

Sara says, "I would just like to say, I am so pleased with our partnership, who would have thought that our two countries would join forces on this endeavor?"

He says, "I agree, I too am very pleased with not only the partnership between our countries but also, the relationship we have built. I have such great respect for you, you have such a vision for the world and an incredible heart that I aspire to duplicate.Thank you for all you have done so far and for everything we will do together in the future."

She says, "There is no other person in the world in our position that I trust more. I too look forward to more progress on our efforts towards world peace."

Chapter 17

Eleven months later-

Gabe, Rai, Hayden, and Sophie are on the back patio at Gabe and Rai's home enjoying some dessert after a dinner Gabe had prepared for them. Gabe says, "Right here, this is where it happened. I accepted Jesus into my heart right here. I might have spoken the words with Gary in his office, but this is where I knew Jesus was real and that I needed Him in my life."

Rai reaches up and rubs his back a little. She says, "I am sure that a miracle was worked on you Sophie, I mean, your cancer was spreading, there was nothing the doctors could do. That night we all prayed for you almost a year ago, that is when it all changed. A month later, the doctors said they couldn't explain the shrinking tumors. Praise Jesus is all I can say."

After a short pause, Sophie says, "Guys, Hayden and I have something to tell you."

Gabe looks at her, and his heart jumps into his throat expecting bad news. She says, "We are going to have a baby."

Rai says, "What, that is great news!"

Gabe almost falls out of his chair. He jumps up and hugs Sophie then Hayden. Gabe says, "That is just great news, when, when is your due date?"

She says, "Eight more months left."

He says, "Holy cow, I'm going to be a grandpa."

Rai says, "Grandma, wow, I never thought I would be a grandma. I am so happy for you both."

They say thank you. Gabe moves to sit next to Hayden, and they start talking about converting the office in Sophie and

Hayden's home into a bedroom for the baby while Sophie and Rai start talking about baby names.

∞

Robert is on the floor in the giant hangar where parts of the device are being built with the rest of it about a mile away on the other end of the site. Everything has gone as planned, and they are on schedule. He gets into the jeep with Bridget Whal driving him. It was part of her security detail; the odd thing about this detail was that she was dating the guy she was protecting. They had started seeing each other about three months after he arrived, and things had gotten pretty serious lately. As they drove towards the site, he could see the large building with the smaller-than-normal nuclear cooling towers, about half the size. Beside it, he could see a crane lifting the large dish to place on top of the building which is why he was coming out here today, to oversee the installation of this piece first hand.

As the jeep stopped, he looked around to see if anyone was looking and gave her a quick kiss. He said, "See you later, baby."

She said, "Ok see you tonight."

He walked up to the building and made a call to Mia, she answers, and he says, "Hello Mia, I am at the site, and the dish is in the air as we speak."

She says, "Great Robert, and the new code I sent you?"

He says, "It is getting installed as we speak. Also, they are finishing up the turbines in the hanger and will transport them to the site this week."

She says, "Ok, everything sounds like it is on track, good job out there. I will let Gabriel know how it is going out there."

He says, "Ok, thank you; I'll talk to you later."

She says, "Goodbye Robert."

He walks into the building where his team is busy with different stages of installation of the state-of-the-art computers and programming them. He has people from all over the world helping him with this project. He had decided to put Wei Yuand a, the programmer from China in charge of getting everything programmed. He had offered it to Virginia from the CIA, but she was not willing to leave her family for an extended period of time. He says hello to everyone and walks up to Wei Yuand a and asks, "So how is everything going?"

He says, "Everything is going well, except one thing, I am afraid we will need to upgrade our memory."

Robert says, "What, already?"

Wei Yuand a says, "I am sorry Robert, but the amount of information we need to put into the systems is proving to be bigger than we anticipated. We knew it would be huge, but we are running low on memory already, and we still have two more systems to get into place."

Robert says, "Ok, do what you need to do."

He says, "Thank you."

∞

Sean says, "Either you hand me the baby, or I pump gas into the room, and I take it from you." Victoria was not going to give him her baby. She crouched in a corner of the room with her newborn baby. She could smell the gas coming into the room through a vent. She got as low as she could and wrapped her baby in a blanket to protect her from the gas. Victoria tried so hard to not go to sleep, but it was of no use. She woke up with no idea how long she had been asleep. She jumped up but stumbled and fell to the ground, she got back up and screamed because she had realized that her baby was gone.

Meanwhile, Sean was just finishing what Lucifer had told him to do. He had done a lot of horrible things overseas while he was in the service, but never anything this horrible. Each time, however, was getting easier, but it still affected him. He finally said, "Why, why do I have to do this?"

Lucifer said, "I will reveal that in time but for now, you must continue your work and you must find the best way to recruit more troops for my army."

Sean said, "As soon as I figure out a way to hide who I am online and my location, I will create a video and post it to every social media platform possible. When would you like me to go back to North Korea?"

Lucifer says, "In two weeks but you need to be careful not to arouse suspicion. There was a close call last trip, but I was able to fix it before anything happened. Now let me rest, our battle is looming."

∞

Sara is in Israel meeting with the Prime Minister. Also, in the meeting is Huan Ji and Gary Manns. Gary is now the Secretary of the office of newly named Christian Global Affairs. He reports directly to the President of the United States and accompanies her to almost all meetings with heads of states, especially as they relate to talks of disarmament and continued normalization of relationships between countries. Sara is speaking to the Prime Minister. She says, "Yes, my goal is one hundred percent reduction of all nuclear arms by the end of the year. We have gotten almost all countries to commit to reducing their arsenal by seventy-five percent, but I think we can be a nuclear-free world."

The Minister says, "I must say, I have no idea how you got the Iranians to the table and got them to reduce by fifty percent, so if you can get them to agree to one hundred percent then we will follow suit."

She says, "That is encouraging to hear sir, and will you be able to make the summit we are planning next month back in Switzerland?"

He says, "Most definitely, I look forward to it."

She says, "Fantastic; we will look forward to seeing you there then sir."

The Israeli guests got up and left his office after some handshaking and other niceties. The three of them are in the car driving back to the hotel, Gary says, "Sara, seemed more tense than normal. Something wasn't right."

She says, "I noticed it too."

Huan Ji said, "I think it was my presence that made him uncomfortable."

Sara said, "Well, we are partners in this endeavor, and people need to accept that and move on because that is not going to change."

Gary said, "Maybe we should invite him to the United States before the summit to try to smooth things over?"

She says, "That might be a good idea, I'll have one of the aids set up a call after we get back home."

∞

"Tehom, that's it," Mia says.

Gabriel says, "What does it mean?"

She says, "Well, it means something like a deep abyss, but as we have learned, we aren't always able to translate literally. So, it could mean something like deep abyss but not a deep abyss."

He says, "Ok, what is your best guess based on what you've learned so far?"

She says, "Honestly it could mean ocean or," she paused for a moment and continued, "universe."

He says, "Ok, and this is the first new message we have gotten since the messages from the device have stopped?"

She says, "Well, aside from the old messages repeating after the device messages stopped, yes, it is the first new message."

He says, "So we should expect more to come, then?"

Mia says, "I would expect more messages, yes."

Gabriel says, "Ok, keep me posted."

Mia says, "I will."

∞

Sean says, "I don't know how he does it, but I have never had any issues coming or going when I travel here to your great nation."

The Supreme Leader says, "We both have faith in the one true Lord. I know he can do great things. He somehow connected us when we were on opposite sides of the world, and now we will rule his new world side by side. You will rule millions with the army of New Babylon, and I will carry out his orders to design a new government of this world. Then there will be peace like we have never seen before." The Supreme Leader asks, "What is our count at right now?"

Sean says, "We are at two million eight hundred thousand people that are pledging their life to the true Lord, the King of New Babylon."

The Leader asks, "What are the arsenal numbers presently?"

He says, "We are at one thousand warheads, we have hit our target on both fronts and are ready to move forward on his command."

The Leader says, "He will tell me when to move forward so wait for my command."

Sean stands up and towers over the little North Korean man and says, "Make no mistake, we are both his servants, but he commands me, not you, we both have roles in New Babylon. You run the government, and I rule the army, we are separate and equal, that is how he wanted this to operate, he says it is most efficient this way. Also, don't forget I was his first chosen, he spoke to me before he spoke to you."

The Leader stood and bowed and said, "You are right, I apologize, Sean. Satan was positioned to finally take this world from Jesus and show the world who the one true God is; he would eliminate all that God had built and would start all over, he would call the world New Babylon and would rule this world supremely."

∞

Huan Ji is meeting with both the President and the Supreme Leader and of Iran. Huan Ji says, "Yes, my flight was good, thank you for asking. I wanted to thank you for meeting with me today."

The President said, "You honor us with your visit to our country, might we offer you a beverage?"

He says," Water would be good."

The Supreme Leader speaks saying, "Might we get on with our talks, I will be needed soon in a dispute amongst our Parliament."

Huan Ji says, "Very well, I am here to talk to you about the process of denuclearization."

The President says, "We have agreed to a reduction by fifty percent, is that not enough?"

He says, "We are grateful for the commitment, but we are looking for one hundred percent reduction and would like a commitment from you."

The Supreme Leader looked him in the eyes and said, "Did the President of the United States send you here?"

He said, "We work as a team towards world peace, and I offered to come to present this to you both."

The Supreme Leader said, "We will only consider it if she comes herself, I don't care if you are present, but she must be here as well."

Huan Ji stood and excused himself. He immediately called Sara who answers with a "hello". Huan Ji said, "Sara, you are still in France, correct?" She said, "Yes." Huan Ji continued to say, "Can you get to Iran as soon as possible?"

She says, "How soon?"

He says, "Sara, I think they are open to denuclearization, but they want to talk directly to you in person."

She said, "Ok, let me finish up here, I have a commitment from the government here for a one hundred percent reduction."

Huan Ji says, "Excellent, I will tell them you will be here before the end of the day."

She says, "Thank you, Huan Ji, thank you so much."

Huan Ji steps back into the meeting room to tell the two leaders of Iran that the President of the United States will be flying from France to meet with them that evening. The president says, "Very good; we will meet here when she arrives."

After Huan Ji leaves, the two men remain in the meeting room, the President says, "Why would you agree to such a thing?"

The Leader says, "First do not question me, I am the Supreme Leader. Second, we will not be destroying our nuclear weapons, we will be sending them to our new partners in North Korea."

The President says, "Has that been the plan all along?"

The Leader says, "Yes, it has, this makes it easier to move them now. You should know that you are now part of something that is going to change the current path that the world is on. I have been working with North Korea to stockpile as many nuclear weapons as possible. Since the rest of the world is disarming, the plan is to wait until every country has decommissioned or destroyed their warheads and we will strike. There is an army that has been building for the last year and will strike once given a signal."

The President says, "Signal, by whom?"

He says, "I have not met him, but they refer to him as their Lord or the King of New Babylon."

The Leader says, "You should know that if you betray our cause, you will be killed instantly; I have been witness to this, I have no idea how, but I have seen men die right in front of me, one minute they are standing talking normally then they are dead on the ground. So, do not say anything to anyone about this."

The President is very skeptical of everything he had just heard but to hear the Leader speak with such fear in his voice made him decide that he would say nothing, at least for now.

∞

Mia is in Gabriel's office, she has a few pages of data, untranslated as well as translated with handwritten notes, scribbled out words, and lines pointing from one thing to the next. She puts the stack on his desk and says, "Gabriel, I am at a loss for words right now, as soon as I get used to the new reality that we live in, something else comes along and makes me rethink that reality."

Gabriel says, "Mia, what are you talking about?"

She says, "Here, look at this."

She hands the pages to him, and he begins looking them over. He skims through them with a puzzled look on his face. Once he gets through them all, he lays them on the desk and starts from the beginning, looking at them slower this time. He turns each page, reading carefully, slowly, then looking up at Mia, then back at the pages, still reading them. After about twenty minutes he sets them down and says nothing at first. He then looks up at Mia and says, "You're sure?"

She says, "Yes, as sure as I can be. I mean we are at the mercy of a computer program that translates data from five light years away into Hebrew and then English. Based on what we have been using up to this point, yes I am sure."

He says, "So, we are not the first they've made contact with and the way this reads, they have been making contact with other worlds for a while now."

She says, "Yes that is what I have come up with, and I am just at a loss for what to think, I mean we go from thinking we are alone in the universe to there are many worlds out there."

He says, "And they call them God's children, meaning what?"

She says, "I can only guess that they are Christians as well."

He says, "Mia, Good work on this, I will put a call into Dan so he can talk to Ben and the President."

She says, "Thank you, Gabriel, I am going back to the message room, I'll talk to you later."

∞

Sara has landed in Iran and made her way to the Palace where she met Huan Ji, and he briefed her more extensively than he had on the phone. He told her that they seemed unusually willing to fall in line with the rest of the world but that he saw no reason not to proceed with the talks. Sara was escorted to a large meeting room that was decorated with great opulence, almost ridiculously so. As she entered, both leaders for Iran entered the room at the other end of the very long room. She met them both at the center of the room, then they all sat down to begin their discussions. She said, "Thank you so much for meeting with Huan Ji and me on such short notice. I am eager to proceed with the previous discussions you were having with Huan Ji."

The Leader says, "I have had a chance to discuss everything with all parties involved in making this decision in our country, and we are willing to move to a one hundred percent disarmament of our nuclear arsenal."

Sara is wary of this new complicit attitude as well, she figures she will take them at their word at present, but she will need to have the CIA monitor their activities. Sara says, "This is outstanding news, I am very humbled by your demonstration of leadership here. Thank you so very much."

After an hour of discussing the fine details of how they would proceed, the meeting was now over, and Sara and Huan Ji were being driven to the hotel they would be staying at until the next morning. Huan begins to talk, but Sara slightly lifts her hand as if to say, not now. They made small talk about their flights and some of the other meetings they had earlier. Finally, they arrive at the hotel where they are escorted into the hotel, but they stop and take a short walk through a small garden and asks the escorts to remain while they walked, which clearly agitated them. While walking Sara says, "I know we are being monitored so I wanted to come to a spot that should be safe."

Huan Ji says, "Good thinking."

She says, "So, give me your thoughts."

He says, "I don't trust them, I think they are up to something…I just don't know what."

She says, "I agree, but we have to at least go through the motions here and move forward, and if something is amiss then we will deal with it as it happens."

The two then walked back to their escorts and went into the hotel saying goodnight and going to their respective rooms.

∞

Robert is at dinner with Bridget, she asks, "When will the device start its testing phase?"

Robert says, "Hopefully tomorrow, but I thought we weren't going to talk shop."

She says, "I know, I was just making conversation, I'm sorry."

He says, "Oh, don't be sorry, it's ok."

Robert was really falling pretty hard for her, but he got the feeling it was not one hundred percent mutual, yet they always had a good time together, and he didn't know many people here still. After dinner, Robert drove her home and gave her a kiss goodnight.

The next morning Robert arrived a little late at the device after battling the traffic on I-95. As he and the driver drove on the runway up to the device, he could see the dish was now secure and in place on the top of the building. He got out of the jeep and said thank you to the driver; he walked into the building, as soon as the door closed behind him. Wei Yuand a said, "Great, am I glad to see you."

Robert said, "Why, what's up?"

He said, "Well, I think we are missing some program data to finish programming this last system."

Robert says, "What makes you say that?"

He says, "We have finished imputing all the data we have and the systems are not coming online."

Robert says, "Ok, show me what you're dealing with."

Wei Yuand a takes him to the massive area that contains all the system's computers as well as the supporting memory. It took up an area that was two stories tall and was one hundred and eighty feet long and eighty feet wide. There was a massive cooling system for the space, and the room was kept at about sixty degrees Celsius. They came to the master control area; while there were many workstations for the separate systems this was the station that could control everything. Wei Yuand a sat down and started typing on the computer with Robert standing behind him. Robert said, "Ok, can you show me all of the systems and hardware on the control panel?"

He said, "Yes, there you go."

Robert looked at everything, and It seemed in order. He said, "Can I see the actual schematic blueprints?" Wei Yuand a turned and asked one of the techs to go up to his office and get the rolls of blueprints for the systems.

After a few minutes, she came back with the prints and handed them to Robert. He spread them out on a table at the center of the room. He spun them around, so they were oriented with the actual systems. Robert studied them for about ten minutes then started walking around and looking at the physical machinery, he was following wires up and down, crawling on the floor and climbing ladders, then he would go back to the prints, study them for a while then start following wires again. After two hours of this Wei Yuand a heard him say, "Ah ha, I think I found it." He joined Robert up on one of the massive computers. Robert said, "Here, there is a crossed wire. The red should go here, and the green should go here."

Wei Yuand a said, "My apologies Robert, I should have caught that mistake."

Robert said, "No problem, we are all human, and we all make mistakes, someday you will find one of mine, I am sure."

Wei Yuand a instructed one of the techs to fix the problem. Once the work was completed the system was turned back on and this time all was working as it should. Robert said, "You see, all of the systems, while they are separate, they also communicate and coordinate with each other as the programs work. Wei Yuand a, you should be proud of the work you and your team have done here, you have all done a great job."

He said, "Thank you, Robert."

Robert said, "Ok, let's start testing all of the systems, once that is done, I will inform senior leadership that we are ready to send our first message."

Chapter 18

Back at Sean's home, Emma is speaking to Nicole; she is trying to console her. All twelve of the women had given birth to their babies, only to have them snatched away and as they all assumed, sacrificed to whoever the hell that crazy man thought he was speaking to. Emma had witnessed it as well; Sean would be talking while no one was around to hear him. Emma says, "Anyhow, he has been gone for a week, and I am worried about when he gets back because I have started my period again. I don't want him to do this all over again; we have to figure out a way to get out of here."

Nicole says, "That would be great, but we are two stories underground."

Emma says, "I know, but there has to be away."

∞

Sara is back in her office in Washington D.C. when she gets a call from Ben; he says, "Madam President, do you have time to meet with me for a few minutes?"

She says, "Sure, come on up."

Once he makes his way through security, he walks into her office and says, "Hello Sara, how were all of your meetings?"

She says, "They were good, we are on our way to a one hundred percent reduction in nuclear arms worldwide."

He says, "Wow that is great. Look, I need to tell you about the most recent messages that we have received."

She says, "Ok, what is it?"

Ben tells her about the messages and how they tell of additional worlds that the other world has contacted. She says in a half-joking way, "Well, why am I not surprised?" She thinks in silence for a moment then says, "I think we should hold off on revealing this to the public. I feel like we have revealed a lot to the world, maybe we should let everything settle a bit. I will give it more thought and pray on it before I make a final decision on it, thank you for bringing this to my attention though Ben."

∞

Sean is sitting in front of his computer, one of the followers of Lucifer had designed a new untraceable application operating on the dark web, that allowed Sean to communicate to the millions that had given their lives to the King of New Babylon. As he opened the new application, all the messages started loading. He closed these messages because he had a new task that he had to complete for Lucifer. He opened the box that allowed him to communicate to all the followers and he started typing. He told them all that it was time to start the battle for New Babylon. He told them to first draw the sign of the King, a pentagram, on their forehead and to take up their arms and begin killing anyone who follows the imposter Jesus Christ. Do not kill one of your own, if they do not have the sign on their forehead, they do not follow the true God, our King, and must be killed. Go now, in the name of our King. He clicked the send button and closed his computer, satisfied that it was finally starting.

∞

Sara's office phone rings, and It is Marvin Steelman her Chief of Staff. She answers, and he says, "Madam, the Secretary of Defense, William Jones, is here to see you."

Sara says, "Oh, ok, I will see him."

William comes into her office, he takes a seat across from her at her desk and says, "Madam President, I wanted to talk to you about some chatter we hear on the web."

She says, "Ok, what's going on?"

He says, "We're not sure, it's not our normal chatter that we hear from the normal groups like Al-Qaeda or Al-Shabaab, who by the way have virtually disappeared since the announcement. This chatter is very hard to pinpoint or decipher; it is coming from somewhere in Asia - that we do know - and it is going all around the world, including the United States."

She says, "Who is working on this?"

He says, "Madam, our normal working groups are on it."

She says, "Ok, if you don't make any progress in the next day or so, let me know, I have some people that might be able to help you out."

He says, "Yes madam, thank you."

William stood and left her office. Sara picked up the phone and asks Marvin to put a call into the CIA and find Virginia Rhodes.

∞

Gary was back in Barstow for a week; while he was spending a lot of time in D.C., his stipulation to taking the job he had there was that he was able to spend weekends at his home. His wife had no desire to move to D.C. and he still had his congregation at his church to tend to. There was no better place in the world than in his own bed beside his wife of forty-five years; all was right in the world when he was there. Because of this, he would get his best sleep, this night was one of those nights. He had gotten home late Friday night and spent Saturday with his wife. He had taken her out to lunch, and they did some shopping. After a good home-cooked meal for dinner and some time on their porch, they decided to go to bed early because he had a big message to preach to his church the next day.

In his deep sleep, he had a dream, and in it, he was talking to God as Gideon. God is saying, "Gideon, you have too many men. I cannot deliver Midian into their hands, or Israel would boast against me, 'My own strength has saved me. Now announce to the army, anyone who trembles with fear may turn back and leave Mount Gilead."So twenty-two thousand men left, while ten thousand remained. Then God said to him, "There are still too many men. Take them down to the water, and I will thin them out for you there. If I say, 'This one shall go with you,' he shall go, but if I say, 'This one shall not go with you,' he shall not go."

Gary woke up startled and soaked in sweat. His wife wakes as well and says, "What's wrong honey, bad dream?"

He sits up and turns the light on and says, "Um, not a bad dream, a disturbing dream, I was talking to God."

She says, "Oh, that doesn't sound bad at all, love."

He says, "No, but he was talking to me as Gideon."

She says, "Gideon? You mean from the Bible, Gideon?"

He says, "Yes, I think I need to pray."

Gary gets up, grabs his worn-out old Bible that never leaves his side and goes into the living room and sits in his old recliner, turns the light on and starts reading his Bible in the book of Judges. As he is reading, he hears a voice, a familiar voice that he has gotten used to hearing. The voice says, "My child, you need not be afraid; I would not ask anything of you that you could not do."

Gary says, "Yes, Lord, I know."

The Voice says, "My child, a battle is coming, and the leaders of this world will turn to their military leaders, but they will need your council as well. When you are called upon, stand with your Bible in hand, and I will be at your side. You will know what to do because I will not leave your side."

Gary says, "Yes Lord, I will do whatever you ask of me."

Gary sat in silence for a few more minutes then gets up, turns off the light and lays back down; he kisses his sleeping wife on the cheek and goes back to sleep.

∞

Robert is on a conference call with Gabriel, Dan, Ben, and Sara. Robert says, "We have completed all of our testings, and we feel we are ready to send our first message."

Sara says, "I would like to be there."

Robert says, "I am not sure that is a good idea, Madam President, we are dealing with stuff here that no one in the world has ever dealt with before. We have nuclear fission happening, and we are using dark matter. It is the first time we have ever been able to produce any, but the information we got from the messages enabled us to produce it and showed us how to harness its energy for the device, not to mention all of the other technology we have never seen before."

She simply said, "I accept the risk, I am not passing this opportunity up." Everyone else on the call said the same thing. It was agreed that the first message would be sent on Tuesday morning.

∞

The President of Iran is at home with his wife Sabra; they had both accepted Christ into their hearts and were now in a difficult situation. He says, "I can ask for asylum in one of the countries that are part of the Christian Coalition or I stay and try to make this right…either way, you must leave. With you here, they will have leverage over me."

She says, "Hamid, I am your wife, and I belong by your side."

He says, "You will be, once I can join you again."

She says, "So, you have decided?"

He says, "Yes, I have to take control of this country, I cannot let our nukes go to North Korea and I can't let Satan rule our country. I am going to make a call to the one person I can trust for this, but if anything happens to either of us, we will be together in heaven my love."

She says, "I love you, husband."

He says, "I love you, wife."

He leaves the room and walks outside; it is a clear, chilly night with few people out. He calls his friend in Turkmenistan, one of the first countries in the Middle East to proclaim their dedication to Jesus. They bordered to the north; he would just have to get there undetected and hand his wife over. The phone rang, and his friend Gulsen answered, he said, "Hello?"

Hamid said, "Gulsen, it is your old friend from the south, I must be quick, but I need your help."

Gulsen said, "What is it, brother?"

Hamid said, "I need to get Sabra out of the country, is there any way you can arrange transport and keep her with your family until I send for her or I can join you all?"

Gulsen is quiet at first, then says, "Of course, but might I ask why?"

He said, "We have both accepted Jesus as our Lord and Savior, and this country is on a collision course with the rest of the world unless I do something about it."

Gulsen says, "Hamid, first, I am so happy for you both to have the love of Jesus in your heart and second, consider it done. I will be in touch with the details."

Hamid says, "I can't thank you enough, brother."

∞

Gabe was in his home at his computer; he had just bought his ticket to Orlando, Florida so he could be there for the first message to be transmitted. The television is on, and he hears KCAL channel nine news out of Los Angeles; the anchor says, "Now let's go to weather with, oh, wait, I am told we have breaking news. There are reports of random murders being committed out in the open all over the world as we speak. Let's go to Brian who is in his vehicle trying to avoid detection. Brian, what are you seeing?"

In a whisper, Brian says, "Andrea, it's the craziest thing I have ever seen. I was driving to a 911 call to cover it when I started seeing people walk out of their homes and start shooting people. They would look into their face, then point and shoot and now I am pulled over and parked between two buildings and, oh crap."

Silence, then Andrea says, "Brian, please be safe out there, Brian?"

Finally, he speaks quietly again, he says, "I just had one walk by the car. I got a good look at her; she had a pentagram drawn on her forehead with a pistol in her hand."

She says, "Ok, Brian, thank you for that report now go find a safe place to hide."

Just then, the doors to the studio opened, it was an intern that several people knew there, only he had a gun, and he started firing at each person he walked up to. Many people got out, except for three of the crew and Andrea, she lay in a pool of her own blood. She had been shot in the neck; she was getting cold and dizzy. Finally, she could not keep her eyes open anymore. Gabe was frozen; then he ran for his phone, he called Rai, she answered, he said, "Where are you?"

She said, "Just pulled into our driveway, he dropped the phone and ran outside, she was getting out of the car, he ran out and grabbed her by the arm and ran inside with her. She said, "What the heck was that for?"

He ignored her, looking for his phone, he said to Rai, "Lock the door and get down."

He then called Sophie; she said, "Daddy, are you guys ok?"

He said, "Yes and you all?"

She said, "Yes we are fine, Hayden just got home, Daddy, what's happening?"

He said, "I don't know baby, I am going to make some more calls, stay inside and stay down, keep your lights off, don't draw attention to yourself, I will call you back, put your phone on silent, bye baby."

She said, "Bye daddy."

Gabe then called Gary, "What is going on Gary?"

Gary said, "Gabriel is everyone ok there?"

He said, "Yes."

Gary said, "Listen, Gabriel, I spoke to God, and he told me a battle was coming, and this must be it, or at least the start of it, they are followers of Lucifer, and they are part of his army. Gabriel, I need to brief the President, be safe brother."

He said, "You too brother."

All through the night, there was random gunfire with sirens all over the city, millions of people all over the world had been killed. Eventually, the hordes of people went into hiding with law enforcement turning the tide. Many people were taken into custody, but not a single person would talk about why they did what they did. Life returned to normal except for the random person repeating the actions of the others. Little did authorities know that the army of Lucifer had been given specific instructions that once law enforcement started to close in on them that they would first hide then blend back in with everyone else and eventually meet in Mexico, Syria or North Korea where they were to gather, organize and train for war.

∞

Robert is at the main station with the giant monitor that was about twelve feet in front of him. There was a sizable crowd in the room that included his team at their different stations, the senior leadership for TASA, and Ben, Gabriel, Mia, Dan, Sara, and Huan Ji were there as well. It had been previously decided by many people weighing in on the decision as to what the first message would be and what messages would follow that. Robert began typing, he wrote, "Hello and greetings from Earth." He then began the protocol for sending a message. Each station played a role in this process with different switches being flipped on making parts of the device activated. Soon, the whole device was humming. There were cameras all over the device, and they could see the light coming out of the dish. As the humming became louder, the light began to change. Finally, the light seemed to disappear, but the building still hummed. Robert turned to everyone behind him as he raised his hand to flip the last switch that would send the message. He said, "God be with us all."

He flipped the switch, after about thirty seconds the humming subsided until there was silence. Slowly people started to applaud until everyone was clapping and cheering, some started shaking hands. Sara congratulated everyone, Gabriel walked up to Robert and said, "Great job."

∞

Abarron had received the first message from Earth and had to tell the Council that they had finally replied. For this, he needed the company of three of the elders in the most senior of the roles. Once they were in the device with him, he was able to answer as soon as he got the messages. They stood behind him in the room as he prepared to answer the first message, so he typed in, "Hello, and greetings from Erets."

After about twenty minutes of different conversations around the room, suddenly there was a noise from Robert's computer; not only was the device capable of sending messages but was far more capable of receiving messages than the system in California. A message had been received, andRobert put it on the large screen so everyone could see it as it came in. The message read, *"Hello and greetings from Erets, I am Abarron."*

There was dead silence as everyone began to realize that they were communicating in almost real time with another world. Gabriel turned to Mia and said, "Erets? Do you have any idea what that means?"

She said, "It's Hebrew for Earth."

Robert asked his team to begin the process again so they could send another message. Again, the building was humming, and Robert typed in the next agreed-upon message. He typed, "Jesus is Lord."He reached for the final switch and flipped it. After the building had stopped humming, it was quiet again. About seven minutes later they received a message that said, *"He is risen."*

∞

With his wife finally safe, Hamid had just returned to his home. His first task was to find and build a coalition to support his efforts. This was going to be a risky undertaking, but he knew he had to do something. He was oddly driven to take the Leader out and take his country to the Christian Coalition. Hamid would start with his Assembly of Experts. He had several people that he suspected had accepted Jesus based on their reactions he had noted at one of the speeches the Supreme Leader had given.

Taavetti Esfand Iar was the first person he approached; he had known him for about seven years, they had worked together on passing some legislation and were fairly good friends. He had asked Taavetti to meet him in his office. Once he arrived, they talked about some of the things going on in government as well as foreign affairs. Then, Hamid said, "Taavetti, my friend, I am going to ask you something that could put a strain on our friendship and force you to report me to the Leader. I am asking you if I may ask you this question."

Taavetti replies, "Yes."

Hamid said, "Are you a follower of Jesus Christ?"

Taavetti was silent. First, he looked at the ground with closed eyes then looked up and right into Hamid's eyes, and said, "Yes, I am a follower of Christ Jesus. I expect that I will be brought in front of the Leader like so many others and drop dead?"

Hamid said, "No my friend, you see, we are brothers in Christ."

Taavetti said, "How did you know I was a Christian?"

He said, "I could see how you reacted when the Leader would speak. Now, I need to tell you something, and I need to know if you will support me."

Taavetti said, "Ok."

Hamid said, "I plan to overthrow the Leader and take our country into the Christian Coalition. Will you help me with this?"

He said, "Yes, I absolutely will help you."

Hamid then asked him, "Do you know of any others like us in leadership positions?"

He said, "Yes, a few."

Hamid said, "Do you think they will support us?"

Taavetti said, "I believe they will help us."

Hamid said, "Very well, let's begin a list of those who we should talk to for support."

∞

Victoria had been a kind of hard knock kind of girl much of her teen life; she had been pretty much abandoned as a teen by her mother and father. Both of her parents had been very successful lawyers in Colorado and were always working, which left her to her own devices. She had fallen into a bad crowd and experimented with drugs and alcohol as well as getting involved with boys, way too young. She had picked up some handy talents though, and one had been picking locks. Since she and all the other women had been alone in Sean's home for what seemed like weeks, she had been working on the locks on her door. There had been several times she thought she had it but then she would lose her grip on her tool and she would have to start all over. Today, though, she was not giving up; she was getting very low on food, and she had been rationing for a few days as well. She knew the others were probably in the same situation. Victoria worked and worked at it for hours and then, just like that, the door was unlocked. She slowly opened the door and walked out; she could see all the other doors, so she started unlocking them and opening them. She was yelling to the other women to come out, that they were free. Finally, all the women were in the hallway, crying and hugging each other.

Victoria then turned to the other door, it too was locked, but was not like the high-quality door holding them in their rooms. All the women started kicking at the door, and it gave way. They ran up the stairs and saw the house was empty. They looked for a phone, but there was no land line. They had been locked up for almost a year and had no idea what had been going on in the world. After a quick search and some success finding food, they ate what they could find and then they decided to leave the home, so out the door they walked, all twelve women walking down the driveway and onto the road.

∞

Meanwhile, in North Korea, Sean had gotten an alert of movement in his house from the security application he had on his phone. He opened the cameras and he saw the women walking around his house and eating his food; then they all left. First, he cursed to himself, then he thought to himself he would not be able to go back home, maybe not even to the states because they would issue a warrant for his arrest. It was just as well, he was living just fine here amongst the wealthy with the Supreme Leader, and he had moved his own money off-shore to several accounts, so he had plenty of money. He cast the issue out of his mind; it was time for all the warriors to gather for battle.

In the remote parts of Syria, Mexico and North Korea over two million people who were followers of Lucifer, the King of New Babylon, had gathered and were preparing for war against the Christian Coalition. Sean's generals and lieutenants were training them. It had been a huge undertaking to find all the people who had any experience in the military as well as organize those people amongst the different countries represented. It was then another colossal task to get the non-military people introduced to the different strategies for battle and trained in the use of the different weapons.

Finally, after a few weeks though, they were able to use their weapons well enough to go to war. The Generals, then reported to Sean, that they were ready for him to inspect all the troops. If they met his approval that would mean the troops were ready for battle. Sean set out first to Mexico to inspect those troops. He started with the majors then lieutenants and worked his way down from there. He then addressed all the troops. It was more people than he had ever spoken to before in his life. Somehow, he was not afraid to do it. It was like a new found gift; once he was on stage in front of them all, he just found the words he needed. He later assumed that the King had been helping him find what needed to be said. Sean was very pleased with how far they all had come in such a short time. He spoke to the crowd; he said, "Followers of the True God, thank you for being willing to give your life to this cause. The King of New Babylon wants you to know that you will all soon live in a world of peace, once the fake traitor who calls himself God is pushed out altogether. He has never been able to show you true peace on earth, but the King of

New Babylon will! Now, continue to train, you will be called to battle soon."

Sean repeated this process in Syria and then in North Korea. Once this was complete, Sean, who was back in his home in North Korea, took refuge in his immaculate prayer room; there were golden statues, ornate rugs, fountains that flowed continually. The room was also connected with huge sliding glass doors to an outside garden with a pond filled with fish and large beautiful plants everywhere. Just inside the room was a large red rug with many candles burning around it, surrounding that was a pentagram. Sean went to the rug and sat, it was here that he would go into a deep state of mind, so deep, he would feel like he had slept afterwards. He called to Lucifer by saying, "My king, the true God, I have news."

Lucifer said, "Yes, what is it?"

Sean said, "Lord, I have returned from reviewing all of the troops. I am here to tell you we are ready for battle at your command."

Lucifer said, "Very good; I will tell you when the time is right. You have done well; you will be well compensated for all of your efforts when this is all over."

Sean said, "Thank you, Lord."

Chapter 19

Gary was in the Oval Office with Sara, she says, "Gary, I want you to accompany me to the summit we are holding in Switzerland, would you be willing to go?"

He says, "Yes I would be honored."

She says, "Great; you will travel with me on Air Force One."

Gary says, "Madam President, I need to talk to you about something that is slightly personal, but I think it will have consequences globally."

She said, "Ok, you have my undivided attention, what is it, Gary?"

He said, "Madam, I know we think that the attacks that happened a while ago were random, but I don't think they were. Madam, I had a conversation with God, and he told me war was coming. I think that these attacks had something to do with the war that is coming."

She said, "A war with whom?"

He said, "I think it is a holy war between good and evil or between God and Satan."

Sara first looked skeptical but then remembered who she was talking to; she trusted Gary. A year ago, there was no way she would believe this, but it was a new world they lived in. She said, "Gary, thanks."

Then a knock at the door, she said, "Come in."

Two men walked in; one was James Black, the Director of the F.B. I., and the other was Fred Mills, the Director of the C. I.A. They approached her and said they needed to speak to her alone.

She said, "This man is my trusted Christian council, and he can stay."

Fred said, "Madam President, we have acquired satellite footage as well as drone footage of massive crowds gathered in different parts of the world."

She asked, "How many people are we talking about?"

James said, "We estimate around two million people scattered between Mexico, Syria and North Korea."

She said, "How did we not see these people moving into these areas?"

James said, "We had some minor chatter, but then everything went silent. Then all of a sudden we found the crowds. It was like they were hidden from us somehow."

Gary interrupted, he said, "Madam, this is what I was telling you about…this is the war that is coming."

Sara said, "Thank you, gentlemen, I will be calling an emergency cabinet meeting, and I will need you both there to brief the members. I will let you know when we schedule it, thank you."

The two men left her office, and Sara sat down looking at Gary, she said, "What am I supposed to do?"

He said, "Pray because God has all of the answers; He will guide you. I should also tell you, Madam President, that God told me I would have a role in this battle. I don't know what that role is, but when the time comes, God will tell me what I need to do." Sara sat in silence and began to pray, not for knowledge but wisdom.

∞

Hamid and Taavetti had spent all their time building their own following of Christians in hopes to overthrow the Supreme Leader of Iran. As Hamid and Taavetti were discussing their next task, about a dozen men wearing all black robes with a type of Al-Amira on their heads and carrying automatic rifles walked into the room and said they were to come with them at the request of the Leader. A short walk and they were in the palace of the Supreme Leader. Hamid and Taavetti stood in the middle of the room with the men still surrounding them with rifles pointed at them. Finally, the Leader walked in and stood looking at them, then said, "Hamid, I have heard a rumor, and I am sure it is not true, that you are planning to oust me from power and take the country over yourself. Now, I am sure this is not true, so, all you have to do is tell me it is not, and we will forget this ever came up."

Hamid looked at Taavetti and said, "I am sorry, but the Bible tells me not to deny my God." Hamid then looks at the Leader and says, "I am here to tell you that it is true."

The Leader showed no reaction, he simply looked at his men surrounding them and said, "Watch as these men fall to the floor, dead before they land." The Leader closed his eyes and prayed his prayer that he had done dozens of times, he opened his eyes to see the two men still standing who were in prayer as well. The surrounding men all looked around at each other, then the Leader closed his eyes again and prayed his prayer only to see the two men still standing as he opened his eyes. The men around them lowered their rifles; one man said, "What is going on?"

Hamid simply opened his eyes and looked at the men and said, "We follow the one true God, we have accepted Jesus as our Savior, our God is all powerful, and the evil one will never be able to defeat him, or us."

The Leader started yelling at the men to shoot, but the men didn't know what to do, they had been terrified of what the Leader had been able to do, but now they were being told that they could have freedom through Jesus Christ. Hamid said, "Just tell Jesus you love him and accept Him and you will have freedom."

Some of the men slowly started praying, when they did, the Leader started his prayers, only to fail once again. Seeing this, the several other men began to pray as well while those men who had just accepted Jesus, ran out and started telling everyone what had happened and that Jesus was the way to salvation. Hamid called for one of the men to take the Leader to a jail cell and keep him isolated. The two men hugged and said, "Peace be with you."

Taavetti said to Hamid, "Go get your wife my friend."

Hamid smiled and said, "I will do that."

∞

Gary was meeting Sara in the lobby, then traveling to the first day of a two-day summit with all the nations that were part of the newly named Christian Coalition. Gary met many people, including the Pope, which had been a bit of a dream of his. However, while it was still an honor, it was a little less thrilling, now that things had changed in the world. After some welcoming remarks by Huan Ji, Sara took the podium. She stood, quiet at first until there was absolute silence in the room. With the audience's full attention, she said, "Ladies and gentlemen, children of Christ, I am here to announce first, that all of our countries are now ninety-nine percent nuclear weapons free…either decommissioned or dismantled. I am so proud of how far we have come. Also, with all the efforts to reduce greenhouse gas emissions, we are starting to see a reversal in rising tides, and regular rains are coming back to the forests and grasslands of the world. Next, I need to tell you about an alarming event that is happening around the world. Our intelligence agencies have found massive groups of people gathering in Mexico, Syria and North Korea. We are convinced that the attacks that occurred a few weeks ago all around the world are connected to the gathering of people in these areas. We have flown some drones into these areas, and It appears that they are camps where military training is occurring. We need to be prepared for an attack."

It was then, that the doors leading out to the lobby flew open. Entering the room was a huge contingent of men, all were dressed in military apparel, and they were surrounding someone as they walked, but it became clear who that person was once they approached the stage where Sara was standing. It was the Supreme Leader of North Korea.

Gabriel had remained with Robert while all the other dignitaries had left the device to tell the world what had occurred; he was interested in learning the operation of it. After about a week he had a rudimentary understanding of how to send a message. Having the other techs there to assist with this task made it easier but it was not necessary, he and Robert could do it just as well. Robert and Gabriel had written a protocol for sending a message; the fear was that sending the wrong message could be interpreted the wrong way and could damage any kind of relationship and communication between them and the other world known as Erets. They had a list of questions they were permitted to ask, however the question Gabriel wanted to send was not on the list. Gabriel was curious. He typed in, "Please tell us about yourselves and your world."

Robert and Gabriel began the process of sending the message with Robert flipping various switches. The humming, like before, grew louder, then Gabriel flipped the final switch, and the message was sent. They waited in silence; they waited longer than the other messages they sent before that were questions about their intentions with their reply stating that they were peaceful and wanted to spread the word of Jesus Christ. Thirty minutes passed, then an hour then two hours. Robert decided they would eat lunch while they waited, so they left the device.

The Supreme Leader of North Korea was brazen, he walked onto the stage, right past all of the world leaders, including Sara, and took the microphone. Everyone was so surprised that no one moved. The Leader spoke in broken English saying, "I'm here to inform you that I will be taking over as ruler of your organization." Sara began to walk up, but his guards blocked her. The Leader said, "As I speak to you now, the army of the King of New Babylon is moving on your countries."

Just then a secret service agent pulled Sara to the side of the stage; he said, "Madam, we have had a major attack on U.S. soil. We have troops marching up from Mexico into Texas, Arizona, New Mexico and California with air attacks on every major city in those states."

Sara told the secret agent to contact the Secretary of Defense and tell him to start a response to the aggression. The agent started to leave when she grabbed him by the arm and pulled him close; she said, "Tell him I want a swift and strong response, immediately."

Sara turned her attention back to the Leader, she approached him again with the same response from the guards, but this time, secret agents from everywhere showed up on the stage in twice the numbers of the Leader's guards. They backed off and let her approach the microphone, she took the microphone and said, "We will continue this conversation in private with all countries involved; now go, we have other work to accomplish here."

As the Leader walked by Sara, he said, "You cannot win, The King will reign supreme over your God."

She said, "Who is this King?" But he walked away, and she left the stage telling her agents to remove the Leader from the meeting, she was determined to be fully briefed on everything going on. She asked Huan Ji to organize a meeting immediately with all parties involved and to meet in the large meeting room provided by the facility. Sara went to the meeting room to make some calls when her phone rang.

∞

Hamid now had his wife back with him along with his children. It was now time to join his country with the Christian Coalition. He was in his new office as the sole leader of Iran. He picked up his phone and called the President of the United States. She answered the phone and said, "Hello."

He said, "Madam President, this is Hamid Mehadifar, the President of Iran. I am calling to tell you that we have just removed the Supreme Leader from our countries' leadership structure, and I am now leading the country."

She said, "That is fantastic, but Hamid, I am in the middle of a situation here and will need to discuss this later."

He said, "I understand, I have one important thing to tell you though. You see, the Leader was involved with a large undertaking. He was involved with North Korea, and someone called the King of New Babylon."

She said, "I was just made aware of this person."

He said, "That's just it though, I am not sure he is a person. He would pray to this King and people would drop dead at his request. Also, he was sending our nuke…"

The phone went dead. Lucifer would not let this information pass to Sara, not yet anyway. Sara tried to get Hamid back on the phone but was not able to reach him. She hung up the phone and asked for Huan Ji to meet with her as soon as possible.

∞

Sean was seated in a large elevated chair in a dimly lit room and was able to command and view all of his troops from one central command station. There was a combination of cameras in the field that were worn by the troops along with drone footage as well as a number of highly classified spy satellites that his people were able to take control of. He had dozens of screens he could view along with a technician that would pull up any footage he wanted on a larger screen that he could view much like a television station. He could see that every platoon and every air attack was not challenged at all. Everyone was being taken by surprise just like Lucifer said it would happen. The damage they were causing to the infrastructure to these cities with the air attacks was devastating, and the carnage the troops were leaving behind was almost hard for him to look at. People were being dragged out into the street and executed if they did not pledge their allegiance to the King of New Babylon. Men, women, and children were being shot in the head and left where they were; there was blood everywhere. Sean breathed deep and commanded his leaders to move to their next objectives. They were to move in all directions until the army of New Babylon occupied every country.

∞

Gabriel and Robert walked back into the device room and could see that a message was waiting for them. It was one of the longer messages they had received. They moved the message to the larger screen so they both could read it easier. They started to read it when Gabriel's phone rang. Normally he would let it ring but he saw it was Rai, so he answered it and said, "Hey baby, what's going on?"

She said, "Gabe, you need to get home right now."

He said, "What, why?"

She said, "That's right, you've been in the device room all day...honey, we are under attack. There is some sort of army that is making its way up from the US/Mexico border. If they keep moving at their current rate, they will be here in a matter of days."

Gabriel had heard Roberts phone and assumed it was Bridget telling him the same thing. Gabriel said, "I am on my way home now baby." He hung up the phone as did Robert; they looked at each other for just a second then Gabriel said, "Let's go."

As soon as they walked out, Bridget was waiting in the jeep to take them back to the main building. Robert kissed her and then said, "Ok, what the hell is going on?" As they drove back, she explained to them how the attacks started from the air followed by hundreds of thousands of people attacking civilians. Gabriel was terrified for his family and wanted nothing more than to get to them and get everyone to safety. He called Rai and said, "I am on my way, have you started packing?"

She said, "Yes, so has Sophie; also, Hayden has access to a large motor home that his parents owned before they passed from the car accident, it has been in storage. He is on his way to get it out and start prepping it for travel. The plan is to head north."

He said, "Very good; I will be there as soon as I can, I love you, Rai."

She said, "I love you too Gabe."

He then immediately called his travel agent and had her book the next flight back to L.A.

Before Sara was to meet with all the leaders, she felt she needed some advice from her now close friend and pastor, Gary Manns; she asked one of her aids to please ask him to come to the meeting room. After a few minutes, Gary walked in and said, "Hello Madam President."

She said, "Gary, I need your counsel. You saw what happened in the meeting out there?"

He said, "Yes, I did."

She said, "I just got off the phone with the President of Iran, they have removed the Supreme Leader and have said they are moving their country to the Christian Coalition."

He said, "That is great news, why do you look so concerned?"

She said, "It's what he said after that I am so worried about, he spoke of why they removed the Supreme Leader. He said that he was working with North Korea and someone called the King of New Babylon."

Gary's Legs gave out, and he had to sit down quickly when he heard this. He said it could only be one that calls himself that. "What did he say about him?"

She said, "Hamid said that he would have people brought in front of him and pray to the King and the person would die instantly."

He said, "I see."

She said, "Gary, who is it?"

He said, "Madam President, Sara, it is Lucifer."

She gasped, and said, "Really. I mean, he is real?"

He said, "Oh very real, think about it, if we now have evidence that Jesus and God exist, that means Satan exists as well."

She sat in silence for a minute. She said, "Gary, I need help, I mean, I can handle war between countries. I accepted that when I ran for this office, but a war between good and evil?"

He said, "Sara, God has put the exact person in the exact position that needs to be there at the right time, you can do this Sara."

She said, "Where would I find words of encouragement in the bible?"

He said, "Ephesians 6:10-17 the armor of God." He opened the Bible that he always had with him and read, "Finally, be strong in the Lord and His mighty power. Put on the full armor of God, so that you can take a stand against the Devil's schemes. For our struggle is not against the flesh and blood, but against the rulers, against the authorities, against the power of this dark world and against the spiritual forces in the heavenly realms. Therefore, put on the full armor of God, so that when the day comes, you may be able to stand your ground, and after you have done everything to stand. Stand firm then, with the belt of truth buckled around your waist, with the breastplate of righteousness in place, and with your feet fitted with the readiness that comes from the gospel of peace. In addition to all this, take up the shield of faith, with which you can extinguish all the flaming arrows of the evil one. Take the Helmet of salvation and the sword of the spirit which is the word of God (NIV®)."

Sara said, "Gary, I am amazed at your ability to know what to say and when to say it when I need you to say it. That was perfect if you think God has put me here to do this job then who am I to deny that? Thank you, I feel I am ready to talk to the rest of the Coalition and address these aggressions towards us."

Gary left, and Sara called Huan Ji. He answered and Sara said, "Have you been able to talk to the rest of the Coalition?"

He said, "Yes, we are all ready to meet now if you would like."

She said, "Yes, please."

After a few minutes, the leaders started walking into the meeting room; once Huan Ji came in he closed the door behind him, and everyone focused on Sara. She said, "As I am sure you all know by now, there is aggression towards our Coalition. I have been in contact with several people, and I have information that will shock you all. First, we have a new member that will be joining our Coalition, Iran has detained the Supreme Leader and Hamid, the President has assumed power and has expressed his desire to bring their country over to the Christian Coalition. However, what he told me about the events leading up to the detainment of the Supreme Leader was very disturbing. He told me that the Leader would have people brought in front of him and would pray to someone he called the King of New Babylon.

Once he would pray to this King, he said the person would drop to the ground, dead before they hit. After some council of my Secretary of Christian Global Affairs, Gary Manns, he informed me that this is not a true king or even a man, but in fact Lucifer or Satan."

Upon hearing this information, the majority of leaders were scoffing at this information, not believing what they heard. After passing along all the information, she learned she was able to convince all the leaders that what she was saying was true. She said, "We have to formulate a response to this aggression."

Just as she made this statement, there was a knock at the door. Secret Service answered the door, then he turned and said, "Madam President there is an Abram Sokolov asking to speak to you all."

Sara was curious about this visit; Abram was the current Prime Minister of Russia whom she had discussed joining the coalition. They had committed to the destruction of their nuclear arsenal but were hesitant to join the Coalition. She said, "Does anyone have any objections?" Everyone's response was no, so she told the agent to let him enter. Abram walked in and stood in front of the members of the Christian Coalition and said, "Hello to you all, I am here to ask for your permission to join you. I have gotten a full commitment from my council of ministers and rushed here to address you, but then the aggression interrupted the proceedings. I only interrupt you now so that I might offer any help my country might be able to offer."

Sara asked him to please step out so they might discuss this matter. He stepped out and immediately some of the council voiced some distrust of Russia, but ultimately, they knew they needed their help to battle the Babylonian army. They asked him to step back in and congratulated him on the new membership.

The meeting then returned to the matter at hand and after Abram had been made aware of all of the information they had, he offered his military assets as well as his head of the Security Council of Russia to assist in any military response. Huan Ji spoke to Sara in a whisper;He said, "Madam, his head of Security Council is probably one of the most decorated and successful generals in the world. His name is Vlad Popov, and we would be very well served to gain his services."

She said, "Thank you." Then she said, "Abram, we would be most thankful to have your head of the Security Council join our response."

He said, "Consider it done Madam."

She suggested that instead of the members forming an immediate response, that all the military leaders of the Christian Coalition countries should communicate with each other and come up with suggestions for the coalition. After everyone agreed, the meeting was concluded but before they all left she said, "Listen everyone, one thing that I have learned is just how powerful prayer is, so I suggest that we all pray over this situation and ask for the steady hand of God to guide our decisions; we will meet back here in the morning. Thank you to you all."

Chapter 20

As Gabe was pulling into his driveway at his home, Hayden had just finished parking the large motor home and was walking towards the house. Gabe got out of his car, the two hugged and then walked into the house together. Gabe and Rai hugged tightly, and he kissed her deeply. Gabe then he hugged Sophie who was starting to show her pregnancy. He then asked Rai what he needed to do. She asked him to start loading everything into the Motor Home. She had boxed up all the groceries they had and filled several suitcases and boxes with clothes she had packed. Sophie and Hayden had packed their belongings into the motor home already. Gabe and Hayden started moving everything into their new temporary home, then they started checking the vehicle. They checked all the fluids, made sure there was enough air in the tires, chose a spot for tools which they moved into the vehicle while organizing them. Finally, Sophie and Rai came out and unpacked all the boxes and suitcases and organized the living space. Before they left, Gabe called Mia, Bobbie and a few of the other people he worked with to make sure they were ok. Everyone he spoke to had an exit strategy to head north.

After a last quick check through the house, the four of them got into the motor home and started driving north and east with no real destination in mind. They just wanted to get away from the hordes of crazy people.

∞

Sean was talking to his top general, Kwon Yushin. Sean said, "What is the problem? We should have plenty of forces to continue our advancement worldwide."

Kwon said, "Honorable Sean, we do not know what to attribute their ability to fend our forces off. We keep sending more forces, and they have been able to keep us from moving, especially in the United States where weaponry is much more available to the average person."

Kwon watched as Sean closed his eyes as if in prayer for a moment, then Sean said, "It is time we add to our forces; I have not told you this, but I have had a secret force hidden from everyone. It is an additional three hundred thousand troops that are just off the coast of the United States and Saudi Arabia; I will signal them to join the battle."

Kwon showed appreciation to Sean, but internally, he was very upset that something like this had been kept from him. He bowed to Sean and left the room; then he heard Sean say, "The King can hear your thoughts, Kwon, just follow orders or face the consequences." Kwon went cold with fear and continued out of the room.

∞

Sara is back in the meeting room waiting for the Christian Coalition Members to arrive. She had prayed much of the night as well as having many conversations with her military leaders. They updated her on the status of the advancing army on American Soil. The National Guard along with armed civilians had virtually stopped the advancement of the enemy troops. They also spoke about their thoughts on a global response. The consensus was that a Christian Coalition Army should be

248

organized to pool all resources to stop the advancement in the Middle East and China.

The Members started to arrive; Sara gave a warm greeting to each person that walked in. Sara took her seat and said, "Good morning everyone, and welcome back, I would like to introduce our newest member who flew in late last night." Hamid stood, and Sara said, "Please welcome Hamid Mehadifar, the President and sole leader of Iran."

Everyone applauded, and Hamid thanked everyone then took his seat. Sara said, "We have much work to get done today so let's get right down to it. I would like to hear any and all ideas for how to move forward."

The German Chancellor spoke up and said, "I have spoken to the members of the old European union, and I can say that we are ready to commit our troops to any endeavor moving against the aggressors."

Huan Ji also said, "The Chinese military is also at your disposal."

Sara stood and said, "Let me stop everyone here, we need direction. I assume everyone here is willing to commit some or all their military to this cause. If there is anyone not willing to commit troops, please raise your hand." After no one raised their hand, she said, "Ok, here is what I think we should do. We need to form a massive army with a single military leader and supporting ranks reporting to this person. I need first to know if everyone is on board with this direction. We need a motion to form a Christian Coalition military."

The Prime Minister of Israel made a motion to form a military, with the King of Saudi Arabia seconding the motion. A vote was called for with all members voting to form the new Military for the Christian Coalition. Sara then said, "We need nominations for top leaders."

Israel nominated their top ranking General Rotem Almen; she was the highest ranked woman in the history of their military. Sara nominated General William Jones, her own Secretary of Defense. He was a four-star General and one of the best strategically minded people she knew. The King from Saudi Arabia nominated their top General Faten Najjar, while Russia offered his top General Vlad Popov. Sara said, "If there are no other nominations, we will break for two hours, take this time to research these folks, we will come back and vote on who will lead this new military as well as what role these other great leaders will take.

∞

Gabe was pulling in to Cedar City, Utah after driving straight through the night. He wanted to get as much distance that he could between them and the invaders. He pulled into a gas station where there was a sizable line; they were not the only ones trying to get away from the fighting. He finally pulled up to the pump and Hayden filled the two tanks, while Gabe checked the oil and the tires. Meanwhile, Rai and Sophie walked inside to get some snacks and drinks. They overheard many conversations about people who watched loved ones get dragged out into the streets and executed. One woman said, "They grabbed my 15-year-old daughter, they raped her in front of us then dragged her outside and shot her. After they did that, about one hundred people, citizens I would say, armed and organized, attacked the ones who killed her. My husband, my son and I jumped in the car and started driving. We had to leave our daughter behind, there in the streets! Why would God let this happen? Why did she have to die?"

The woman was clearly in shock and was crying inconsolably. Rai walked up to her and took her into her arms and hugged her.

She never spoke, she just held the poor woman who had gone through something that Rai hoped she would never have to witness. A few minutes later Sophie and Rai were walking back out to the motor home when they heard a massive amount of noise. First, it was a long distance away, but the noise got louder and louder. Then they could see it, coming from the north and the east heading south and west were thousands of military trucks, jeeps, and tanks on the road and planes, jets and helicopters as far as the eye could see in the sky. They were headed to the fight; they were going to meet these evildoers and stop them. Everyone ran out into the streets and cheered and screamed. Saying things like, go get em, and God bless you. People were high fiving and hugging each other. For the first time, people felt like there was hope and that hope lay in the hands of these young men and women who were there to defend their freedom. Gabe thought, thank you, God. Then quietly he said, "God bless the United States."

∞

Sara was back in the meeting room; the members were coming back from the two-hour break. Sara said, "Ok, is everyone ready to cast their vote for our military leader?" The group said yes. Sara went through each nominee with the members raising their hand in favor of that person. In the end, General Popov was the one with the most votes, so it was noted that General Popov would be leading the Christian Coalition Military. They decided to separate the branches by air, land, and sea, with General Rotem Almen heading up the new Air force, General William Jones would be leading the new Christian Army and General Faten Najjar would lead the new Navy.

Sara thanked everyone for working on all of this and wished them safe travels home. Sara was exhausted and ready to get home and deal with everything going on there. She had been briefed on what was happening along the southern border and how much success the military was having as they were trying to stop the enemy from advancing.

Once aboard Air Force One, she was alone in her cabin thinking about everything that had happened when she got a clear thought. No, it wasn't a thought; this seemed to be coming from somewhere else, almost from her heart and her brain. Her initial thought was that something didn't make sense about the attacks on the different countries. She heard something, a voice, what was it saying? Then as she waited and relaxed the voice became clearer. My child, you have done well. At first, she was terrified then she remembered Gary recounting his conversations with God, she realized she was talking to God. She said, "I am not worthy to speak to you, God."

He said, "You are worthy, you are My child." He continued, "Sara, you will be my hand that brings this world to peace. Listen to those closest to you and be ready for anything, the dark one will do anything to create hell on earth but do not be afraid; I am with you always. You must also know that the answer in defeating the dark one is not with armor but with faith and prayer."

She opened her eyes with no idea how long she had been like that. She knew the sun had been in the sky when she closed her eyes and it was dark now. For some reason though, she was at peace, more so now than in months. Then she thought, "I need to figure out what this King of New Babylon is doing."

Sean was cursing and screaming at his generals, saying, "Get more troops in there and get more planes in the air." He could hear Lucifer telling him something, but he was too pissed to listen to him. Then Lucifer screamed, saying, "You are failing, but I knew you would, which is why I have the Supreme Leader in place. I will have him take over this battle. The world will now know true power."

Sean had gone from screaming at everyone, to complete silence. Everyone was looking at him as he left his chair; he walked outside, looked into the sun for a moment, pulled out a pistol, and aimed it at his head. He felt the warmth of the sun and could hear a bird off in the distance. A fly was buzzing over his head. He could hear some kids playing in the distance and he thought, how could I have been so wrong about Lucifer? He had done everything Lucifer had asked of him, it was his last thought because he had pulled the trigger and a bullet traveled through his brain, killing him. General Kwon had watched him walk outside and take his own life. Everyone had no idea what to do so they looked to him; Kwon hesitated but then took the seat Sean had been sitting in.

∞

A few weeks after the initial attack, the Christian army had been able to fend off the attackers. The new Coalition force was too powerful for the unorganized and poorly trained troops that the King had set forth. While the invading troops had caused a massive amount of damage and killed hundreds of thousands of people, it could have been much worse.

Sara was in the oval office meeting with Huan Ji and General Jones to discuss what was left of the dwindling army that was now on the run from the Coalition forces. There was a knock at the door, she said, "Come in."

One of her aids walked in and said, "You need to turn on the television madam President."

She did that, on the screen was the Supreme Leader of North Korea, she said, "What is he doing on TV?"

The shot then switched to a shot of rows and rows of rockets. She turned the sound up, and the Leader was saying. "The world has 48 hours to surrender to me, or I will destroy every large city in the world."

Sara stood and said, "What did he say? Why would we do that?"

Huan Ji said, "Madam, those are nuclear warheads."

The Leader was back on the screen, he said, "I have been stocking piling these weapons for years. We now have eleven hundred warheads aimed at every major city in the world. We will destroy all that you know and love, the way you can avoid this is to dismantle all governments in the world. I will assemble a single government and rule the entire world; there will be one bank, one currency and one army under the rule of the King of New Babylon which will be the new name of this world. You will have one day to decide what you will do, or the missiles will be launched, and I will still rule the world."

Sara was clearly shaken, her knees buckled, and she fell to the floor. William grabbed her and stood her back up and then helped her to a seat. She said, "How, after everything we've been through, how can this be?"

William said, "I am not sure Madam, but we need to figure out what we are going to do."

She said, "We have no choice, you heard him, he can kill millions of people, and we have no way to retaliate or protect ourselves. I made a huge mistake in destroying our arsenal."

Gary walked into the Oval office and said, "Madam President, are you ok?"

She said, "No Gary, I am not alright, look at what I have gotten us into."

He said, "Madam, listen to me please, remember that God has a plan. He always has a reason for what He does."

Sara yelled, "Well what's his plan now?"

Gary stood looking at her; she said, "I am sorry Gary, I fear I am buckling under the pressure."

He said, "It is ok Madam we are only human."

Sara walked to the window and looked at the trees and the birds that were gathering in the branches. She sighed and reflected on everything she had been through as well as everything the country and its people had endured. It was almost too much, but she remembered that Gary said God never gave us more than we can carry. She stood straight; it was that moment that she became a true leader. She would not back down; she would not let this man terrorize the world, she didn't know what she was going to do, but hiding or giving into his demands was not an option. She turned, and Gary could see it, the change that had occurred in that little bit of time. The look she had in her eyes was a look that would drive anyone to follow her. She simply said, "No."

William said, "Madam, no?"

She said, "We will not bow to this fool, gather the members of my cabinet and see how many members of the Coalition we can get on a conference call and Gary, pray, pray as you've never prayed, we need it right now."

∞

Gabe and his family were finally getting back home. Gabe parked the motor home; he could see that their house had been ransacked. At first, he began to get angry and want revenge but then he thought to himself, it could have been much worse. They all walked into the house, the door was off its hinges, and the house was a mess. Rai was speechless then quietly started cleaning up the mess. At first, Gabe wanted to tell her to wait, that they could start cleaning tomorrow. However he could tell that she needed this, she needs to erase this. So instead of protesting, he started helping her. He and Hayden fixed the front door and turned the furniture back upright and moved them back into place. After a few hours they had things roughly organized, it was the start of the healing they needed. Sophie and Hayden left to see what their home looked like. Gabe said, "We will be there to help in just a bit."

Hayden said, "No, that's ok, I have a few buddies that said they would meet us there and help out." They all hugged, then Sophie and Hayden left. Later after a dinner of cold cut sandwiches and chips they decided to go to bed early, Rai would continue working on the house, Gabe wanted to see if he could catch a flight out to Orlando to get back to the messages they had never been able to read. Gabe and Rai laid in their own bed after weeks of being on the run. They were finally able to hold each other with no worries that at any moment one, or both of them, could be killed. It was a deep and blissful sleep they got that night.

∞

Sara was in her meeting room with her entire cabinet. Several of the monitors around the room were split screens with members of the coalition as well as others conferenced in on the phone. Sara said, "Thank you, everyone, for making time for this meeting. I know you are all very busy dealing with the aftermath of the tragic attacks. As you know, we are being threatened with nuclear attacks now; I would like to hear everyone's thoughts so we can make a good decision on how to move forward."

Huan Ji, who had been a close friend and ally to Sara spoke. First, he said, "Madam President, with all due respect, what do you mean? Is it not obvious what we need to do? We are at a serious disadvantage right now. The Supreme Leader has virtually all the nuclear arms that exist in the world, save for a handful that has not been destroyed yet. We have to dismantle our governments and hand power over to him." Most of the others agreed while some remained quiet. Sara was hurt that the man she had grown close to as a friend would voice this without any discussion. But he was entitled to his opinion and so was she.

Sara said, "I see that most have spoken to this option, but some are silent. Do some of you need some time to think this over?" About a dozen people said they needed to consult with some of their experts. Sara said, "Before you all make a decision, I would like to propose an alternative choice to just giving up. You see, I believe, I believe in the one true God, and I have given my life to Jesus. I have spoken to God; He said that Satan would do whatever he had to do to create hell on earth and that armor was not the way to defeat him. I think that the mighty hand of God is our weapon. We have ways of stalling him, we could probably send up missiles to intercept the warheads, but success with them would be less than fifty percent; I think the answer to this problem is prayer."

Nearly every person could not believe what she was saying. They were incredulous with what she had said, scoffing her, even yelling at her. She simply sat there and took it. She looked at Gary, and he instantly jumped up, most people didn't even notice he was in the room and even if they had, he was always poised and quiet. Not today, not this moment. Gary had been told by God that there would be a moment that he would need to convince the world that God was the way. He had been in deep prayer with God, he was not even fully aware of what was being said in the room, it was God who said, "Your time is now, Gary, the world will change forever if you do not move these people, right now, right this instant, if you do not, my children will be lost. Now, Gary…NOW!"

That is when he jumped out of his chair, with a yell. His first word was "Listen!" even Sara was taken aback by this. Gary said, "People, the Lord our God sent his Son to save us, we have clear evidence that Jesus is real, that God is real. So many times, in the Bible, prayer has been the answer. Faith is more powerful than a rocket, the hand of God will save us. We must pray, every person around the entire world who is a believer in Jesus Christ must pray. If, and when, the missiles are launched we must pray that the hand of God protects us all."

Sara was quiet at first, and then she said, "I will be praying, I hope you all will as well. We will reconvene in two hours to discuss what everyone's decision is."

∞

Gabriel landed in Orlando, Robert and Bridget had picked him up. Gabriel said, "When did you all get back to Cocoa Beach?"

Robert said, "Yesterday evening, we were in Canada with Bridget's aunt and uncle."

Gabriel said, "So have you been back to the device yet?"

Robert said, "No, I haven't had time, we came back to a mess in the house. But I am not too worried about it; the President ordered the Army to protect it at almost all costs."

Gabriel said, "Good, I figured she would."

Robert pulled off the highway at an exit and made his way to the compound where the device was. They all had to show their identification, they were admitted, then they were on their way to the device. As they drove across the expanse, they could see the device was intact and safe, but there was clear evidence that there were forces that tried to make their way in. Thank God for the Army, who protected this area. They pulled up to the door, and Robert unlocked the door, and they entered the device after weeks of not being there. Robert was very proud of this machine, and It was a good feeling to get back in to continue the work they had started. As they walked in and got settled, they started the process of rebooting the computers as well as bringing the power sources online.

This took about an hour; once this was complete Robert brought the last messages up on the big screen so they could both read it. It was so efficient with the device able to translate the messages to English; this was an added feature as the original design didn't call for this. Robert was able to add it with the help of a team of incredible computer science experts. The last message appeared, and they began to read. It said *We have been asked this before by others we have contacted. We are a people that are solely committed to the service to God and spreading a message of love for all that God created. Other worlds we have contacted have been very curious to know what we look like, I have prayed to God to show me a way to show others what we look like so I have been able to, with God's wisdom, insert a likeness of my family and me. You will need to produce the message in a compressed manner and view it from far away. My next message will be very large and will take a long time to transfer. It will be the history of our world and will describe how Jesus saved us. God bless you all.*

Gabriel and Robert finished reading at about the same time, and they looked at each other. Gabriel said, "We have to forward this on to the senior staff and the President."

Robert said, "Can we send it to Mia as well? I have been keeping her and her team in the loop because of everything they contributed to the success here."

Gabriel said, "Sure thing, that's no problem."

Robert said, "And now, the picture, I am not sure what he means."

Gabriel said, "Let's start by printing out the message."

Robert did that, and they laid it down and stood back and tried to find the picture he was talking about, but they couldn't see anything. Robert said, "What if we print what was sent to us before the translation, the raw data?"

Gabriel said, "Crap that is a great idea, Robert."

Robert had to pull up the original message and displayed it, he highlighted all of the data and moved it to a simple word document and printed it. They laid it down on the ground but still couldn't make anything out, then Gabriel said, "Let's move it over to the floor under the balcony."

After a few minutes of making sure they had moved it correctly, they both went up to the second floor; once they looked down, they were able to see something, but the order was not right. Robert said, "You stay up here, and I'll go rearrange the pages."

Robert was on the first floor and started moving the pages, Robert said, "Move the second row up one." He did that then Robert said, "Ok I am starting to see something, move the next row up, then the next row to the top." After about thirty minutes of this, Robert said, "That's it, holy cow, it's amazing." Robert hurried to the balcony and looked down to see what Gabriel was looking at, he looked down and couldn't believe what he was seeing.

Chapter 21

Young Ra-il was talking to Song Mi-Hyang, he said, "Direct orders from the Supreme Leader, we are to mobilize the majority of the arsenal of nuclear warheads. Start the process of loading the missiles onto the trucks. We also need to send the operators with them. This is the reason Dear Leader wanted so many operators trained. No one will be able to detect remote detonations. There will be no warning; the rockets will be in the air and on their way to their targets before the Coalition knows they have been sent." Song Mi-Hyang had learned just to follow orders but she was terrified right now, she had not thought it would get to this point. Young Ra-il said, "is there a problem?"

As he reached for his pistol at his side, she said, "No Great Director, I will see to the operation myself."

He said, "Very well, carry on." She turned with tears in her eyes, she knew millions and millions of people would die if these missiles were sent to their targets but she had no choice, she had already been threatened by having to watch her family executed in front of her. She would carry out the plan of the Supreme Leader.

∞

Sara was in the Oval Office about to go back to the meeting room when she got a call on her cell phone; it was a number she vaguely recognized, so she answered it.
She said, "Hello."
Gabriel said, "Madam President, this is Gabriel Dane."
She said, "Gabriel, hello, how are you and how can I help you?"

He said, "I am great madam President, my entire family made it through the invasion safely, but the reason I am calling, is to tell you first-hand that we broke protocol and sent a message to Erets that was not our list."

She said, "I see, and what did you ask them?"

He said, "I just asked about them as a people and about their world."

She said, "Well, I prefer you follow protocol, but that seems like a pretty harmless question. Why are you calling me about this?"

Gabriel said, "Madam, they devised a way to send pictures using the data to form a picture. Madam, they are actual people. They look very similar to us; the picture is of what I assume is Abarron and his family."

She said, "That is amazing."

He said, "Madam they look very similar to Native Americans, Cherokee to be exact."

She said, "That is just amazing Gabriel."

He said, "I know, I just wanted to tell you first-hand."

She said, "Thank you, Gabriel, I am sorry to do this but I need to get to a meeting, there is a very disturbing development, and I need to deal with it."

Gabriel said, "So sorry Madam, I will let you go then."

A thought occurred to Sara, and she said, "Gabriel wait are you still there?"

He said, "Yes."

She said, "If I want to send a message to Abarron can I call you directly?"

He said, "Certainly Madam, any time."

She said, "Thank you and goodbye."

Sara walks into the Cabinet meeting room where all the members are waiting as well as the coalition members. She says, "I am sorry to keep you waiting, I was on the phone with Gabriel Danes, he was telling me of some developments with the messages with Erets. Anyhow, let us get back to our order of business. Where is everyone with how we move forward with the decision on how we respond to North Korea?"

Huan Ji spoke. First, he said, "Madam President, you know that I am one of logical thinking, I have never been religious but this last year has certainly challenged me on that philosophy. This last year, I have been so very impressed with your leadership, and I am thankful for our friendship. I must also report that my intelligence team has observed a massive amount of movement in the north central part of North Korea. There appear to be thousands of trucks with a large payload undercover. I am confident that these are the warheads he said they had. I think that no matter what we do, he will launch these missiles. I am now convinced that we must put our faith in God, but it must be a massive movement of prayer. Israel, Ireland, India, Australia, and Iran all said they agreed. Germany was skeptical but said they would get behind the effort and support it." Huan Ji continues, "I would like to make a motion that the Christian Coalition support a day of prayer to protect the world from the harm of a nuclear attack from North Korea."

India said, "We second the motion."

Sara said, "I will put it to a vote then, all in favor of the motion say aye." All members voted with aye; she said, "All members voting no say no." There was silence, so she said, "The motion carries with all votes yes. Everyone should start getting the message out to your countries; I plan on plastering it everywhere I can, TV, Social Media, and print media, that we should be in continual prayer and that if and when the missiles are launched that we will all pray at the same time. Thank you, everyone."

Faizan and Anahita were cuddled up on the couch together; Anahita shared a house with several other girls that were going to the same school. Faizan also attended the same school but stayed at his parent's home to save money, yet he had a car and was able to spend time with Anahita when their schedules allowed it. This was one of those times, and they were watching a movie with a few of the other roommates. Faizan had accepted Jesus into his life the day that he left the backpack with the bomb inside it behind at the capitol and was reunited with the love of his life. They had found each other the day the invasion happened and decided to stay together at his parent's house. He knew that day that he would spend the rest of his life with her.

As they were watching the movie, everyone started getting an alert on their phones. It was a presidential alert telling everyone to turn their televisions on or go to the presidential video channel. One of the girls turned the news on just as the President came into view. She said, "Ladies and gentlemen of the United States, I come to you with alarming news but please do not panic. We have the love of Jesus and the awesome power of God on our side. As you know the Christian Coalition has been confronted by the North Korean regime with a threat of nuclear war. They have over one thousand warheads and are aiming them at our major cities. I have met with the Christian Coalition, and we have reason to believe that North Korea is going to use the missiles no matter what decision we make. We have no way to defend ourselves with armor, but we have something even more powerful. I have asked Pastor Gary Manns to explain our strategy."

The camera panned to the right to find Gary sitting not far from the President. Gary says, "Brothers and sisters in Christ, I will always consult the Bible for wisdom and direction. When the President asked me for advice that is what I did, I went to the

Bible. While many verses explain how faith in God will always lead you to the place you need to be, I thought this one would be the best fit for our needs. If you have a Bible, turn to Ephesians 6:10-17, the Armor of God. 'Finally, be strong in the Lord and in His mighty power, put on the full armor of God, so that you can take your stand against the devil's schemes. For our struggle is not against flesh and blood, but against the rulers, against the authorities, against the powers of this dark world and against the spiritual forces of evil in the heavenly realms. Therefore, put on the full armor of God, so that when the day of evil comes, you may be able to stand your ground, and after you have done everything to stand. Stand firm then, with the belt of truth buckled around your waist, with the breastplate of righteousness in place, and with our feet fitted with the readiness that comes from the gospel of peace. In addition to all this, take up the shield of faith, with which you can extinguish all the flaming arrows of the evil one. Take the helmet of salvation and the sword of the spirit, which is the word of God (NIV ®)."

Sara said, "Thank you for that Gary. Ladies and gentlemen, what I ask next, I do not take lightly, and I know it will sound fanatical, or maybe not. The past year has changed many of us, mostly for the better. Today I am asking you to pray; I am asking you to do nothing but pray for the remainder of the twenty-four hours we were given to make a decision. Then, if and when the missiles are launched, I want us all to pray specifically for the protection of God's hand over his children as one voice. I will close with this quote from John Newton who was and English Anglican, clergyman and abolitionist. He said, "If the Lord be with us, we have no cause for fear. His eye is upon us, His arm over us, His ear open to our prayer, His grace sufficient and his promise unchangeable."Sara continued, "Thank you, ladies and Gentlemen, God bless you, God bless the United States and the world in which we live, Good night."

Faizan said, "What is next? This is unbelievable how many things are going on."

Anahita said, "I know, but it is all God's plan, we must have faith. Now we should all pray as the president asked us to do."

∞

The Supreme Leader of North Korea still felt odd talking to Lucifer. He knew he had great power but he himself had told so many that he was a God for so long that he had actually believed it himself until he saw what Lucifer could do, then he made adjustments with his own perspective of how things really were. Lucifer was telling the Leader where to place the missiles and what coordinates to use. By now, the Leader had proven himself to be more loyal than Sean had been. Sean had been too compassionate to do the things Lucifer needed him to do. Lucifer said, "I can trust you to follow through with this action? I don't care what those stupid people do; they will all die."

The Leader said, "I have no problem doing this and anything else you need me to do great King."

Lucifer said, "Very good, for your dedication to me I am making you the commander of the military as well now."

The Leader said, "Thank you, my Lord. I will not fail you."

Song Mi-Hyang arrived at the office of Young Ra-il; as she walked into his office she said, "Most honorable Director I felt it was important to tell you in person that all of the missiles are in place and ready to be launched at the Great Leaders direction."

He said, "Very good, and the operators are in place?"

She said, "Yes, they are prepared to arm the warheads and fire them as they are commanded."

He said, "Good job, Song Mi-Hyang, I will be directing the men watching your family to stand down. Your family is safe now."

She began to tear up and said, "Thank you most honorable and great Director, thank you so much." She backed out of the room and started to make her way down to the road to go see her family. As she walked down the steps, she got a phone call from an unknown number, she answered the call, a voice said, "Do you really think that your dissidence would be rewarded? The King knows your thoughts, you were not loyal to the cause, here is your mother."

Her mother said, "My daughter, why are these men here? You said you would do whatever you needed to do to keep us safe."

A gun fired, she could hear her father scream, "No!" Then four more shots followed. There was silence, and the strange man said, "Dissidence is not tolerated."

She stood on the steps in shock, she had done everything asked of her, and then she thought, "The King knew her thoughts, what did that mean?"

She heard a pop off in the distance, and she felt a searing pain enter her back and exit her chest. Suddenly she could not breathe, she fell forward. She realized in an instant that she was moments from dying, she had heard that you could be forgiven of your sins if you just prayed to Jesus and accepted him as your savior, something she was going to do, but now she thought she was too late, she decided to pray. She said, "Jesus, I am sorry for everything I have done. I am sorry for everything I have done against God, and I ask you to forgive my sins, I love you, Jesus and I accept you as my Lord and Savior."

Another shot rang out, and everything went black for her. The beautiful and intelligent Song Mi-Hyang lay on the steps, her blood spreading all around her. A group of men drove up, lifted her into a black bag, zipped it up and carried her to the van they had pulled up in. Just like that, she and her family were eliminated from this world.

Sara called Gabriel; he answered the phone and he said, "Hello?"

She said, "Gabriel, it is Sara."

He was taken by surprise; it's not every day the president of the United States calls you. He said, "Madam President, hello, what can I do for you?"

She said, "Gabriel, did you see any of the press release I did earlier?"

He said, "Yes madam, I did, and I will be praying. I am in Florida with Robert working on our next message to Erets, and he will be praying as well."

She said, "That is great, but that is not why I called."

He said, "Oh, what do you need then?"

She said, "Gabriel, I feel that we need all of the help we can get, we need faith on an unprecedented level."

He said, "Ok, what are you thinking?"

She said, "How long does it take for a message to get to Erets and for us to get a reply?"

He said, "Well, it depends on how much data is going and coming back. For a short message, it could be as quick as about seven minutes to get there and seven minutes to get back so a total of about fourteen or fifteen minutes."

She was quiet for a moment, then said, "Ok, here is what I would like you to do, can you send a message explaining our situation and ask them to pray for us and for the missiles to have no effect on us? Then when the missiles are headed towards us, message them again to pray with us as a massive unit of faith?"

Gabriel said, "Great idea madam, I will send the message now, then when I get word from you, if and when the missiles are in the air, I will message them again."

She said, "No, don't wait for me, if you hear the missiles have been launched send the message right away, I think that it is crucial that we all pray at the same time."

He said, "Very well madam, I will set it all up."

She said, "Thank you Gabriel, goodbye, and God Bless you."

He said, "Goodbye Madam and may God Bless you too."

Gabriel walked back into the room where they sent the messages from and said, "Robert, we need to put the message you are working on to the side, and we need to start a new message."

He said, "What new message?"

Gabriel said, "That was the President, she wants us to craft a letter to Erets, we are to explain our situation and ask them to pray with us as she described in her address to the nation earlier."

He said, "Ok, but they will not get the message in time if the missiles are launched."

Gabriel said, "We are going to set it all up so that all they have to do is get the message then go right into prayer, they will not need to reply because we will have it all set up beforehand."

He said, "Got it, ok, what do you want to say?"

∞

The Dear Leader was in deep discussion with Lucifer, Lucifer said, "In eight hours you will launch the entire arsenal to the coordinates I gave you. All the people we want to protect need to be in the deep bunkers before that. You have everything prepared for a year in there, correct?"

He said, "Yes my Lord, I have enough rations for a million people in the underground bunkers the missiles were in."

Lucifer said, "Very good, and after the world is cleansed of the stupid Christians you will sit by my side, you and only you will have the power to rule New Babylon."

The Leader said, "I will not fail you."

∞

Abarron was alerted to an incoming message from Earth; as it came in, he too had to translate it. By the time it finished he had several pages to read. He gathered everything and took them with him. It was dinner time, and he was looking forward to sitting with his wife and children. He walked from the device into his home; he kissed his wife on the cheek and smelled the fish she was cooking. His children came running in screaming, "Daddy is home." He knelt down, and they dragged him to the floor and hugged him as he lay on his back. The papers were spread around on the floor; his wife was picking them up, and she started reading them. She looked at him with a puzzled look on her face. He said, "Liala, what has alarmed you?"

She said, "Have you read any of this?"

He said, "No, I wanted to be on time for dinner."

She said, "You need to read this."

He started to read the pages; his heart broke for the people he had been conversing with. He knew he had to call an emergency meeting with the Elders in the sanctuary. Before he left, his wife said, "You have to help them, no, we have to help them, husband."

He said, "I agree, but it is up to the Elders and God. They will pray on it and seek an answer."

She said, "Abarron, you have the clearest voice with God, I wish we could change the ways decisions were made."

He said, "Wife, you are right, I have the clearest voice with God, but I also know that the way we make decisions is according to how He wants us to do it. He does not want one man to have all the power to make decisions. He says it could corrupt that man, so it is for a good reason it is set up this way my love." He kissed her and his children and left to meet with the elders.

∞

Gary Manns is at Wembley Stadium; he is going to preach to a capacity of 90,000 people. It is also being televised by every possible station available and is on all social media platforms. It is expected to be viewed by over seven billion people in the world. Gary said, "Today is the day we change the course of the future of this world we live on. Today, I want to tell you about the power of God. God, you see, works in some strange ways. He used a murderer to lead the people out of slavery in Egypt, Noah was a drunk and David was an adulterer and a murderer. You see, God is not looking for the perfect person for a particular job. No, you see, He wants you to believe. He wants you to ask for forgiveness and give your life to Jesus. Over the last year, we have learned so much about God and His Son Jesus, that he is indeed real and that he loves us all as his children. You might be asking yourself, why I am speaking to this at this time. It is because God loves you, each and every one of you. He knows your thoughts and what is in your heart. He knows the good and the bad about you and loves you anyway. At this time, we need faith; we need every person in this world to believe that He can stop the missiles that are sure to be launched. I would like to read from Psalm 91: 1-16.'He who dwells in the shelter of the most high will rest in the shadows of the Almighty. I will say of the Lord; He is my refuge and my fortress, my God, in whom I trust. Surely He will save you from the fowler's snare and from the deadly pestilence. He will cover you with his feathers, and under his wings you will find refuge; His faithfulness will be your shield and rampart. You will not fear the terror of the night, nor the arrow that flies by day, nor the pestilence that stalks in the darkness, nor the plague that destroys at midday. A thousand may fall at your side, ten thousand at your right hand, but it will not come near you, you will only observe with your eyes and see the punishment of the wicked. If you make the most high your dwelling-even the Lord, who is my refuge-then no harm will befall you, no disaster will come near your tent, for He will lift you up in their hands so that you will not strike your foot against a stone. You will tread upon the lion and the cobra; you will trample the great lion and the serpent. Because he loves me, says the Lord, I will rescue him; I will protect him, for he acknowledges My Name. He will call upon Me, and I will answer him; I will be with him in trouble, I will deliver him and honor him. With long life will I satisfy him and show him My salvation (NIV®)."

Chapter 22

Young Ra-il is at the command center for the launch of the missiles; he waits for the word from the Dear Leader to give the order for the operators to arm the warheads and launch them. The Leader was in a dark room in deep meditation. He was waiting for Lucifer to give him the word to launch the attack. Finally, after what seemed like hours of waiting, Lucifer said, "My right hand is waiting for me, which is good because today is the day we take this world away from these Christians."

The Leader said, "Yes my Great King, my Lord, I wait for your word and it will happen."

Lucifer said, "Very well, make it rain fire on them, they will die a horrible death all because they choose the wrong side, they could have chosen me, and they would have had favor with me, but now they will die screaming in pain."

The Leader opened his eyes and said to himself, "It is time."

∞

Abarron has made his way to the sanctuary. As he entered, he removed his foot ware and made it known that he was entering. The elders were made aware of his need to speak, so they gathered at the meeting place in the sanctuary. When they were ready, they had him brought before them, he knelt before them and said, "Wise elders, I am in need of your wisdom and your council. I have been made aware of a situation on the world I have most recently contacted. They are preparing for a war against the evil one and are in need of our help."

One of the Elders said, "The evil one? He never gives up does he?"

Another one of the Elders asked, "Could you explain the situation and their request?"

Abarron said, "This world has a weapon that is capable of killing thousands of people at one time, they call it a nuclear weapon. Apparently there were thousands of them all over the world, but they have destroyed all of them, or so they thought. It seems Lucifer has been able to have one of his own fallen angels, stockpile and hide enough of these weapons to defeat the followers of Christ."

The Elder said, "Understood, what do they ask of us?"

He said, "They ask us to pray that God protects them from the missiles that would be launched and blow up their cities all over their world."

An Elder said, "We need to pray here first."

Abarron knew they would do this, so he left and sat in the garden outside of the sanctuary. After about fifteen minutes he was summoned to the sanctuary where the Elders waited, the senior of the Elders said, "You must go now and tell them we will pray, God is clear in His message. You must hurry though, this is of the greatest of important battles, and we must all pray for their success."

Abarron said, "Thank you."

He stood and left, he went home and told his wife that they would be praying. She said, "Thank God."

He walked to the device and started typing the reply. He flipped the switches and pressed the last button, and the message was sent. He went back to his home, he knelt with his family, and they began to pray. Meanwhile, the elders had sent messengers far and wide to spread the command of God. Everyone on Erets was to pray for Earth and the defeat of Satan, for this was a battle between God and Satan.

∞

The Dear Leader came out of his darkened room; it took a few seconds for his eyes to adjust to the light, he walked to the

274

command center where Young Ra-il was stationed and said, "It is time, send the message to fire the Missiles."

Young Ra-il breathed in, held his breath for a second and let his breath out, he picked up the headset and said, "Attention all operators, this message is not a drill, you are to fire your missiles now."

Young Ra-il was almost sick knowing he had just given the order to kill millions of people. He stood to salute the Dear Leader, but before he could raise his hand, he dropped dead, Lucifer whispered in the Leader's ear, "He had regret." While this happened, each of the operators armed the warheads, which required climbing to the top of the missile, opening a door and manually arming the missile; they then climbed back down and pressed the button that fired the missile.

∞

Gabriel had waited on pins and needles, but finally, there was an indication that there was an incoming message. After the message was received and processed through the system to be deciphered and translated, he and Robert were able to read the message. It read, "We are all God's people and are to stand as one with you all, the Elders have prayed and spoken to God, and he was clear that this battle was of most importance and that all should pray to defeat the evil one, Lucifer. We will wait for your signal to begin the protection prayer."

Gabriel was relieved. He and Robert gave a sigh of relief at almost the same time, shook hands and Gabriel said, "I need to call the President." Gabriel pulled his phone out and stepped out of the building to get a better signal. As soon as he did, he got a Presidential message via text. First, he heard a loud peeping that lasted for about ten seconds, then a text appeared on his phone. Robert came running out, the text said in all capital letters,

'ROCKETS HAVE BEEN LAUNCHED AND WILL ARRIVE AT THEIR DESTINATIONS IN 10 TO 15 MINUTES. TAKE COVER AND RECITE PSALM 91 AS A PRAYER. REPEAT THIS PRAYER AS LONG AS POSSIBLE.'

Gabriel yelled, "Crap."

First, he called the President and told her he was sending the message to Erets and that they had agreed to pray for Earth. He then called Rai as he was walked into the building. She answered, she was crying. He said, "Baby, I wish I could be there, but I have to send this message to Erets. It could be the thing that turns the tide for us, yet know that I love you."

She said, "Gabe, I love you too."

He hung the phone up and started the process of sending the message indicating the need for them to pray. He flipped the last switch and pressed the key on the keyboard that would send the message. As soon as he did this he joined Robert who was already on his knees praying. Gabriel placed his hand on Robert's shoulder as he knelt next to him and began praying as well.

∞

Sara and Tim were in their residence, kneeling in the bedroom. Tim had his Bible opened to Psalm 91; Sara and he were reading the words in earnest. Each saying, "He who dwells in the shelter of the most high will rest in the shadows of the Almighty. I will say of the Lord; He is my refuge and my fortress, my God, in whom I trust..." Every person in the world had their Bibles out, reading Psalms 91. It was the single largest human effort ever in the history of the world. Over seven billion people on Earth were saying the same prayer from Psalm 91 over and over.

Abarron was waiting at the device for a while when he suddenly heard the indication of a message coming in. Instead of waiting for the message to actually be processed, he immediately jumped up and ran for the door. He ran as fast as he could to the Elders sanctuary and yelled for them to begin the prayer chain. As they sent the message out, within minutes, another three billion people were praying for the protection of God on earth as well.

∞

In a staggered sequence, eleven hundred nuclear warheads were in the air headed for all the major cities of the world. Every believer in Christ was praying for God to protect them. As the missiles flew it was clear that they were not being diverted by God's hand. Five minutes passed, and the missiles were still armed and headed for their targets. The first city that was targeted was Beijing, where Huan Ji was kneeling with his wife, deep in convicted prayer. The missile came closer and closer; it was at thirty thousand feet and headed straight down to the middle of the city, then twenty thousand, then ten thousand feet above the city. Not a single believer was aware of the missile headed toward them. Those who had their eyes open had not given their life to Christ; they accepted the impending death and they knew that they would have favor with Lucifer. The missile was now five thousand feet above the city…one thousand feet…five hundred feet, then…impact. Those that had watched the missile come down; shut their eyes just as it hit the ground. Waiting for the heat to hit them, the massive wave of energy would hit, ending every life for at least fifty miles in every direction. As they stood there, waiting, it seemed like it was taking a while to hit, so they opened their eyes, and nothing happened. Everything appeared as normal as it had before the missile hit. It appeared this missile had malfunctioned, but surely the other missiles would have success. The next missiles were expected to hit Tokyo and Melbourne, Australia. Again, the missiles just fell to the ground without detonating. This repeated time and again all over the world; every missile had failed to explode.

∞

Sara and Tim, still in deep prayer, were startled when they heard a knock at the door of their residence. Sara stood and opened the door. Her Secretary of Defense was there, he says, "Madam President, we have tracked every warhead, and each one hit its target, but failed to detonate. Madam, God, has laid his mighty hand on us and protected us."

Sara was amazed, it had worked, and thankful none the less. She said, "Thank God." She then thanked William, and he left. She turned to Tim and threw her arms around him and hugged him knowing they would live to see another glorious day, God willing.

∞

Gabriel and Robert had been kneeling for what felt like thirty minutes when a loud tone sounded on their phones followed by a text saying, "Missiles failed to detonate, God has protected his children." They jumped up and hugged each other, and then they each started making phone calls to their loved ones. Once they got off the phone, Gabriel told Robert that they needed to send a message to Erets to tell them God had won the battle. They did this and waited for a message back. Abarron was clearly pleased with the success and congratulated everyone for not losing faith in the almighty Lord God.

∞

A week later, the army of the Christian Coalition finally tracked down the Leader of North Korea and arrested him and all the people that had helped him. The President of the United States suggested a trial for each of the offenders, other leaders agreed and the "Dear Leader" was now a prisoner with many others he had failed. It would be a miracle if he were alive long enough to stand trial.

∞

Gabriel and Robert were alerted to a new message coming in from Erets. The message had started loading hours ago, and it was taking longer than any other message to come through. Finally, the system indicated it was finished. Gabriel sent it to the big screen so they could both read it easily. Robert said, "What the heck? We asked for the history of their world, but this looks like a...Bible, at least it starts out like our Bible."

About the Author

Jeff Bolling was born in Sandusky, Ohio but left his home town to pursue a career in animal training; this is something he has done for over thirty years. During this time he has published several articles in an industry related journal. He has also co-authored several scientific research papers. Today Jeff lives in Florida on the Treasure coast with his wife and three kids. He enjoys listing to music while he writes fiction stories on his property with the family dogs and their horse. Jeff was baptized in 2006 and attends church regularly.

References

John Glenn Quote from American Marine and Astronaut, b. 1921
MERE CHRISTIANITY by C.S. Lewis Copyright © C.S. Lewis Pte.
Ltd. 1942, 1943, 1944, 1952. Extract reprinted by permission.
Scripture taken from the HOLY BIBLE, NEW INTERNATIONAL
VERSION®, NIV®. COPYRIGHT © 1973, 1978, 1984, 2011 by
Biblica, Inc.®.   Used by permission.   All rights reserved
worldwide.
Editing by Gail Melnick
Additional revisions by Kerri Bolling